Tate

Hockey Royalty

Victoria Denault

For Los Angeles, my former home. I miss you. Stay golden.

Author's Note

Trigger Warning:

This book contains frequent mentions of a car accident which causes the death of a friend. It also touches on survivor guilt, and the child in this book has lost his mother. These issues can be very personal, and although I tried to treat the topics with respect and sensitivity, this might not be the book for you if you have experienced a traumatic loss.

HOCKEY ROYALTY
Garrison Family Tree

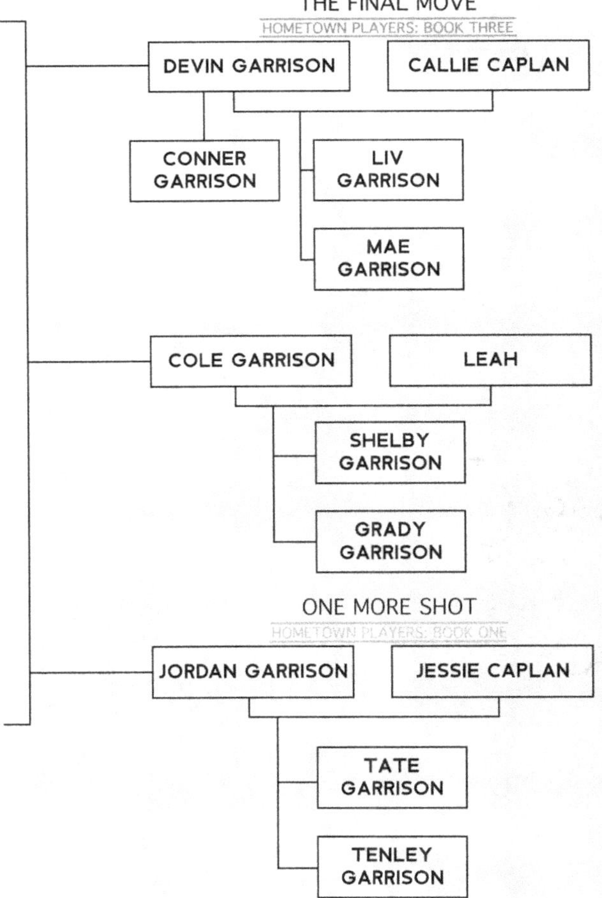

HOCKEY ROYALTY
Echolls Family Tree

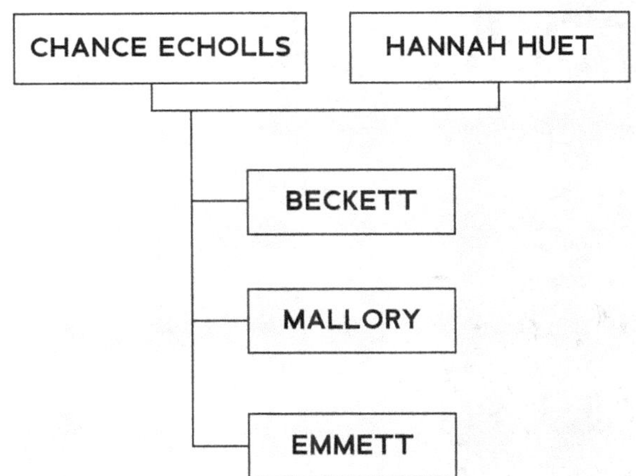

Prologue - Mallory

I always realize I'm not a good drunk after I've gotten drunk. It's not that I get sick, or become a blubbering mess, it's that every single one of my inhibitions melts like ice cream in a broken freezer. And this impromptu vacation is the last possible place I should be letting down my guard, let alone losing all common sense.

And yet, here I am in the fanciest lobby, in the fanciest hotel in Beverly Hills, waiting for my best friend's boytoy to book a room for the three of us because we got day drunk and can't drive back to his house in Venice Beach. The hotel room costs over a thousand dollars for the night, by the way. Not that Tate Garrison even blinked at that price tag. He didn't. He's rich. And talented, and funny, and charismatic, and sexy, and built like a book cover model. See? I shouldn't be drunk right now. With him. And Diana. His bed buddy and my best friend.

Diana is cool as a cucumber and without a care in the world. Being day drunk makes her cute and confident like she belongs in a five-star hotel with marble floors and a chandelier bigger than my car. She's currently got one of her long slender arms draped across Tate's broad shoulders and she's holding my hand with her free one. I'm standing like I always do when I'm with these two, off to the side.

The hotel clerk, who looks like she should be on a runway for one of those designer brands lining the Rodeo Drive, isn't fazed by a professional hockey player and two small-town girls in Target dresses booking a room for one night with no luggage. Maybe she's seen this before but I haven't. And it's weird enough that it registers in my brain, but the tequila from the margaritas and the vodka from the martinis is numbing my ability to care. I need to sleep this off, even if it means sleeping in the bathtub while these two bang in the bed.

The clerk slides two key cards in a delicate paper envelope toward Tate. "Enjoy your stay at the Beverly Wilshire, Mr. Garrison, and do not hesitate to contact us if you need anything."

"Thanks." Tate winks at her with those ridiculous eyeballs of his. They were the color of my favorite crayon when I was a kid. Robin's Egg Blue, which is really equal parts green and blue like the Caribbean Sea. I once drew him a Valentine's Card and colored in the eyes of the guy on the front with that color. I never gave it to him, though. I wonder where it is?

"Where what is?" Tate asks.

I blink and realize we're in the elevator and both Diana and Tate are looking at me quizzically. I guess I said that last bit out loud. God, I hope that's all I said out loud. I ignore them and look around the small, yet glamorous elevator. It has old-fashioned mirrors and a carved wooden bench to sit on. "This elevator is fancier than my parents' house."

Tate laughs. Diana pulls me into a hug. "Wait until you see the room."

"For eleven hundred bucks it better be a freaking palace," I mumble as the elevator doors slide open and we all stumble out into the lushly carpeted hall.

The room, is in fact, designed like a palace with fine furniture, a marble bathroom bigger than my current bedroom in my teeny Silver Bay rental apartment. The bed looks like a freaking cloud, with a million pillows and a thick duvet. Too bad I won't be able to find out how it feels. The bed is their domain.

I walk over to the blue velvet chair in the corner by the window that overlooks Tiffany's on the corner of Wilshire and Rodeo. I lean over and push on the cushion. Seems comfy...

"What are you doing, Mal?" Tate's drunk voice is better than his sober voice, and his sober voice is deep, slightly throaty, and warm like he's got some sexy secret he's sharing with you every time he speaks. But his drunk voice is all that with this tremor of... something dark. It's delicious.

Just wondering if I crash here or the bathtub, I want to explain but I can't because it would make things awkward. Even drunk me knows that. So instead I flop down on the chair and throw my legs up on the matching ottoman. "I need to sit."

"Fair." Tate chuckles and wanders away from me. Diana kisses his cheek as he passes her and then he disappears into the bathroom.

Diana flops down on the bed, like she's belly-flopping into a pool, and immediately lets out a sinful groan. "Oh my God, this thing is beyond comfortable."

"Cool," I mutter and my eyes flutter shut.

"Get over here and try it out," Diana insists. "Especially if you're going to pass out."

"Beds are for bed buddies. I'm just a plain, old, regular buddy," I explain.

"You are ridiculous." Diana giggles. "It's not like Tate and I can do anything anyway. You're right there."

"I'm a heavy sleeper," I reply because I usually am when I'm drunk. I wasn't drunk enough most nights on this trip though, and despite being across the hall with the door of my bedroom firmly closed, I could hear Diana's moans while she was hooking up with Tate the last two nights. Last night it sounded like she orgasmed *three* times.

"What?" Diana asks and her voice is closer, but I'm too tired to open my eyes and see if she got off the bed. "Why are your cheeks pink?"

"I'm drunk." Which is true but also a lie. I'm blushing because I know that on the final round between her and Tate, at four in the morning last night, I masturbated to the sounds of them fucking, imagining it was me under him. "Anyway, sorry I'm crashing this potentially romantic night in a fancy hotel. I can Uber it back to his place alone. I'm a big girl."

"How many times do I have to tell you," Diana laughs, "Tate and I don't do romance. We do sex. Sex with zero attachment or commitment."

"Mmm... if you say so," I murmur because sleep is tugging hard at my consciousness. This chair is actually pretty comfortable. "If someone made me moan that loud when I orgasmed, I wouldn't take it casually."

This time the chuckle is deeper and directly above me. Sobriety shoots through me like a bullet as I realize that one, I said that out loud, and two, Tate heard it. Luckily I have the common sense not to let my eyes fly open. I pretend I'm still sliding into sleep. My heart is racing with embarrassment, though.

"Mal? Mallory?" Diana calls to me but I act like I've died and don't respond or even move. "She must have passed out."

"I can't believe she said that." Tate chuckles and I hear him move across the room. "We should have been more quiet."

"Whatever," Diana replies airily. "She knew we were going to hook up when she agreed to come visit you with me."

"Still. I don't want to embarrass her," Tate replies.

"Why did you never hook up with Mal? Is it because your

parents hate each other?" Diana asks and I hear a sound that might be kissing as the conversation stalls for a second or two.

"I don't care what ancient grudge my parents have with Chance and Hannah Echolls. We aren't the Hatfields and McCoys. I have always liked Mallory. She's fun and sweet and hilarious when she opens up."

"Also easy on the eyes," Diana adds helpfully.

"She's pretty," Tate agrees. "There is nothing not to like about Mallory Echolls. But I think she's the strings type, which is cool. It's fine. It's great, even. But I'm not... and can we stop talking about this. It's fucking weird."

The conversation stops and I let those words sink into my brain. I'm strings. He's stringless. But he likes me. He thinks I'm pretty. I like that much more than I should.

"I bet if you tried, she might be down for just one night with you. After all one night is better than no nights," Diana states and I can't control it. My eyes fly open. The room is dark. Someone has drawn the black-out curtains across the window. Neither of them is anywhere near me, at least I can't see them, but I don't dare turn my head and alert them to my eaves-dropping.

"Diana..."

"No, listen, I'm not being silly or stupid or even playing a game here," Diana says and there's a firmness that seems to over-ride the drunkenness in her tone. "We've said all along we aren't anything exclusive and never will be. You can be with whoever you want, whenever you want. I won't be offended."

"Stop," Tate commands and there's a kissing sound again. "Let's sleep off the booze, like Mal."

There are a few more kissing sounds and a giggle and a slap and another soft giggle but nothing else. At least not while I remain conscious, but I drift off suddenly, alcohol finally winning the war.

I don't know how long I'm out but I wake up feeling like I'm floating, while also pressed against a very firm, very solid wall. My eyes flutter open. The room is still dark and now even the late afternoon sun that had breached the corners of the curtains earlier is gone. I'm moving through the room in a horizontal position and I realize that Tate is carrying me.

"What's happening?" I whisper, wondering if this is some drunken dream.

"You're sleeping in the bed," he whispers to me. "You looked like a pretzel in that chair. I'll take the... floor."

"The three of us could share," I say, showing once and for all why drunk Mallory is a danger to herself and others. "I mean, the bed is more than big enough, even with you being the size of a small house. We can all play nice, right?"

"I can if you can." Tate lifts both his chestnut eyebrows. "And you always do, don't you, Mallory?"

"Play nice? Yeah, I do. I'm the nicest nice girl you will ever meet," I ramble and then he's leaning over and placing me gently on the bed. "Marriage material. Sweet and serious and all those things hot guys like you don't find attractive."

"Mallory..." he whispers my name.

"Shh!" I scold. "I'm drunk. Nothing I'm saying is supposed to be acknowledged... or even remembered."

The bed is as comfortable as I thought it would be. It feels like being bear-hugged by a cloud. I moan as my whole body relaxes and I start to drift off again. Then I hear Tate's voice in my ear and his breath against my cheek. "Tell me I can share your bed, Mallory."

"You are welcome in my bed anytime," I murmur.

He crawls over me, to the center of the bed. Now he's the filling in a Mallory-Diana sandwich.

"Oh baby girl, if only that were true," is the last thing I hear before I slip back into a deep, drunk sleep.

I wake up hours later, with a thick, slightly throbbing head. I've got my back to the rest of the bed and Tate's big heavy arm is draped over my waist. I'm his little spoon, curled right into his torso like a needy cat, and it feels... like a desperate, irrational, impossible dream come true. I don't move a muscle. I just close my eyes and enjoy the feel of his breath tickling my neck. But then, after a few minutes, I feel him inhale deeply and stretch a little, without really moving positions. His hand also stretches and flexes, his palm now flat against my abdomen, just below my belly button.

And he flexes his hips and oh my God his erection pushes into my left thigh just under my butt cheek. Desire floods my veins. I just felt Tate's dick. I shouldn't have, but I did. And, like it or not, I'm over the moon with happiness about it.

But then his lips are on the base of my neck, pressing purposefully. His hand, fingers extended across my abdomen, is sliding lower, toward the hem of my long sundress, which has bunched up under the covers and is gathered at the tops of my thighs.

Alarm, as thick and heavy as the desire I feel for him, courses through me. He thinks I'm Diana. That's what's happening here and I have to stop it. My hand moves to cover his before he can slip under the bunched-up fabric. "Tate. It's Mallory."

His fingers still. His breathing stops and then his lips lift off my skin so he can speak. I'm expecting an 'oops' or a 'sorry' but what I get are two words that will change my life forever. "I know."

Prologue - Tate

This is crazy. Full-blown, deep-end crazy. I mean, I am breaking *all* my own rules. I don't fuck around with women who don't do one-night stands. Mallory doesn't. She made that clear once in high school. We were all hanging out at Diana's house. Diana and I weren't hooking up yet, there were like ten of us just hanging out, playing cards, and being lazy bums eating crap food and drinking beers we snuck from Diana's mom's boyfriend's stash.

Grady had just gone on a date with a girl and he was saying there was no spark. I said there didn't need to be a spark to hook up. Mallory flat-out, in total seriousness, asked why you would want to hook up with someone you didn't have feelings for. I said, "Because it feels good. Sex is fun without feelings and I don't have time for feelings. I've got a career to start."

She looked away from me. Diana announced that Mallory wanted, "Sparks and butterflies and true love."

And that's when I realized Mallory was off-limits.

I never let myself entertain the thought of being with her again. When she would join the gang at the lake in a tiny bikini, I would remind myself of that conversation. When she would smile at me and the light from a summer bonfire would make her hazel eyes glow amber, I would remind myself of that night. When she would say something so witty or downright funny that it made me grin so hard I could feel it in my chest, like my heart was smiling too, I would repeat that night in my brain.

She is not on the same page as I am. We want different things. She's hot, smart, and sexy and I would love to fuck her, but she wants more and I don't have more to give right now. Maybe never. I am yet to see myself as the settling-down type. Mallory is long-term or no-term, as her dating history has proven.

So why did I just kiss her neck and why are my hands all over her? And why am I harder than a steel pipe right now? I could blame the alcohol but that would be a cop-out. I'm a big boy and I know how to handle my booze. I also have a rule, which I have yet to break, that I don't hook up with drunk girls (at least not the first time). I want their brains at full capacity so they know what they're agreeing to. Mallory is not sober. And I know she isn't agreeing to this.

That thought sobers me instantly and I start to pull away. But then she grabs my hand and presses it to her stomach again, keeping me in place. I freeze. She seems frozen too, like she may even be holding her breath.

"I... we shouldn't," Mallory finally whispers. "It's crazy."

"Stop overthinking it, Mal," Diana says, and Mallory and I pull apart instantly.

Mallory sits up, turning her head to look at Diana, who is on the other side of me on the bed, on her side with her head on her elbow. Diana looks ridiculously calm and unbothered. "He's attracted you, and lord knows you could use a great lay. Tate did you know in two years, Owen never made her come."

"Di!" Mallory barks and immediately covers her flushed face with her hands.

"Oh come on, Tate is the closest thing you have to another bestie," Diana replies, sitting up. "You confided in me, you can confide in him."

This is definitely a powder keg of complications, but yet somehow I'm doing nothing to stop the situation or change the conversation. I feel like, deep down, something is shifting between us and if I play my cards right, I'll get what I want. And what I want is Mallory. Right or wrong, I want her. Just once, of course.

"You never came with Jones?" I question, my eyes laser-focused on Mallory. Dear Lord, she looks hot as hell with her mussed hair and the spaghetti straps on her sundress hanging off her arms.

I always call her ex by his last name. I think she assumes it's just a hockey player thing, she knows we all call each other by our last names a lot, but the fact is I never liked Owen Jones enough to call him by his first. Dude irked me from day one. And they didn't date for two years. It was only twenty months. I know. I counted. Because he annoyed me.

"I did come," Mallory confesses in a strained whisper like it physically pains her to tell me this. "Just not *because* of him."

Now I find myself sitting up too. This is too interesting of a plot twist to take lying down. I turn my torso to face Mallory, blocking out Diana who is stretching her arms above her head.

"She had to play with herself or it was a no-go."

"Jesus, sober you are going to have a lot of apologizing to do to me," Mallory hisses at Diana and covers her face with her hands, again.

Diana reaches across me and tugs Mallory's hands away. "Enough with this bullshit. I'm telling you, Tate's a remarkable lay and I'm down with sharing. I mean, he's not even mine to share but if I'm what's making you say no, don't. Watching you and him could be fun."

Mallory's mouth drops open and she stares at her best friend like Diana's lost her fucking mind. I don't because Diana and I have had a threesome before. This past summer with a girl who worked at Last Call, my uncle's bar in Silver Bay. Diana is bisexual and told me flat-out, but I realize now she may never have told Mallory.

"What are you on?" Mallory asks Diana. "Because at this point, you must have taken more than a margarita to be suggesting this."

Diana laughs and I glance over my shoulder to see her hands sliding down her body provocatively until they settle between her thighs over the dress' fabric bunched there. "Life," Diana announces. "I am high on life. And I think it would be fucking hot to touch myself and watch you two mess around."

My head flips back to Mallory. And that's when I see it. The way her pupils dilate. The way her hands twist in the duvet. The way her skin gets pink and almost dewy. The way she won't look me in the eye and digs her top teeth into her bottom lip. She's turned on by what Diana said. She wants me. This. Now.

I smile and a chuckle rumbles up. The sound is low and comes out of me in a way that isn't funny. It's... feral. Finally, Mallory lifts her eyes to mine.

"Are you seriously considering this?" she whispers, a tremor shaking her tiny voice.

"Considering making my gorgeous, fun, incredible friend, come?" I ask, and a prideful smile flickers across her lips before she bites it back. "If Di is right and you didn't come from someone else's touch the whole damn time you were with Jones, I would be honored to fix that for you."

Mallory's eyes flicker to Diana and I glance over and see my bed buddy's fingertips are dancing across her thighs, on an upward trajectory to the apex between her legs.

"Mallory, eyes on me," I say in a soft but commanding voice. She obeys. "Do you want me to make you come?"

"I... but I ... I mean... you're with her," Mallory whispers, her face flaming red now.

She shifts her hips and I have to believe it's because her panties are wet. Because she wants me so bad she's already aching for it. Please, dear God, let that be the case.

Diana gets up stands at the foot of the bed, and says, her voice strong, "He wants to. I want him to. And you do too, Mal. Just admit it. Just this once."

I reach up and place my hand against Mallory's cheek. Her skin is hot and soft. Our eyes lock. I don't rein in my hormones, I let them dance all over my face—the desire, the need, the lust I've had on the back burner for her since the day we first dared to break family protocol and talk to each other at the summer town fair where both our Dads were playing in a street hockey charity tournament.

She finally sees it, and more importantly, *believes* it. But she doesn't say anything. Mallory just leans in and kisses me.

God, it's good. Needy and urgent and fuck me, if the first touch of her tongue doesn't make my blood pressure spike so fast my heart flutters in my chest. I don't think I've ever wanted anyone more. And the truth is I won't even have her tonight. Not the way I want. This has to be just a taste. It may be all I will ever get, so I better do it right.

I respond, full throttle. My hand growing possessive and wrapping into her hair at the back of her neck. I lean my whole body into her, pushing her back onto the mattress. Somewhere in my brain, I know Di is watching this, but it doesn't really register. All I can concentrate on is how good this feels.

We spend a long moment just making out, with my body over hers, my hips pushing down into her and hers pushing up into me. Her hands roam my back until they find the hem of my shirt and then she urgently tugs it off of me. When it falls to the floor, she shoves her hands into my hair and lets out this mewing sigh that lights every last hormone in my body on fire.

I grab her and move us in one bold, rough movement. Now she's straddling me, sitting up. Her eyes dart to Diana who is on the chair Mallory had been sleeping on earlier—which feels like a decade ago now. I don't want her to think about Di. I don't want her to think about anything but me and how I make her feel, so I grip one of her thighs with one hand and lean up and cup a breast with the other. She gasps and arches into my touch, her eyes snapping closed. Good. Block out your friend in the corner, baby girl, this is only about us.

I want so badly to pull down the top of her dress, reach into her bra, and pinch her nipple between my fingertips, but I don't want to expose her to Diana. I know they've been best friends since grade school, and have probably seen each other naked a million times, but this feels different. And I don't want to share my first sight of what I'm sure are Mallory's perfect pink nipples and round, perky tits with Diana.

So I fight that urge and instead slide my other hand under her bunched-up dress and press into the thin fabric of her underwear covering her hip. I hold her still and rub my hard aching cock against the space between her legs. She snaps her head down and stares at me with wide, wondrous eyes. I pull my upper body off the bed and move my hand from her breast to the back of her neck, pulling our heads together.

"You feel what you do to me, Mallory?" I move my mouth to her ear and against the shell I whisper, "Wanna know a secret? This isn't the first time you've made me hard, baby girl."

"Baby girl." She whispers it, shocked, awed, enamored. I don't give my bed buddies nicknames. It's too intimate, so I have no idea where that just came from, but I have to admit I love the way she reacted to it. "Say it again, Tate."

"Tell me I can make you come, baby girl," I whisper in between licking and sucking the column of her neck. "Tell me you want me to make you come."

"I want you to make me come, Tate."

Oh my God, this is everything. Wrong or right. Good or bad. This is everything. Her fingers lace into my hair and her hips buck against my shaft making me ravenous with need for her.

Both of my hands are under the hem of her dress now, moving swiftly, fingertips skirting the lace edging of her panties. I want to slip my hand right into them, but I fight the urge and slide around to cup her ass in my palms instead. Her butt fits in my palms like it was sculpted to be in my grip.

"You okay?" I hate myself for asking but I have to know for sure this is still okay. "Say stop if you want this to end."

"I don't want this to end," Mallory huffs out in a needy breath.

Diana giggles. She sounds far away. My head tilts and for a second I see her. She's in the chair by the window, her legs spread, her dress hiked up and fingers dipped under the thin material of her black thong.

Diana is fingering herself while her bed buddy fools around with her best friend. The reality hits me with a start but then Mallory leans down and covers my mouth with her own. Her tongue seeks out mine and all I can do is flip her onto her back and kiss her until I can't even remember my own name let alone where we are or who is watching.

My ache now is growing physically painful. I know I can't fuck her here, now, probably ever, but my dick wants what my dick wants. I'll have to give it a stern talking-to later. For now, though, I shift so I'm lying on the bed beside her, my back to Diana, and I reach for my button and fly. Mallory watches me and I can feel her tense up beside me. She might want to fuck me too, but she doesn't want it here, like this, either. "He just needs a little more space. I promise he isn't joining the party. This is about you getting off, not me."

Undoing my pants gives me some relief and my cock pushes only against the fabric of my boxer-briefs, which helps a little. Mallory is staring down at the outline of it and she reaches over slowly with her hand, a fingertip pressing into the wet spot from my pre-cum.

Her eyelashes flutter and her tongue slips out across her bottom lip as she stares with abandon. She is fucking mesmerized by my cock and I swear to God something inside me sparks and catches fire like a faulty wire burning any hesitation to ash. I grab the back of her head and yank her into another kiss. She throws her leg on my hip and I grab her ass and grind against her like my life depends on it.

This horizontal humping session goes on for a while, and by the time I move my lips to her collarbone, Mallory is panting and, like me, has lost all sanity. "Touch me. Hurry. I already feel like I might come and you haven't even touched it."

"Touched what?" I ask, panting, playing dumb, but my hand moves over her hip and dances under the edge of her underwear just below her belly button. I make sure to keep the dress from moving too much, so it still covers her from Diana's view.

"You know."

"Say it."

"Tate..."

"Say it, baby girl."

"You haven't touched my pussy," she whispers feverishly. "Please, touch my pussy. I want to come from your touch."

Mallory Echolls is my new favorite lay.

My lips bite down on her collarbone as my fingers dip into her underwear. I hear a muffled moan from the corner but I don't dare look at Diana. I don't want to think about her, only

Mallory, and the wetness on my fingers as I explore the most private part of her beautiful body.

When my first finger slips into her she moans my name in a way that I will remember for the rest of my God damn life.

I have lost all rational thought. All self-preservation. All logic. This is going to ruin everything but I'm too greedy and horny to care. I push a second finger into her and slide my thumb over her clit. "This is too good to be true," I whisper against her ear. "You're too good to be true."

Mallory responds by gripping my shoulder and lifting her hips, pushing into my hand. I rut my erection against my thigh, seeking any kind of contact I can. We kiss again, my mouth more urgent and demanding, whereas my hand is gentler but just as demanding somehow. My thumb keeps a steady rhythm of circles against her swollen clit. I have never wanted to taste a girl as badly as I want to taste Mallory right now. I want to yank those panties down, shove that dress up, and bury my tongue deep into her hot, wet heat. I want to worship her perfect cunt and let her come all over my face.

But the soft moans from the corner of the room make that impossible. Jesus, this is sexual purgatory. I'm caught between heaven, which would be having no audience and just being able to have my way with her, and hell, which would be not having Mallory at all. If purgatory is all I'm being offered, then I'm not turning it down for hell.

Her nails dig into the skin of my shoulder blades and she mews and cries my name. A whimper really. Her eyes are pinched close, her head tilted back, and I pump into her again and press my thumb into her clit, and growl in a voice I don't recognize. "Break apart for me, baby girl. And look at me when you do it. Look at me, I need you to see me. And watch when I suck you off my fingers afterward."

Her eyes fly open. So does her mouth. And a moan escapes

as I curl my fingers inside her and rub that spongy spot... the one that so many men never bother to find. She goes rigid all over and then liquefies all at once. "Tate, oh God, you... I... yes..."

I watch her writhe and pant and whisper incoherent prayers and enjoy the feel of her body pulse and pull against my fingers. My cock jerks and shudders and I punch my hips against her thigh one more time and come. I come. In my underwear. Jesus Christ this woman just made me come like a middle schooler having a wet dream.

Mallory watches as my fingers slide out of her body. She follows my hand as it travels up to my lips and I open my mouth and suck her come off my fingers. She lets out a shaky breath and I savor the only taste I will ever have of her on my tongue and wonder how it will ever be enough.

And then I feel hands on my shoulders. Diana's voice in my ear. "Boo. I wanted to taste, too."

Diana's undeniable presence is a cold bucket of water on this steamy dream we just lived. It hits me hard, and Mallory even harder judging by the way every muscle in her body tightens and she pulls away from me, scurrying off the bed like a scared kitten.

Mallory looks at Diana, blinks, and rushes into the bathroom. I turn and find Diana, her dress straps half down her shoulders, her breasts exposed, standing beside the bed. I roll off the bed and stand up. Diana cups the front of my underwear. "Ooh! What the... did you come? Was she touching you too? I couldn't see. You guys didn't give me a good angle."

I slap her hand away, less forcefully than I want to, and turn away from her, racing to do up my pants. "Diana, stop."

"Stop what?" Diana whines. "I just want my turn."

I ignore her and rush to the closed bathroom door. I lean against the frame. "Mal? Please don't freak out. Please."

The door flies open and she storms past me before I can stop her. She grabs her purse and shoes, which are by the foot of the bed and walks quickly to the door. No, not walks, jogs. *Runs.*

"Mallory! Wait!" Diana calls.

"No." Mallory's voice is hard and unfamiliar.

"Do not freak out, okay?" I say again calmly, which is absurd because my heart is bouncing around my chest like a prize fighter dodging punches and I feel so filled with panic I'm light-headed. "This was fun. That's all. No need to lose it."

"I am aware that you..." Mallory pauses and for a heart-wrenching second, I think she might cry. "I know that this probably isn't the first time you've given a woman an orgasm in front of witnesses, but it's the first time I've done... anything like this and... I just... it's not who I am. I don't... I... I regret it."

"Don't say that," Diana whines.

"I didn't... please don't say you felt forced." I think I might puke.

"No. I did it willingly and now I'm leaving willingly. Alone." Mallory yanks the door to the hotel room open. "I don't want to see... either of you again for a while."

She disappears down the hall and I stand there, filled with nausea, watching the door slowly swoosh closed behind her. I cover my face with my hands before raking them into my hair. "Fuck."

"She'll get over it," Diana promises.

But I know in my heart she won't. I know in my heart I've ruined my friendship with Mallory Echolls. And any faint, silly, far-off hope that one day, when and if I was ever ready, the friendship would turn to more.

Fuck.

Chapter 1

Tate

18 months later

I barely have my gloves off when my phone buzzes from the pocket of my suit jacket hanging behind me in my locker. I rush to grab it, but it's Conner and not my dad so I send it to voicemail and continue undressing. Nash Westwood is grinning at me from across the dressing room.

"What?" I ask, a smile playing on my mouth. "It's no big deal."

"You liar. It's the biggest deal for guys like us," Nash replies as he brushes his dirty blond hair, damp with sweat, off his forehead.

I smirk and shrug. He's right, of course. Our eyes meet and he knows I appreciate his understanding. Being the son, or daughter, of a famous athlete is a club we both belong to. Being the only son of arguably the best hockey player in the last two decades is an honor and a curse, Nash shares with his twin brother Crew. Their dad, Avery Westwood, was the league's number-one golden boy when he played. He set a lot of records that still stand today but not the record for the most short-handed goals in a season. That's held by my dad, Jordan Garrison. And, after tonight, I'm so close to beating it, I can taste it.

My phone is beeping and buzzing like it's having a software meltdown. I ignore all of it, not even glancing at it. Nash's eyes keep darting to it, though, as it bounces and buzzes on the bench beside me and I shrug. "Family group text. They're brutal when you have eight cousins, three aunts, three uncles, and two grandparents."

"And all of them know or play hockey and all of them have big opinions," Nash adds.

I grin. "Big, well-meaning but annoying opinions."

"Remind me to thank my Uncle Seb and Aunt Shayne for having puppies instead of children," Nash quips.

My phone rings again. The name on the screen is "The 'Rents". I pick up this time and fight like hell to sound as nonchalant as possible. "Hey."

"Hey my ass," Dad says, and I fucking love the sound of his voice. I always like talking to my dad. We've never even had a rough patch in our relationship. Not even when I was a cocky, brash, hormonal teenager. But now, listening to his voice thick with pride, it's the best sound in the entire world. "You are just three goals away from not just matching my record, but breaking it. You little, amazing shit. I am so proud of you."

"Three is a lot when there's only ten games left in the regular season," I remind him. I can get three goals in seven games with one arm tied behind my back, blindfolded. But this isn't about just getting goals. It's *short-handed* goals. We need to be on a power play, down one person, on the defensive, for me to score a goal that will count against my dad's record. Short-handed goals are this magical clusterfuck of circumstances, talent and luck.

"Well, if you don't score three shorties in that time, you'll have to focus your energy on getting your name on that Cup," Dad replies with a chuckle. "There are worse problems to have, Tater Tot."

"Yeah, like getting called Tater Tot at twenty-freaking-two," I complain, but I'm smiling and I know he can hear that in my voice.

"Oh to be twenty-two again and think I'm an actual grown-up." Dad laughs like I'm a toddler asking if I can drive the car. He doesn't mean it in a patronizing way. It's more whimsical like he misses being young.

"Those were the days, old man?" I ask, snarky as usual. Dad's not exactly geriatric. He's in his fifties.

"Hell no," Dad replies. "I was a disaster at your age. Ask your mother. But I was in the process of making the history you're trying to re-write."

Dad got his first short-handed goal record, tying the previous record-holder, when he was twenty-one, and then, seven years later, after being traded from the Seattle Winterhawks to the Brooklyn Barons, he beat that record by two goals and no one has beaten it since. But I'm going to.

Fifteen goals is all I need. I'm at twelve.

"What are you up to after the game?"

"Beers with the guys and food, I think," I tell him. "We have a local spot by the beach we love. They have pool tables and great wings."

"Cool. Mom was hoping you'd have a date." We both groan a little and he adds, "She means well."

"You just pointed out that's not even old enough to stop being called infantile nicknames," I say and grin. "Tell Mom to cool her jets."

"Will do," Dad says. "I'll let you go sow your oats. Just wanted to say if someone has to wipe away my legendary record, I'm happy it might be you."

"*Will* be me. And thanks Dad," I refrain from adding 'I love you' because Nash and now his brother Crew are staring at me as they peel out of the last of their gear and get ready for the showers.

"Night Tater Tot."

"Argh! Night."

I hang up and shove my phone in my jacket pocket. Nash smiles at me as he wraps a towel around his waist and walks by on his way to the shower. "I hope my dad is that big a supporter when I eventually crush his records."

"I'll let you know how he reacts when I do it first," Crew adds. They're not identical twins, although they look similar with dirty blond hair and matching brown eyes, but Crew is stockier, and Nash is taller. Crew has a wider jaw and nose and Nash has a narrow nose and he can barely grow a playoff beard whereas Crew looks like Grizzly Adams by the end of the first game. The most glaring difference is their personalities. Crew is brash and cocky and aggressive. Nash is quiet and mellow and almost shy. Crew is covered in tattoos, recently getting two full sleeves, and Nash doesn't have one. On the ice, though, they're exactly the same—skilled, fast, with an incredible slap shot, and face-off wins that always lead the league. But they haven't beat their dad's face-off record. Yet.

Nash gives Crew the finger for that comment as they proceed to the showers, and I strip out of the last of my gear and join them. A few other guys congratulate me on inching closer to the short-handed goals record and I just nod and change the subject to who wants to go out for beers and food. I don't want to jinx this by making everyone hyper-focused on it. Or acting like I care about it. Even though I do care. A lot. I scored my first short-handed goal in the first game of the season and it was somehow the easiest goal I ever scored. It just felt so simple. And then I scored another in the next game. By the mid-point in the season the media was buzzing. I was more than halfway to my dad's record. The second half of this season hasn't been so easy, but I'm still managing to score the shorties.

"What was your dad ribbing you about?" Crew asks as he turns on his shower and I step into the stall beside him.

"My mom wants me to go on dates instead of out with you goons after the games," I tell him.

Crew groans. "Oh God, I'm sorry. I'm lucky because my mom was relieved when things ended with Anne-Marie and me. She never let me know it when we were together but she thought I was too young to settle down."

"You were. You are." Crew is one year older than me. He got married at nineteen for crying out loud. No wonder it didn't last. "I don't want to settle down until my late thirties, at the earliest, if at all."

Mom might want me to settle down and fall in love and have something outside of hockey, but that sounds like a living nightmare to me. I just want to live, breathe, and be hockey. Inside and out. Sure, I have needs and urges and I meet them with very lovely, fun, willing bed buddies, which bugs Mom too. But it's archaic and misogynistic to think that women can't also want to have a primal, no-strings friend. I told her that last summer when she lectured me about Diana's potential feelings.

Diana Hutchens had no issue having a little naked fun with me. She had ambitions and priorities that were bigger than a relationship too. We got each other. We could also make each other come pretty easily. It was a great arrangement for a while. Diana never once hinted at making it more than it was. I was actually kind of bummed when her dream of moving to England panned out for her because the arrangement we had stopped. And because I never got the chance to smooth things over with Mallory Echolls, who also went to England.

Mal and Di and I were inseparable until they came to visit me in Los Angeles and Mal and I fucked around. It got awkward fast after that, even though Diana didn't care. I never got to see them again because they haven't been back to America since. Last I heard Diana was working in London for some social media marketing firm and was in an actual relationship with some guy. And Mallory was putting her early education degree to work as a nanny. I felt their absence last summer. I had emailed them both, but never heard back from either of them, so I made the best of it with a random hookup here and there.

"What are you thinking about. You look... weird," Nash notes.

"Some old friends," I mutter as I turn off the water and grab my towel. "You coming for wings or you gonna be your usual party-pooper self and go home and read a book or something ridiculous."

"Reading is life, bro," Nash says without a hint of mocking in his tone. Man, how is this guy a star forward like me? He'd be better suited to a job in a basement sorting files or, like, working at a library. If I was into setting up my relatives, I'd set him up with my cousin Mae, who we all call Mayhem. She reads all the time too and is as anti-social as him.

"Wings and beer and bonding with your teammates beats any book, bro," I say and give him a friendly shove.

"Can we order teriyaki wings?"

"Yeah. Gross but yeah."

Nash grins at me. "I'm in."

* * *

Two hours later we've consumed our weight in various wing flavors. Crew is still sweating from the Inferno sauce on his. We're ordering our fourth draft beers and Collingwood, our goalie, is trying to beat Nash at pool. Two women at the bar have noticed us and aren't even being subtle about it. Crew and I are deciding which one of us will buy them a round first.

My phone buzzes in my pocket. I've been getting a lot of group chat notifications with the family chat and the male cousins' WhatsApp group. Everyone is psyched about me inching up on my dad's record. Also, the fact that if my team, the L.A. Quake, win just half the remaining games they clinch top spot in the division going into the playoffs. This is the shit that gets my family riled up and I wouldn't have it any other way.

I glance at the messages between pool rounds but never respond because it drives some of them nuts that I don't and I love pushing familial buttons.

> TENLEY: What are you too cool to talk to us now?

> GRADY: You know my team is gonna make the playoffs too. You ain't special.

> THEO: He's special. A special kind of egomaniac. FYI I'll break your record next year kid.

I add a laughing face to Theo's comment. He's the second youngest cousin and he's been in the league for all of seven months. He's scored three goals, none of them shorties. I am *so* not worried.

And as I'm waiting for his response, which will likely be a 'fuck you', which will send his mom, my Aunt Rose, into a rant about language, I get another message. This one is from some weird number I don't know. It's not even American. It doesn't have a three-digit area code. I figure it's some kind of spam or something but I open it anyway.

> Tate? It's Mallory.

I blink and re-read it three times. I was just thinking about her earlier tonight and she's messaging me? My heart starts galloping because fuck, I've missed her. If she's contacting me, then she's no longer angry at me for that night in the hotel room, right?

> Echolls.

Echolls? Does she think I wouldn't remember her? That I have a long list of Mallorys in my life? I type back quickly.

'I don't need a last name, baby girl' is what I type out but then I erase it. Too much, too soon. Mallory is like a skittish deer on a good day and this, after what we did, probably isn't her feeling super comfortable or confident.

> I don't need your last name Mal. I've missed you! How are things? Is this a UK number?

> Yeah. I'm in London.

> Cool. With Di? You guys must like it a lot. :(
> Missed you guys here though.

It feels like a normal thing to say right? Small talk between old friends. But it also feels ridiculously awkward because we haven't spoken a word in so long that small talk isn't normal. I furrow my brow as I look at the message. Should I have said 'you guys'? She knows I'm referring to Diana, right? Does she think I want Diana again?

> Heard Di's got a BF. That's great!

There. That helps, right?

There are a few typing bubbles. Then nothing. Then Typing bubbles. Nothing. Typing bubbles.

I am coming to Los Angeles.

What? I'm immediately excited but also equally apprehensive.

Cool! Let's get together. Do you need a place to stay?

Yes. That would be good. Thanks.

Holy shit. I just went from not knowing if I would ever see Mallory again to inviting her to stay with me. Wait... for how long? And why? Why does she suddenly want to see me, but her texts are almost cold and distant like she doesn't actually want to see me.

Everything alright?

Bubbles. Nothing. Bubbles. Nothing. Bubbles. Nothing. Bubbles.

I'm fine. I have a flight booked for Thursday.

Shit. That's in forty-eight hours.

I have a home game that night and leave the next day for a road trip.

Bubbles. Nothing. Bubbles. Nothing.

"Dude! More family texts or something good?" Crew asks, grinning. "You making plans for later? What's her name? Christine again or you finally gonna score with that neighbor of yours?"

"An old friend is coming to visit," I mutter and turn my back to the boys to continue the conversation with Mallory in private.

I have to come Thursday. And I have to see you.

My stomach lurches and drops, like a kid on a swing who jumps off on the upswing.

K. Will make it work. Something wrong?

See you Thursday. Thanks.

Mallory… can you call me? Let's talk.

Can't. Will talk Thursday.

"Fuck this," I mutter and I immediately hit the call button on my WhatsApp. The phone goes straight to voicemail without even ringing. She's turned it off.

That's fucking weird. What person under the age of thirty ever turns off their phone? I get an uneasy feeling in my gut as I turn back to the guys. Nash is eyeing me thoughtfully. "You try one of my brother's taste bud-destroying wings or something? You're making a face."

"Did your booty call deny you?" Crew jokes.

"Nah that was an old friend who is coming to visit," I explain, shoving my phone into my pocket. "But she was weird about it. And we didn't exactly leave things on great terms the last time we saw each other."

"Wait. This is a female friend?" Crew's eyebrows lift. "With benefits?"

"Does Garrison have any other kind of female friends?" Collingwood quips and the Westwood twins snicker.

"Fuck off and get me a beer," I mutter and Collingwood trots off toward the bar.

Crew follows. "Let's see if those girls are thirsty too."

Nash starts racking the balls for another game. I can't get the texts with Mallory out of my head so I grab my jacket and turn to Nash. "I'm gonna head."

"Seriously? You're the one that bullied me into coming out and you're ghosting me?"

I smirk. "That's not what ghosting is, dude. And I didn't bully you, you pussy. Besides, you've got your brother and Collingwood."

I point to the bar, where Crew and Collingwood are buying drinks for the two women. "And now you've got some women too."

"Ah fuck." Nash drops his pool cue on the table and grabs his own jacket off the chair at the high-top table. "I'm out too."

I don't argue with him. I just head to the door and he follows. "Text your brother and let him know we bailed."

He nods. "I will when I get home. Trust me, he probably won't even notice. All he cares about since Anne-Marie left is getting laid."

"I guess that's to be expected after a life-changing break-up," I surmise but honestly, I have no fucking idea.

We walk together up Abbott Kinney Boulevard because Nash lives just off it, and I live on it and we've both had too many beers to drive. The owner of our wing bar will always let us leave our cars overnight. Nash looks over at me. "So why did you want to bail? You're usually Crew's wingman."

"The friend who is coming to visit," I explain. "Her text was weird. Something is up and I don't know what but, I don't know, I just lost the mood."

"She a friend with benefits like Collingwood said?" Nash asks.

"No. Yeah. I mean... once." Nash rolls his eyes and I shake my head. "I know. It was a bad decision and that's why I haven't talked to her since."

"This that tall blonde who came to visit from your home-town? The one with the short blonde friend?" Nash asks.

"It's the short blonde. Not the tall blonde."

He stops on the sidewalk, a foot from the crosswalk where he'll turn left and I will continue straight up Abbott Kinney. His brown eyes are so wide you can't see the whites at all. "Wait... you messed around with the short blonde? While you were also messing around with the tall blonde? Aren't they best friends?"

"Yes, they're friends. And no, not at the same time or anything, but Diana—the tall blonde—wasn't, like my girlfriend, and she not only didn't care she urged me to mess around with Mallory. The short blonde." I know defending myself to him is futile because no matter how I word it, it sounds bad.

"Shit, dude." Nash shakes his head and starts walking again. "You are reaffirming my decision to stay home and read instead of dating. So thanks for that."

"I wasn't dating!" I remind him. "I was in a mutually benefi-cial arrangement."

Nash stops as he reaches the crosswalk and turns to stare at me, his face growing serious. "Could she be pregnant?"

"Fuck no!" I snap confidently. "Not a possibility. At all."

"No birth control is foolproof, fool."

"Not putting your dick in someone is pretty foolproof," I reply flatly, and Nash just shakes his head and keeps walking away.

"See you at practice tomorrow, you non-penetration stud."

I make it home a few minutes later and get ready for bed. Once I'm under the covers I stare at my phone, scrolling Instagram. My account is run by an assistant who works for my agent but I also have the password. I send her photos that I think are cool and she posts things she thinks fit my brand. I just can't be bothered to do it myself. Also, I don't know what the fuck my brand is, and have no inclination to learn.

I don't follow anyone except hockey and sponsorship-related accounts, so like ESPN, Trader Joe's who I did a paid partnership with, Bauer, Under Armour, the league, and my team of course. But I know the socials of some of my Silver Bay friends and of course, my relatives who dare to be online. I scroll to those first. I don't know why, or what I'm looking for, but I feel like there's a missing piece with Mallory and this visit, and for some reason, checking in with other Silver Bay people feels appropriate.

I see nothing overly interesting from most of my relatives. Tenley posted a work shot of her behind the camera and a bunch of professional lights on some school project. My cousin Liv posted a picture of some meal she ate. Grady posted his legs bulging as he did a leg press.

"Thirst trap," I mutter and punch in Diana's account. She still hasn't posted since the day she left for England. Her last photo was sixteen months ago and it was a picture through the window of a plane, with Portland, Maine, below in the distance. The caption was "Leaving on a jet plane. Don't know when I'll be back again."

Why she dropped Insta as soon as she got to Britain is beyond me. Maybe Mallory can enlighten me when she's here. I scroll to her account and see nothing has changed. She stopped using it the weekend they came to visit. Her last post is the three of us at that Mexican restaurant we got drunk at in Beverly Hills. Right before we rented the hotel room. It's just a picture of our three hands clinking our margarita glasses together. No caption.

I drop my phone on the charger turn off my light and try to push down the uneasy feeling in my gut. Does Mallory want to tell me how hurt she was by what we did? Does she regret it? Or worse does she not and she's coming here to confess feelings or something insane? I mean, she's great. I miss her in my life, but I don't want to date anyone right now. I have one responsibility. Hockey. And that's exactly the way I want it.

Chapter 2

Mallory

I never thought that the first time I flew first class it would be with a nine-month-old, bruised ribs, and a court-ordered temporary custody agreement. But yet, here we are. And spoiler alert, if you think the angry stares you get when your child wails in economy are embarrassing, you should see the ones you get in first class.

"Dyllie Bear, these people didn't pay thousands to listen to your lungs," I whisper against his ear as I pat his back and pray to any and all powers that be for him to stop wailing.

The man in the pod-like seat across the aisle gives me a sympathetic smile. "He was excellent most of the flight."

"Thank you," I whisper back, which he probably doesn't even hear because Dylan decides to raise the decibel to migraine levels with his next scream.

Someone sighs, annoyed. I think it's the woman behind me who either has never had a kid or doesn't remember what it's like. Or maybe rich babies don't scream on flights. What do I know?

Luckily we are seconds from landing, which is probably why he's screaming. His ears are likely popping up a storm.

Dylan has had a lot of ear trouble. He's only nine months but he's had three severe ear infections. Diana and Felix were discussing possibly putting tubes in his ears.

Now that will be his father's decision. If he wants Dylan.

My eyes fill with tears and I blink them back because the last thing I need is to look as lost and hopeless as I feel. We have to get through customs and the situation is already precarious. The baby isn't mine. Dylan's mother is dead and I was given temporary custody by a foreign court. Also, Dylan doesn't have a US passport yet. The man Diana wanted to raise Dylan, the man who promised to, swore everything would be fine as he shoved a stack of paperwork, and a first-class, one-way ticket at me.

I look at Dylan's blotchy, wet face and cradle the back of his head. He's got silky blond hair. Thicker and lusher than I would have expected him to have. He hasn't lost any either like some babies do. I know the color is from Diana, but the thickness and texture are from his dad. I had my fingers laced through that hair only once in my life but I remember how thick and soft it felt.

I shake my head to rid it of the memory that has so many mixed emotions still attached to it. It was a mistake. The biggest of my life. It changed the course of everything, for Tate and Diana and me. And I've spent a good chunk of each day since that ill-fated night to think about how wrong it was. I don't think Tate or Diana thought about it much at all.

To be fair, Diana had been busy trying to string together an entirely new life for her and Dylan. And Tate was busy being the prince of the hockey rink. I googled him, for the first time in months, while I sat in the hospital bed after the crash. Tate was having an epic year on the ice. The L.A. Quake were guaranteed a playoff spot, maybe even top of their division. He's also about to beat some record his dad has held, which knowing Tate the way I do... I did... it's gotta have him buzzing with excitement and pride.

I know Tate's personal success hinges on beating his dad. It's a rivalry he takes seriously and lives entirely in his own head. Mr. Garrison would love nothing more than to see Tate crush his own career, so it's not an actual rivalry. I've always thought Tate's attitude created a slight level of toxicity. One that he should be grateful isn't there naturally, like it is in my family.

My dad also played hockey professionally. Not as long or as well as Jordan Garrison, and so I know of what I speak. My father, Chance Echolls, constantly feels threatened by my brother Emmett who plays and at the very same time makes both me and my brother Beckett feel inadequate for not being involved with, or obsessed with, hockey.

Dylan sniffles loudly. I kiss his forehead, warm with the exertion of crying, and the landing gear slams into contact with the ground. Dylan wails again. "It's okay buddy. That means we're on the ground again. Your ears will be fine soon. I promise."

They better be because we don't have healthcare here, I think to myself. We technically don't have anything.

My blood chills with the weight of what I have to do. Present Tate, my unrequited former crush, with a baby that is his, but isn't mine. A child he knew absolutely nothing about. A child I helped keep from him. And then I have to beg him to accept Dylan. Because the poor kid has no one else in this God-forsaken world.

Okay. Yeah. I'm tearing up. I sniff and blink as people begin unbuckling their seatbelts and yanking down their overhead baggage. The kind middle-aged man across the aisle leans in. "You're doing great, Mom. Do you want me to hold him while you get your bag?"

I nod, not bothering to correct him about the mom part.

This story is too horrendous to burden a stranger with. I wish I was Dylan's mom because I love him, unconditionally, just like Diana did. And if I was his mom, he would have someone. Right now, he has no one.

I quickly unbuckle as the kind man plucks Dylan from me and puts him on his hip like a pro, then stand and grab my bag from the overhead compartment. I have three extra-large suit-cases to pick up and a car seat, but I will deal with that later. I can strap Dylan to my chest for that part. The carrier is in my bag. I quickly take him back and he blabbers something in his baby language. "He says thank you for the help. You're too kind."

"I'm just kind." The guy shrugs. "You look like someone who would do the same."

If only you knew.

I smile, grateful, and he motions for me to go ahead of him as the flight attendant opens the door and people begin to disembark. I have a new task to deal with and luckily Dylan has stopped wailing. He's tired now so he rests his chubby cheek on my shoulder as soon as I get him strapped into his carrier. I didn't bring a lot of his stuff because there just wasn't room. If Tate agrees to accept him, he'll have more than enough money to buy Dylan new toys and baby items.

By the time we get to the front of the customs line, I'm almost quaking with anxiety. I mean, I'm not doing anything illegal, but I've never crossed into another country with a baby before, let alone one that isn't mine. The guy glances at us and his face lights up at Dylan's still-red face with wet cheeks and droopy eyes.

"Rough flight?" he asks and shoots me a sympathetic smile.

I nod. He takes my passport and Dylan's, which has his back stiffening because Dylan's is a United Kingdom passport and mine is American. "I'm the nanny."

I hand him the file folder the lawyer gave me at Felix's law firm. He opens it and glances at the paperwork inside. "I have to call my boss."

I nod. There's nothing else I can do. If they deny Dylan entry I will just take him back to Diana's sister in the UK. She said she couldn't take him. Told Diana flat-out not to make her a guardian or Godparent, so Diana didn't. And when she found out about the accident, and that Felix was not going to adopt Dylan like he'd promised when he asked Diana to marry him, Stephanie cried with me on the phone. "I'm pregnant with my own kid. I can't... Jonathan says it would be unfair to our baby. I'm sorry Mal. But if you want him, I will support you in the process. Adopt him yourself and we will help you. I promise."

That was tempting but also not the right thing to do. Dylan had a biological parent and I had to do what Diana refused to do when she was alive—give Tate a chance to be a dad if he wanted it.

Now I rock from foot to foot as I wait for the customs agent to return with someone who can decide what happens next. My brain goes straight into panic mode. I will not let them take him from me. There will be an international incident if they try. It would be a shame if I survived a car wreck just to die at the hands of customs and immigration, but I will risk getting shot to keep Dylan out of the system.

The customs agent comes back and hands me the documents, with an additional stamped thing he staples into Dylan's passport. "He can only be in the country for three months."

"Okay yeah."

"When do his parents join him?"

"His dad is already here," I say. "I'm delivering him and his dad is an American citizen so he'll get the baby's US passport. He was just born in the UK."

"Okay." The guy doesn't seem to give a shit, which is fine by me. "If he gets that passport, he can stay, obviously. You file the paperwork online."

Next hurdle, baggage claim. I immediately head straight for a cart, so I can load up all the bags I have to collect. But I am stopped by the crowd at the exit door from customs. It's all friends and family of the arriving passengers, and a few drivers holding signs with names. And one of those signs says Mallory Echolls.

I walk over to the guy in the black suit and cap. "Hi. I'm Mallory."

He looks at me and blinks. "Oh. I wasn't informed there would be a baby. I... I don't have a car seat in the limo."

"It's okay. I brought one," I reply and then his words sink in. "There's a limo? For me? Why?"

He smiles, and I realize this is Los Angeles. The dude has probably driven actual real-life celebrities and now he's got some country bumpkin with a baby and he thinks I'm adorably naive. "Mr. Tate Garrison hired me to drive you to the Quake Arena. You'll arrive after the game starts but apparently, if I drop you at Gate E, the player entrance, they'll escort you inside and you will be able to watch the game from the friends and family lounge."

Oh. Wow. I blink and nod and then freeze. Oh shit.

"I don't want to watch the game," I say. He stares, more confused than ever.

"Umm... okay well I was paid to deliver you to the arena."

"He didn't tell me that he was doing this."

"Probably a surprise." The driver is starting to look slightly disgruntled. "Look, I would say call him but if he's a hockey player and there's a game... I mean I don't watch hockey. I'm a basketball fan myself, but I don't think they answer phones during games, right?"

I nod. Dylan lets out a heavy, exhausted sigh. Okay so this is unexpected but the driver part is a blessing. One step at a time, Mallory, I repeat the mantra I've had echoing in my head since I woke up in the upside-down car. "Okay well, we need a cart. I have lots of bags."

He nods, drops his sign, and marches to the carts. Forty minutes later my bags are loaded in his limo, which is actually a blackout SUV, not some eighties stretch job. I had to put one of the bags in the front passenger seat because they didn't all fit in the trunk, but the driver doesn't seem to mind. I get Dylan strapped into the back of his car seat and belt myself in next to him. The ride is long because of the traffic, but the driver is nice, and after a little bit of small talk leaves me alone. He's stocked the back with water and I plug in my phone to one of his charging cables sip water and watch LA's scenery fly by.

I've only ever been here once before, but I was and still am amazed by how flat and grid-like it is. Until it isn't. Los Angeles can feel like blocks and blocks of concrete buildings and boulevards and then suddenly, bam, there's a breathtaking ocean. Or bam, there are rolling hills and jungle-like canyons. It's chaotic and beautiful, overwhelming and Zen. It's one extreme or the other, which is why I've never met anyone who says Los Angeles is just okay. They either love it or hate it.

Tate loves it, which when he first came back to Silver Bay after his rookie season, surprised me. He's a small-town Maine boy through and through but loved LA. The way his eyes lit up when he talked about it was why I agreed to go when Diana wanted to visit him. She wanted sex. I wanted to see what made his eyes light up.

"Okay, so I was told to deliver you to this gate. They're expecting you," the driver says as he pulls into the parking lot for the arena, which is in downtown Los Angeles. "I will unload the bags while you talk to security. They should have a badge for you, and the kid I guess."

"Not the kid," I mutter as I unbuckle my seat belt and reach over to undo Dylan's harnesses. "The kid is a surprise guest."

"Oookaayyy..." He clearly thinks something is utterly sketchy about this now, and I don't blame him.

I leave the driver to unload my stuff and walk to the big dude in a black security shirt at the barrier at the entrance. "I'm Mallory Echolls."

"Right. Guest of Tate Garrison." The guy nods. "Sadly you missed the whole game. The third ends in two minutes, but you can still go in and wait for him in the lounge. He will be expecting you."

He glances up at the sleeping blob that is Dylan. I've strapped him to my chest again in his Baby Bjorn. "I forgot to mention I was bringing a guest," I say.

"He's too little to get his own badge anyway," the guy replies and slides a badge at me.

I take it with tentative fingers. "I don't want to go to the lounge. Is there somewhere private I could wait for Tate?"

"I... I mean..."

Who turns down VIP access to a friends and family lounge? No one. I remember when my dad was still playing it was like a wonderland. There was a gleaming free bar for the adults and a candy table for the kids filled with bowls of colorful sweet treats. There were TVs on every wall, expensive comfy furniture. And I'm saying no. Why? Because too many people will ask questions when they see me with a baby.

A baby that undeniably looks a lot like one of their star players. Add my last name to that list of red flags. My dad and Uncle Beau played hockey and although they weren't record crushers or even Stanley Cup winners like the Garrisons, they are still active in the league. My dad is the General Manager for the Brooklyn Barons and my uncle coaches for the Quebec Nationals. And die-hard fans on message boards still talk about how

Jordan Garrison once punched Chance Echolls in an off-ice incident.

"Where do the players park? Can I wait by there?"

He twists his face up like I'm insane. "You want to wait in the garage? With your baby? Instead of the lounge?"

"Yes please."

He stares. The driver rolls my bags, with the car seat balanced precariously on one of the suitcases, over to me. The security guy's eyes widen at the pile of bags. He pulls up a walkie-talkie. "I'll get someone to help you to the restricted level where the players park. And I'll let Mr. Garrison know."

"Thanks. Appreciate it."

After a few minutes, a guy appears with a flat trolley. He stacks my luggage and ushers me into an elevator with him and my stuff. It opens onto a floor with a security guard who nods and asks me if I want a chair. He doesn't have one but he can find one.

"No thank you. I've been sitting for a very long flight. I need to stand." I smile shakily. The fact is I'm too nervous to sit. This is it. Tate is going to know the truth in a matter of moments.

I am about to blow his world up forever. Having a son might be a good thing, in the long run. I fully believe Tate will become a great, responsible dad. But right now it will feel like I'm ruining his life. He will hate me and that may not go away, ever. I own that. I accept it. I would accept anything if it meant Dylan gets to be safe and happy with a family who loves him. And the Garrisons will love him. I know my parents hate them, but I don't. I see how much they love each other. Dylan will be fine once Tate accepts him. "Please accept him, Tate," I whisper to myself.

Chapter 3

Mallory

I t takes forty more minutes for players to start trickling out to their cars. Dylan is wide awake now and fussing so I grab his trusty giraffe stuffy and sing a stupid song to him while shaking the toy and he is entertained enough not to cry. I also tuck myself behind the beast of a security guard so no one notices me.

When the door into the arena opens again and Tate walks through it, everything freezes for me. I watch him like he's in slow motion, striding confidently, a cocky smile on his lips, his rich blue and gray plaid suit hugging and tugging on all the right parts of his extremely fit body. His eyes are focused on his teammates walking ahead of him. I recognize them as the Westwood twins. He yells something at them, but for some reason, I can't hear what he says. My brain is making too much noise.

He looks so confident and comfortable in his own skin but he has never looked anything but that. I've known him since middle school when his dad retired and his parents moved back to Silver Bay full-time. He walked into school, the new kid, with a family reputation and expectation that would have weighed a lot of other kids down, but not Tate. He didn't even have the normal new kid jitters. He looked like he knew how lucky we all were for getting him as a classmate and potential friend. And man, I know I felt lucky when he finally talked to me one day and didn't blink when he found out my last name.

Dylan lets out a frustrated squeal. I've been frozen in the past, and in the present, the baby in my arms has had enough.

"Mal?"

I find the courage to look up. He is grinning that gregarious, infectious grin that he's had his whole damn perfect life. The one that says he knows he won the lottery being born Tate Garrison. Only for the first time, it doesn't make me smile back. And when his eyes slip down to Dylan that smile evaporates entirely. I watch it fade, searing it into my memory because I honestly don't think I will ever see it again.

His jaw goes slack. His face loses color. He starts towards me slowly, almost like he's scared of me. Like I'm an aggressive dog. Or, you know, his worst nightmare.

With every step he inches closer I feel my anxiety ratchet higher and higher. He doesn't know the bottom is about to drop out of his world, but I do. "You have a baby?"

"Not exactly," I reply. My voice is barely over a whisper and it's hoarse. The emotions clogging my throat are trying to tear the words to pieces before I can get them out. I blink and shake my head. Tears flood my eyes and tumble down my cheeks.

"Mallory, what the hell is going..." Tate says softly and takes another few steps. And then I pull Dylan out of the carrier on my chest and turn him so his back is against my front. His face toward Tate.

Tate stops moving mid-step. His eyes scan the length of Dylan, resting for a long moment on his chubby little face. He sees the dimple in the baby's chin that matches his own. He takes in the color of Dylan's eyes, the same green color swirling in Tate's own, that match his mother Jessie Garrison's eye color perfectly. There is a baby picture on the wall by the staircase in his parents' house. I saw it the one time I was there. It's Tate, under a year old, sitting in the Stanley Cup because his dad won it that year. If you put Dylan in that Cup today, you would have a hard time telling them apart, except for the hair color.

More color drains from his face. He's the color of chalk now. He tears his eyes from Dylan, gives the security guard a curt nod and tight smile, and with a hand on my back, he guides us away, towards the line of very fancy and expensive parked cars.

Once we are away from anyone who could overhear he asks, "Mallory, whose baby is that?"

"Di's," I croak out.

"Why do you have Diana's baby?" Tate's voice is low and hard and angry. "Is she with you?"

"Tate..." I wondered if somehow he would know. I hoped he would so I wouldn't have to tell him.

Diana's death must have hit Silver Bay by now because, although she doesn't have any family living there anymore, my family knows. It's a small town and news, especially bad news, travels fast. Silver Bay: Home to Hockey Royalty and Fast-Moving Gossip.

"Where is Diana?" he snaps as we stop and he pulls me in between two luxury SUVs.

"She died, Tate," I finally managed to choke out as I wipe at the tears on my face. "There was a car accident and she didn't make it."

Tate steps forward, his arms reaching for me. I think he's going to hug me but then his eyes land on Dylan again who is staring right at him with this look of contemplation. Like he's trying desperately to figure out who Tate is. Tate turns to me with a look very similar, only there is fear fluttering his eyelashes because deep down he is scared to know the answer to the question that flies out of his mouth next.

"Why did you bring Diana's baby here?"

I don't say it. I can't. But I don't have to. Before I can, the security guard is back. He's pushed all the luggage we left behind and is standing with it in front of the cars we're tucked between. "Sorry Mr. Garrison, but do you need me to load this for you?"

Tate nods, pulls a fob from his pocket, and tosses it to the guard. The guy keeps wheeling the luggage farther down the aisle.

"Mallory. Talk."

I open my mouth but nothing comes out. Why am I such a fucking wuss? This is hard. It's ugly and brutal but Dylan needs me to be strong, not a fucking coward. I run a hand over Dylan's thick hair and meet Tate's eyes. "You know why I brought him here. Look at him. You *know*."

"Diana... she's dead," Tate whispers and steps away from Dylan and me. He begins pacing in the narrow space between the cars. His hands rake into his hair and his eyes stay firmly on the gritty pavement.

I fight the tears pricking at my eyes. "Yes. Eight days ago."

"And you have... you have this baby..." His voice cracks and he swallows. He still won't look at us. "Why? Why do you have this... her baby?"

He wants me to lie. Say anything but the truth. I know. I almost get it. I mean, this is going to flip his world upside down. Change it forever. No matter what he chooses to do. Even if he rejects Dylan and tells me to adopt him or put him in foster care, his life will never be the same. This isn't something you move on from like an impulse buy you later return.

"Mallory!" he growls my name and stops pacing, but his eyes are still rooted on the ground. "Fucking talk."

Dylan lets out a whimper and I adjust him on my hip as I

take a small, ragged breath. "Because I agreed to bring him to his only living parent."

Tate's eyes finally snap up from the ground and lock with mine. I stare at him until the tears swimming in my eyes make it impossible to focus. "Oh my God." The words rush out of him in a hoarse whisper.

"Mr. Garrison?" the guard calls out and Tate jumps. "All this stuff ain't gonna fit in your car."

He rakes his hands through his hair again and brushes past me in the tight space. I turn and watch a couple more players walk by. They call out goodbyes to Tate and he waves but focuses on the security guard and the two bags sitting on the ground.

"Okay. I'm going to call an Uber to take the extra bags to my house," Tate tells the security guard. "Hold on."

He pulls out his phone and I slowly walk over to his car, which is a very fancy sports car. A Mercedes so sleek and low and compact I'm not even sure it has a back seat. Dylan and I may also have to ride in that Uber. If he lets us go home with him that is.

"Can you walk them up to the gate and have the gate security give the bags to the Uber with this license plate," Tate asks and shows the guard his phone screen. The guard pulls a notepad and pen out of his back pocket, jots down the plate number, and nods.

"I can go and do that. And we can take the Uber with the bags," I interject. "He has to be in a car seat. In a back seat and I don't know if you... this car has one."

"It does." Tate grabs the car seat off one of the suitcases where it is balanced. He stares at it for a second like it's an alien life force before glancing back up at me. "You know how to install this?"

"Yeah. Of course." I nod and take it from him.

The security guard walks away with the extra luggage. I walk to the passenger side and open the only door. The car only has two doors, not four, which is going to make installing this a bit of a bitch. And I can't do it with Dylan strapped to my chest or on my hip.

I look at Tate who is still the color of a bleached bed sheet. "I need you to hold him a sec."

Then I hand him Dylan, but he doesn't take him. The baby is just dangling between us. "Tate! Either hold him or I have to put him on the ground. And he can't walk yet so he's just going to sit on the disgusting pavement and cry."

Tate steps forward, puts his hands under Dylan's armpits, and holds him. Out in front of him like he's some kind of rancid garbage. Good, great. We're off to a fabulous start. Now I'm getting angry. Dylan is squirming and his little face bunches up and I open my mouth to snap at Tate but before I can he pulls his arms in and tucks Dylan against his left side. Dylan's face is still bunched up and turning red like he's about to wail. He is staring at Tate like 'Who the fuck are you stranger?' But that's fair.

I duck into the tiny back seat with the car seat and focus on getting it secured as quickly as possible. It's a bit annoying and takes longer than normal due to the cramped space but I get it done before Dylan really starts crying.

As soon as my body is upright and out of the car, Tate is handing Dylan back to me like he's a hot potato. I take the baby and smile at him reassuringly. "It's okay Dyllie Bear. We'll get you settled soon, I promise."

Tate is already getting into the driver's seat and has the engine going by the time I get Dylan strapped in and give him his giraffe for company. I scurry into the passenger seat and click my seatbelt but Tate doesn't drive out of the spot. He stares straight ahead through the windshield. A couple more players walk by on the way to their own cars.

"Tate?" I say quietly with a deep inhale. The car still has that new car smell.

He swallows so hard I can see his Adam's apple strain against the skin at his throat. Tate's eyes flick up to the rearview mirror and I know he's watching Dylan through it. "I'm his only living parent."

It isn't a question. There's no confusion in his voice. Not even shock. There is a strong tone of resignation and it both breaks my heart and brings me a weird sense of calm I wasn't anticipating. Tate may not like this, but he accepts it.

"Yes. You."

He drops his head into his hands.

Chapter 4

Tate

"Look, Tate, I don't mean to interrupt your processing. I know this is a lot," Mallory's voice cuts through the silence in the car. "But he's had an extremely long day. And a rough couple of weeks. He fell asleep and he is going to wake up hungry and disoriented and it would be best if we weren't in a car when that happens."

She is so calm about this. How? How can she be so calm? Nothing about this is anything less than a vortex of chaos. But one last brain cell, buried in the back of my head, which is rioting with this news, knows she is right. That kid deserves better, after all, he's been through and is going to continue to go through, than to wake up hungry and confused in the back of a stranger's car. And that's exactly what I am. A stranger. Even if I know, in my heart, that DNA will say otherwise. I mean... *look* at him.

My mom is obsessed with family photos. She says it's because she didn't have a real family growing up, she just had her sisters, and no one really took pictures of them. So we went, and still go, for yearly family photos. We have a wall of them in the living room, peppered across the bookcases on either side of the river rock fireplace. And there's a bunch of candid photos on the wall all the way up both staircases, the one to the second floor and the one to the attic rec room. I've stared at enough pictures of me as a baby to know this kid is a fair-haired replica of me.

My eyes were just as green at his age, the blue tint in there now came later. My cheeks just as pudgy, that's how I got the nickname tater tot because I looked as round and plump as one. And that dimple, well it's still in my chin, just like my dad's. His hair is lighter than mine was, almost wheat colored, like Diana's. His nose seems to be a miniature replica of hers too. Not only is there no reason for Mallory to lie, there's an avalanche of evidence in his appearance that she isn't.

Holy fuck. How did this happen and why didn't anyone tell me before now? All these questions need to be addressed but not here in the parking lot of the arena. We are literally the last car left. I have been sitting here with my head in my hands just trying to come to terms with this and Mallory has patiently waited it out. Until now.

I lift my head and realize she must have turned off the car. The engine is no longer running. I punch the button again and it purrs to life. Without a word, I ease out of the spot and toward the exit. Even security is gone now. I pull the pass from the center console and swipe the machine at the gate and the bar glides upward. And then, I drive the twenty minutes back to my townhome on Abbott Kinney on autopilot.

Usually, as I approach the building, just the sight of the palm trees that line the front garden area brings me peace and happiness but not tonight. I love Los Angeles. I didn't think I would as a small-town East Coaster, but I was wrong. Before I was drafted the New Englander in me thought California was an excess and stupidity dipped in ridiculousness and covered in sunshine. But it's exactly the perfect vibe for a young, rich athlete who never loved snow or cold unless he was playing a game of hockey.

Venice is where I decided to settle because it's got the beach, a banging nightlife, and a great daytime energy, and it's close to the arena and practice facility. Bonus, it's nowhere near UCLA, or West Hollywood where my sister currently lives with my cousin Liv. I love my family, but I like my independence, a lot. This two-bedroom, two-bath townhouse within walking distance to bars, restaurants, and the beach, with a bright multi-level open concept main floor and sunlit patio on the back, quaint porch on the front was worth every cent of the two-and-a-half million I paid. But is it kid-friendly? That's a question I never thought I would have to ask.

And now, as I pull into my parking spot I'm contemplating that very thought as I stare out the window again. I hear a gentle coo in the back. Was that a coo? Do kids his age coo? What age is he anyway? Oh, I am so beyond fucked.

"I get it. This is a lot. Is there any way we can go inside?" Mallory asks. Again she is insanely calm. "I need to feed him something and let him stretch his legs."

"Stretch his legs? Like, walk around? Run?" I pull my eyes from the Reserved sign nailed to the wall in front of my spot and look at Mallory—*really* look for the first time since she appeared at the arena.

Mallory Echolls looks exhausted. The skin under her eyes is puffy and holds a grayish tinge. Her eyes are bloodshot. Her hair... well she's had better hair days. "You both must be exhausted."

"Yes," she says and twists in her seat so she can see the kid. Her shirt pulls a little, exposing her collarbone, which is blue. Well, actually more of a dark, angry purple.

"Fuck. What happened to your—"

She moves like she's been jolted with electricity, quickly

facing forward and yanking at the collar of her shirt and then she winces. Loudly. But she changes the topic. "Tate. He needs to get out of this car. He needs space and food. And no, to answer your earlier question, he isn't walking yet. He's only slightly over nine months old but he can pull himself up to a standing position and he loves to do it and kind of bounce. Like he's listening to music we can't hear."

"Oh. Okay. Yeah. I mean, I can let him bounce," I say stupidly because I have been rendered absolutely brain-dead by this news.

Like a robot, I get out of the car. Leaving their suitcases, I walk around to the trunk and grab her shoulder bag as she gets him out of the car seat. "I'm going to need the other suitcases the Uber was supposed to deliver."

"Ray should have them."

"Ray?"

I point to the small box-like building by the entrance gate. "Our night security guard for the complex."

I leave her by the car and jog over to the booth. Ray is happy and friendly, like always, and I try not to cut off his small talk too much. He glances out his booth door as he hands me the suitcases. "You want me to bring these to your door?"

I shake my head even though, yeah, that would help since I have two other suitcases in the car. But then I have to introduce him to Mallory and the kid, and I would lie. Say this is my friend and her kid and that feels shitty and also, if he catches one look at the kid... "I'll do it. My friend just got here from Europe and she's... they're exhausted."

"Okay. Well, have a great night, Tate."

"Thanks. You too, Ray."

I walk back over to Mallory, wheeling her suitcases beside me. She has the kid on her hip now and she's staring at me. Her bottom lip quivers. "Look, I don't know where you're at with all of this. I don't think you even know, so let me focus on what I do know."

The palm trees rustle in an ocean breeze as traffic zooms by on the busy, popular boulevard on the other side of the gate. She takes a breath that I can see, even from a few feet away, is shaky. "I have nowhere else to go right now. Eventually, I will make my way to Silver Bay, once Dylan is settled, legally. I don't have much money that is mine. Diana's former fiancé gave me some money to get him settled, for my troubles he said, but I'm trying not to spend it so Dylan can have it, as a trust or whatever. And I have paperwork for him that I can pass on to you so you can organize custody. If you don't want him... well, I can help you deal with that, but I can't do that tonight. So can we please just stay with you? Just tonight?"

Wow. I thought this development had knocked me on my ass but her speech was a drop kick on top of a roundhouse. "You can both stay with me as long as you need to. Without question. Did you really think I was going to send you away?"

"I don't know what to think about anything anymore, Tate," Mallory confesses, her voice weary.

"Come on."

The entrance to my townhouse faces the interior courtyard of the building. It's a few feet from the freeform pool, which thankfully is gated. Unattended pools and babies don't mix, even I know that. As we climb the stairs to my front porch, I pull open the storm door, unlock the main door, and instantly realize there isn't much about my space that works for a nine-month-old.

There are stairs off the entry down into the living room and dining room. The kitchen is open to the rest of the space with top-heavy bar chairs he could tip over. Nash once got hammered and tipped over in one so I'm sure the kid could knock it over.

I'm not a slob, and I have a maid that comes once a week so the place is clean, but are there sheets on the guest bed? Have they been changed since Crew hooked up with some girl there two weeks ago, too drunk to make it home to his house at the Venice Canals? Did I tell my housekeeper about that? Because she doesn't tend to do more than dust the guest room unless I tell her I've had or am having guests. I can't be sure I've told her, all of a sudden. I definitely didn't tell her Mallory was coming because I didn't get a chance.

Mallory brushes by me, familiar with the space because it's where she and Di stayed when they visited, and scoops a suitcase from my hand. The brush of her fingertips is cool and brief. With one hand around the kid's waist on her hip and the other on the suitcase she walks straight into my living room and gets to work.

She plops him on the floor and hands him a toy. She opens the suitcase while he plays and starts pulling out stuff. Juice packets and baby food in jars, all bubble-wrapped. I watch, amazed and stunned, waiting for her to tell me what to do. I wish someone could tell me how to *feel* about all of this.

"If you keep him, we will have to baby-proof this place," she surmises and it feels almost like she's making an internal thought to herself public and not telling me, specifically. "I can help you before I leave."

"Yeah. I... I mean I have bigger things to sort out than baby-proofing, right?" I sound as panicked as I feel and she stops on the way to the dining room and turns back to me. She's holding this seat contraption with, like, poles sticking out of it that she pulled out of the suitcase. "Like, I mean, how do I keep him. Legally? Am I even on his birth certificate?"

"No. No one is listed as the father," Mallory says as she marches to my dining room table, slides a chair out of place, and replaces it with the contraption in her hands. Is it a... seat? It doesn't look all that safe but I trust she knows what she's doing.

"Mal, this is all... I can't... I mean what the fuck?" I swallow and start to feel lightheaded, which it takes me a second to realize because I have never been lightheaded a day in my life. "Were you just going to keep this a secret forever if Di didn't..."

"It wasn't my secret," she reminds me, her tone defensive.

"Was she never going to let me know?"

"I don't know," Mallory admits and sighs. "I was... encouraging her to tell you before Felix adopted him."

"Who the fuck is Felix?"

"Diana's fiancé," Mallory replies.

"He wanted to adopt my..." I can't say it. "Where is he now?"

"In London. Grieving, I guess," Mallory's tone sounds less than empathetic. She shakes her head as if dismissing a thought before she can express it. "He loved Diana and he wanted to be Felix's father, but I guess not without her. But he got us here. He made sure I got Dylan to you."

"Well, fuck him," I mutter, not sure if it's because he was going to steal my child or because he changed his mind and dumped him when he needed someone the most. "Whoa!"

I swear we just had an earthquake. Everything starts to move to the left, like the *entire* room.

The next thing I know Mallory's grabbing my shoulders, tightly, and guiding me down onto one of the couches. "Just sit there and take some deep breaths. Do you want me to call anyone? Tenley?"

"No!" Okay, that flew out of my mouth with the force of a jumbo jet taking off. Mallory looks appropriately shocked. I lean back into the couch and close my eyes. "Sorry. I just. Yeah. I need to process."

The kid lets out a wail. "You do that. I'll feed him."

I don't respond. I just sit there, head thrown back, eyes closed, and think. This is actually happening. This kid is mine. Diana never told me. Not one fucking word. Where has she been this whole time? What was in London that was more important than telling me about my offspring? Or letting me meet him before this? If she hadn't died, would she have told me about him, like, ever?

And how the hell do I tell my family about this? About him? And how the hell do I travel for work if I have a kid? And no wife? And who is even going to let me have him? Is it just, like, a given? Because I share his DNA? I must need paperwork or something, right? Oh God, what the fuck do I do?

I hear some gurgling and giggling and open my eyes to see Mallory sitting next to the kid at the table, facing the living room. He's in the contraption hanging from the table. His legs are swinging and he's grinning with green crap all over his cheeks. The green crap is from a jar that Mallory is shoveling into his open waiting mouth with a smile on her face. She looks... well still as exhausted as she looked before but also happy. Content.

"Can you tell me how this happened?" I ask.

She keeps her eyes on the baby as she wipes his face with a paper towel and shakes some rice puffs from a small container onto the table. His chubby hands grab them immediately and he brings them to his open mouth. "Well, you and Diana had sex. A lot of it, and I guess you weren't always safe."

"We were. As far as I know," I reply quickly. She frowns and glares at me with the wide-set hazel eyes. "I mean we used condoms. We had two break, but she said she was on something."

"She was," Mallory admits. "But that time we came to see you out here..."

The memories flick through my brain like snapshots. Most

of them involved that last night where we did things that maybe we shouldn't have.

"That was... a great weekend. Mostly. Except you getting weird at the end," I mutter and I know the second I say it I shouldn't have.

"Sorry I couldn't cope with fooling around with my bestie's boy toy while she watched," she snaps. "Anyway, he was conceived that weekend. Diana had just gotten over a sinus infection. Just finished a course of antibiotics and so her birth control was weakened. Some drugs do that. Of course, she didn't figure that out until she got a positive pregnancy test the day before she moved to London."

"Oh." I take a deep, slow breath and look at the back of his blond head, and his chunky legs swinging in contentment as he eats his rice puffs. "And she went anyway? Without even telling me?"

"Diana had a job waiting for her in London and her sister, and she knew I was moving there too, and she wasn't going to give that up to tell you about a baby she thought you didn't want."

"And now she's... gone and I'm a dad."

"If you choose to be, yeah."

I glare at her now. "I don't have a choice. It's fact. He's mine, right?"

"Yes."

"Then I'm his dad."

"Dads are more than sperm donors," Mallory counters. "And you didn't ask for this."

I stand up and run my hands through my hair, still damp from a shower. A shower that feels like it happened a lifetime ago. I was joking with the guys, high off the win and the anticipation that I would beat my dad's record. I scored yet another shorty tonight. Now smashing the record is a mere two goals away. One if I was just to tie with Dad, which wouldn't be horrible.

And now... I'm sitting here with a long-lost frenemy and a child. My child. "Diana didn't ask for it either, but she kept him. And I would have stood by that decision and been there for him and for her if she had fucking told me. Why didn't she tell me?"

Mallory's face softens with compassion. So she doesn't totally hate me, I guess. Or at least she can relate to how I feel. "She knew that you would be there for her, but that it wasn't what you wanted. Or needed. She knew what she was and wasn't to you, and she didn't want to force you into making her into more than what she was just because of Dylan."

"Dylan," I say my child's name for the first time. It feels weird on my tongue. I hate that it feels weird. I like that his name is Dylan though. It's nice. "Why didn't *you* tell me?"

Mallory frowns. "Diana and I... we both moved to London at the same time but not together, as we originally planned. I didn't talk for a while after the weekend here. I changed my flight so we were on different ones. I didn't reach out to her. I ignored her emails. By the time I knew about Dylan, she was all settled into this new life, with a fiancé who said he wanted them both. She did promise me she would tell you this summer. Before the paperwork with Felix was signed in case you did want to claim parental rights. She promised me she would give you the option."

"When's his birthday?"

"July twenty-fourth."

I nod. My son's birthday is July twenty-fourth. What was I doing while he was entering the world last summer? I was in Silver Bay. I was probably at my uncle's bar, joking around with my cousins, drinking some beer, or maybe playing golf with my dad and uncles. I was doing nothing of any kind of importance and something incredibly important was happening without me. I have a wave of anger toward Diana that is drowned out only by a wave of guilt. Whatever her reasons for doing this to me, she's gone and she didn't deserve to have her life cut so short. God, this is so fucked.

Dylan lets out a bit of a high-pitched noise and slaps his hands on the table. "Okay Dyllie Bear, just need you to drink more for me, okay?"

She hands him a bottle she has filled with what looks like milk. I have no idea when she got that. Did she bring milk from England? Mallory must see me eyeing it, confused. "Powder formula. He was still being breastfed but... well, she was weaning him anyway."

Oh my God. She's dead. Diana is dead. The revelation keeps pounding me, like a hammer. I just stare as Mallory goes about unpacking other stuff from her suitcase. She glances up at me. "He's going to need to go straight to bed after this, to try and regulate him to this time zone."

"I don't—I have a guest room but, like, no crib."

"Of course you don't." She smiles, but it's not happy. It's full of woe. "I have a portable sleeping pod for him."

"A what?"

"It's like a crib-tent thingy." She doesn't elaborate further. "It's in the yellow suitcase still in your trunk."

"I'll go get it now." She winces as she picks Dylan out of the chair thingy. "Are you okay?"

"Yeah," she says, focusing her attention on Dylan and wiping his face with the paper towel she's holding. "It's just been a long flight. And day, and well, it's been a long everything for the last eight days."

I nod and walk up the stairs to the entryway and grab my keys off the console table. "I'll be back with your bags in a second. The guest room is second door on the right. It has an ensuite. Make yourself at home."

"I remember," Mallory replies. "Thanks."

Right. I nod and head out the door and she heads upstairs. I grab both suitcases and head back toward the house. I'm moving on autopilot. I bring them inside and straight upstairs. Mallory is in the bathroom, the door slightly ajar and I hear Dylan making noises and splashing sounds but I don't go in. I leave the suitcases in the bedroom and go back downstairs where I clean up the mess he left on the table and then bring her other suitcase upstairs.

Then I head into my room and change out of my suit. I'm accomplishing tasks without thinking about what I'm actually doing. My head is still swimming with confusing, painful emotions.

"Oh. Oops!"

I turn to the door. I'm wearing nothing but sweatpants, having peeled out of everything, including my underwear, and not having managed to get a shirt on yet. I didn't close the door to my room because I never close the door to my room. I live alone. Or at least I did until twenty-five minutes ago.

"Mallory, you've seen me in less," I remind her, which once again was a mistake judging by the dark look that suddenly blankets her delicate features.

"Can you please close your door while I'm here?" she requests calmly but also coolly.

"Yeah. Of course." I clear my throat. "Where is he?"

"Crashed out in his sleeping pod," she informs me and motions for me to come into the hall.

I grab a T-shirt out of my dresser throw it on and join her in the hall. The door is cracked to the guest room and I glance in and see what looks like a little mini tent. "These things are genius," Mallory informs me. "They have a built-in battery-operated camera with a microphone too so I can... we can keep an eye on him and hear him if he makes a noise. The app is on my phone but I can put it on yours too."

"Okay. Maybe, like, tomorrow?"

She nods. We stare at each other in the dimly lit hallway. "Okay. Well, I am going to go to sleep, if that's fine," she announces.

"Yeah. Whatever you want," I say.

She stares at me another full second and then disappears into the guest room and I panic.

"Mallory!" I whisper her name as loudly as I dare. The door opens a crack and one of her hazel eyes is staring at me. "The sheets... need to be changed in there. I had some guests and... I forgot to change them. Let me grab a new set."

I rush to the small closet in the hall with the extra sheets and grab a gray pinstriped set. I walk back over to the door which she's opened a little more. Just enough to take the stack from me.

"I can put them on," I volunteer.

"I've got it. See you in the morning," she says and shuts the door firmly. I hear the lock click and for some reason, it feels like an insult.

But I have bigger things to deal with. I'm a *father*. And, despite having hands-down the best dad in the world, I never took notes. I don't know how to be a dad myself. And then it hits me, I'm going to have to tell my family. And that's when I find myself kneeling in front of my toilet puking my guts out.

Chapter 5

Mallory

I'm dreaming when Dylan's cries wake me up. It's more of a nightmare actually. I'm unable to get air in my lungs. My chest feels like it's caved in. My head is pounding and my shoulder is aching. Diana is making an awful gurgling sound beside me, but I can't turn my head to see her. She keeps pushing out the same words. "Dylan. Help. Dylan. Help. Mal. Help. Dylan. Promise."

That dream is not new and it's not, sadly, made up. But the part of the dream where, instead of a set of policemen rushing toward the car, there is one man. Tate. And he looks right at me through the cracked windshield and says, "Stay."

And then Dylan's cry gets shrill and I bolt up from the tangled mess of sheets, sweaty and confused. "Coming Dyllie Bear."

I shove the sheets off me and get him out of his sleeping pod. He is warm and still groggy and wraps his pudgy arms around my neck and nuzzles his face against mine. My heart hurts, and it's hard to breathe but not from my lingering injuries or the terrors of my sleep. Because I'm going to have to leave this kid, and I love him so much.

I was there when he was born, holding Diana's hand and motivating her to push. I cut his cord for her. I've been his one and only nanny, although Diana refused to call me that in front of him. She called me Auntie Mallory. My eyes get damp. I miss her so damn much. Dylan tugs on my hair. Snuggle time is over. He wants breakfast.

"Okay. I'll get you some food," I promise and lift him to sniff his diaper. "But first things first."

As I lie him out on a towel and change his diaper, I hear a noise in the hall. Tate must be up. The heavy awkward feeling that filled me last night comes back full force. God, this is not at all how I'd hoped to see him again. I mean, to be honest, there were times when I hoped to never see him again, but I knew that would be impossible. Like it or not, I would end up back in Silver Bay eventually. My family isn't the most functional, or likable at times, but they're mine and I love them and the little town I grew up in. Unlike Diana, I didn't have any intention of living in England forever.

I figured one day Tate and I would run into each other once I moved back home in a few years. I was hoping I would be over everything that transpired on that night in that Four Seasons hotel room by the time our paths crossed. My cheeks flame as I think back on it. In this fantasy reunion, I'm engaged to some perfect, dashing man, and happy, and I don't turn pink at the thought of Tate, and what almost happened. And what *did* happen. When I'm tipsy, or feeling particularly desperate, the fantasy is that I'm not engaged. I'm single and he is thrilled by that and tells me he wants me, still —in all the ways I want to be wanted, not just the physical way.

I pick up Dylan now and smile at him. "Okay, let's hope there are eggs in this place. I know it's your favorite."

I throw my cardigan over my pajamas for a little bit more modesty, even though it's not remotely cold here, and head downstairs. Tate is sitting at the dining room table staring into a cup of coffee that looks untouched. He doesn't move a muscle as I walk from the stairs to the dining room.

"Morning."

"Hey. Everything go okay last night?" He still sounds shell-shocked, but that isn't surprising.

"Yeah. He sleeps really well, in general," I explain. "Has since he was two months old."

"Must get that from me," Tate murmurs. "Mom says she used to have to wake me up to feed me. I slept more than a geriatric cat. I still love my sleep."

"Who doesn't?" I smile a little but he doesn't look up from his coffee to see it. And he doesn't look at his son. "Do you happen to have eggs? Any veggies in the house?"

"He eats eggs?"

I nod even though he still isn't looking up. "Yeah. Eggs, veggies, pasta without sauce, drinks a little juice, water, and milk too but we need to keep giving him a bit of formula to help ween him off the breast. I don't want to end that abruptly. The formula is a good substitute."

"Okay." He reaches for his phone, which is on the table, and I frown, not sure what he's doing. "Every veg or only certain ones? Does he like cauliflower because I hate it."

"He doesn't like cauliflower actually," I reply. "Or asparagus. But he loves broccoli and carrots and is kind of indifferent about peas and peppers. He hates oranges. Adores pears."

"Cool," Tate says, but it doesn't actually sound like he thinks it's cool. "I have eggs and some veggies. Help yourself to anything."

He goes back to typing on his phone and I fight the urge to ask him what he's doing and head into the kitchen.

With Dylan on my hip, I get busy poking around Tate's immaculate space trying to find all the ingredients I need. Then, before I start cooking, I walk out of the kitchen and settle Dylan on the ground in the living room. I place him on his back and put his hanging toy apparatus above him. He giggles and reaches for the plush crane toy swinging above him.

Tate is watching us and typing on his phone intermittently. I stand up and stare at his glass and brass coffee table with all the sharp corners. "Can we move this somewhere else? Dylan needs the space and he's started pulling himself up and he might hurt himself on this."

"Sure. No problem." Tate types on his phone.

"Can you pay attention please!" I bark and his head snaps up, aquamarine eyes on me with guilt swimming in them. "I'm sorry if that's your girlfriend or whatever."

He twists his face in confusion and shakes his head with a huff of laughter. "You don't know me at all do you?"

"Still the chronic bachelor?"

"Of course," Tate says like I'm insane for thinking that might have changed. "And for the record, I'm not texting anyone. I'm taking notes."

He holds his phone screen out to me and I blink to make sure my eyes on playing tricks on me. The note is titled Baby How To. And he's got stuff like Cauliflower = no. Carrots = yes. Can pull himself up. Hide sharp-angled crap.

I almost smile at how ridiculous it is, but he did it in earnest so it would be cruel to laugh. He's trying. And now he's tossed his phone on the couch and is bending to grab the bulky, heavy coffee table all by himself. "Wait, I can..."

I stop speaking and just watch him as he squats and lifts it all by himself. Every muscle in his arms flexes. His veins pop. His ass flexes hard against the fabric of his sweatpants. And damn, it's hot. I can do nothing but stare as he somehow manages to carry it all by himself up the three stairs to the landing. He places it on the ground there. "I'll bring it out to the storage locker I have at the back of the building, next to my parking spot."

"I can help with that after I feed him."

He shakes his head. "You just work your magic on his food. And please, can you write down the recipe for me for whatever you make? In my notes app?"

"Yeah."

"Password is 2-0-2-4-1-5."

And then he shoves his big feet into some shoes, opens the front door, and disappears with the coffee table again. I take his phone off the couch, make sure Dylan is still occupied, and head back to the kitchen. I can't believe he just gave me the password for his phone. Who does that?

Tate Garrison. That's who. I shouldn't be surprised. Tate has always been the most authentic, honest person I know. He has never pretended to be someone or something he isn't. That's why I'm the fool here. I was the faker. I pretended I wasn't attracted to him. I pretended it didn't bother me when my best friend started sleeping with him. I acted like I was down with non-committed orgasms with an audience. It nearly cost me my friendship with Diana and it definitely damaged my friendship with Tate.

I shake my head, trying to clear the bad memories as I finish mixing up some formula in his bottle and walk over, pick up Dylan, and place him in his travel highchair. I hand him the bottle and he immediately starts sucking. I head back to the kitchen to dice some chives and spinach I found in Tate's fridge for the omelet. I keep tabs on Dylan through the breakfast bar opening that looks directly into the dining area.

I reluctantly open Tate's phone. Thankfully the notes app is still open so I don't see anything else on his device. Not a call history, names, or text messages, nothing. I don't want to know what is going on in Tate's life. I just want to settle Dylan and get the hell out. I jot down step-by-step instructions like he's never made food himself before, which I know he has.

By the time the omelet is made and broken up in a Tupperware I place in front of Dylan, I'm deep into two new notes for Tate. I make a list of things he needs to buy for this place for Dylan and a list of things he needs to baby-proof. This townhouse is quite possibly the worst place I could imagine for an infant about to start walking. So many stairs and virtually no outdoor space. If I were Tate, I would move. But I'm not and that's too big a suggestion to make. If he asks my opinion I'll tell him though.

Where the hell is Tate anyway? It shouldn't take that long to store a coffee table. As Dylan finishes his omelet I wet some paper towels and clean up his face and hands. Tate's phone rings and I see a WhatsApp video chat request come up with this dad's name. A jolt of panic hits me and I take Dylan and back away from the phone like it's dangerous. It is. I don't want to hit the wrong button by mistake and end up face-to-face with Mr. Garrison. That is *not* how his dad can find out.

I decide to go outside and hunt down Tate. With Dylan on my hip, I walk out the front door. Southern California hits me full force. I have only ever been here once before, but the feel of the Los Angeles heat is unforgettable.

It's barely nine in the morning and it's hot. Not sweat-inducing but close. The traffic is zipping by at a relentless rate on Abbott Kinney just past the metal fence and palm trees. The air swirls with scents of tar from the heated pavement and salt from the ocean a few blocks away. And yeah, it's hot but the sky is full-on slate gray. Tate told me, that first morning Diana and I visited, that the locals call it June Gloom, but that it's actually year-round in the coastal areas like Santa Monica, Malibu, and Venice. I liked it. I still like it.

I see him wedged in between the bumper of his fancy car

and the closed door to the storage locker. His shoulders are hunched and… moving. "Hey."

He startles. His hands move up to his face but he doesn't turn to face me. "What?"

Did he just snap at me?

"I was just wondering if you needed help," I lie, my tone a little sharp but nothing like his. "You've been gone a while. Where is the table?"

"Already in the unit," he barks. *Barks.* Yeah, I am not deserving of this attitude.

"Well, your dad tried to video chat you," I add.

Now he spins to face me. He looks… weird. His skin is… red. From the exertion of dealing with the table by himself? But something twists in my gut.

"Tell me you didn't answer it."

"No," I spit out, confused by the fact that he is still coming at me like an angry animal. All bite and bark. "I am not going to be the one to tell your parents about any of this."

"Neither am I," he replies, and before his words even register he brushes past me.

"What?" I heard what he said, I just can't believe it. I start to follow him back to his townhouse. A car pulls into the parking and slowly drives past. It's a cherry red Porsche. I swear everyone in Los Angeles spends more on their cars than the average American makes in a year. "What do you mean you aren't going to tell them? Today? Or… ever?"

Tate keeps stomping toward his house. I follow, ignoring the rustling palms, the hot air blowing them, and the sun finally trying to push through the gray haze above us. Tate's hair has a rusty tint to it when the sun hits it a certain way. He gets that from his mom who has auburn hair. "I can't lock him away in a dungeon and pretend he doesn't exist, Mal. So obviously they'll find out eventually. Everyone will."

"So when?" I demand as we round the corner on the flag-stone path and reach the steps to his front patio.

Tate stops and turns to face me. He's much taller than me. It wasn't always the case. Back in fifth grade, I was taller than him by half an inch. I miss those days when my biggest worry was my crush was shorter than me. Instead of whether this gorgeous, talented, rich man was going to reject this child I love so much. And how I was going to get over losing my best friend. And what the hell I was going to do next with my life. And if my ribs would ever stop hurting or my head would ever stop pounding. I've had a low-grade headache since the accident.

"I... I will... tell them. Everyone. I just need..." Tate's stuttering pulls me from my reverie. "I just need to figure some stuff out. And a lot is going on right now with the team and my career."

"Sorry, his mother couldn't die at a more convenient time."

Yeah. I said that. And as soon as it comes out of my mouth I regret it. His face goes ghost white and his light eyes somehow darken and his whole body goes rigid. And I open my mouth to say something else, but I have no idea what to say so it just hangs open, wordless. He turns and storms into his house, not bothering to wait for us. I throw open the metal storm door and step inside, pausing to lock it because that's who I am. He is standing in the middle of the living room just staring straight ahead at nothing. He's breathing so heavily I can see the rise and fall of his chest across the room.

"You can keep judging me, Mallory," Tate says, his voice so hard and venomous it's unrecognizable. "I can learn very easily not to give a fuck about you or your opinions of me, so do your worst. But the fact is, this is a catastrophic level of shock and I am doing my best to figure out how to cope with it. You don't like it, then perhaps you should have picked up the fucking phone and told me I was a father before showing up here.

74

Before Diana died. Before he was even fucking born. I had a right to know *before* this."

The guilt I feel over my comment grows as heavy and thick as concrete in my gut. "I begged her almost every day to tell you until she told me if I kept asking she would never speak to me again."

"*You* could have told me."

"It wasn't my place." I swallow and feel tears sting the corners of my eyes. "Her body. Her baby. Her choice. I know you know that."

"I wouldn't have asked her to get rid of him," Tate snaps, and now his eyes look glossy like he's fighting his own tears. "What the fuck, Mal. Do you think I would have done that? I just... I would have been there."

"She had found someone else." My ribs are starting to ache from holding Dylan who has been extremely patient throughout this. I move to put him back on the floor, by his toys, but the motion makes me wince as sharp, stabbing needles of pain attack my side.

"What is wrong with you?" Tate asks. "You wince a lot."

I turn to face him. "It's nothing."

"Clearly it's something."

And then his phone rings. He breaks our little stand-off to walk into the dining room where I left it on the table. His eyes flare as he glances at the screen. "I have to take this."

"Is it your dad?"

"Yeah," he replies and without another word leaves us and charges upstairs.

I hear his bedroom door close more forcefully than necessary. I bet he's locked it too. Because he thinks I'm some kind of raging lunatic that will, what? Barge in there and reveal his secret like some trashy ex on an episode of *Jerry Springer*? A show my mom still watches when repeats are on late at night after she's had a huge fight with my dad and spends her night on the couch in front of the TV. That happened every couple of weeks of my childhood.

I sigh and lower myself to the floor to play with Dylan. That's when I realize he's got his face all scrunched up and his cheeks are pinking. His tells that he is dropping a post-breakfast poop in that pristine diaper. I let him finish the task and then lift him up immediately and start toward the stairs. "Whew! That's quite the stinker, Dyllie Bear."

I feel my eyes watering and pray I have enough wipes left to clean this up. I remind myself to make a list of everything I need and ask Tate to pick it up, or at least take me to a drugstore or Target so I can get the stuff myself.

I place Dylan on a towel on the bed, next to a new diaper and my remaining wet wipes. Oh boy, it's his worst poop yet and I quickly go through all the wet wipes, but I get the job done. As I'm wrapping the new diaper on him he squeals in delight. I smile and fight the urge to shush him. I am not going to teach him to hide because his dad is too scared to admit he exists.

I pick up Dylan, ignoring the pain in my side, and put him on my other hip and carry him, and the toxic waste that is his diaper, into the bathroom. I toss it in the ridiculously small garbage and make a note to add a proper disposal for diapers to my list for Tate.

When I enter the bedroom Tate is there, looking pissed off. "You had to come up here? You couldn't keep him quiet downstairs? My dad heard him!"

"He needed a diaper change and the supplies were up here," I explain, anger simmering like boiling water under my skin. "He gets excited when he gets a new diaper. He hates being dirty. Loves being clean. And fuck you for shaming me for tending to your son."

"I didn't mean it that way it's just—"

"You're hiding him. I'm not," I snap. "And I won't make him ashamed for existing because you are ashamed—"

"I'm not ashamed!" Tate yells so loud it bounces off every corner of the room and I swear the walls shake.

He turns and storms out of the room as Dylan bursts into tears. Tate scared the shit out of him, and me if I'm honest. Tate has never been anything but the fun, easy-going, golden boy that he was born to be. Even in games, and I've watched a lot of his games both when he was a junior and as a pro. I have the NHL Network app just so I can watch him, even in England. My parents and Diana thought I had it for my brother Emmett, but I never missed a Quake game. And even on the ice, when pests try to mess with his game, try to force him to get angry and throw a punch, or try to take a swing at him, he just smiles. Literally grins, like he's just been told the best joke ever. He doesn't engage, ever. Nothing gets under Tate's skin. Except me, apparently.

I bounce Dylan in my arms give him soothing words and head into the hall to find Tate and fix this, somehow. I assume he went downstairs but I didn't hear his footsteps on the stairs. His bedroom door is open and the light from the bathroom is spilling out and glancing off the hardwood floor.

Dylan's face is buried in my neck, making it damp with his tears, as I rub his back. But he's stopped wailing and now I can hear a different sound. Something deeper, more anguished. Ashamed. I follow the sound into Tate's bedroom.

It smells so much like him in here it's like a punch to my heart. His woodsy aftershave. His crisp deodorant. It floods my brain with memories of the night I buried my face in his neck, threaded my fingers through his thick hair, felt his skilled fingers between my legs.

My skin heats. And then I turn to look in his bathroom and everything gets cold. Tate is standing there facing the marble vanity. His shoulders slumped and shaking, his face tilted down, his hands in balled fists on the countertop. Tears leaking out of his shut eyes. He's crying. No sobbing.

I rush to him and touch his shaking back with the flat of my hand not holding Dylan. "I'm sorry."

"No. Don't," he chokes out and tries to move away from me. I grab onto the fabric of his shirt, trying to hold him in place. It works even though I know he could yank free if he wanted to.

"I'm sorry, Tate. It's going to be okay," I promise blindly.

"I can't do this alone," he confesses hoarsely. "Please don't leave. Please. I promise I won't... I'll do my best for him but I just... please help me."

He turns his head toward me finally, fixing his watery bloodshot eyes on me. Dylan is still whining and fussing in my arm and he reaches out and cups the back of his son's head, gently threading his fingers through his downy hair. "I'm gonna do right by you, Dylan. I promise."

All the fury confusion and pain in me just melts into a puddle of nothing. Because none of it matters. All that matters is helping this amazing man be an amazing father. I step closer to him and he steps into me, wrapping his arms around both me and Dylan.

With Tate's head on one shoulder and Dylan's on the other, my neck now saturated by both their tears, I fight my own and vow, "I've got you both. I promise."

Chapter 6

Tate

"Garrison!" Coach Braddock barks as I hop over the boards to take my spot on the bench. "Can you get your brain in the game now, for fucksake!"

I give him a solid nod. Crew shoots me a wary glance as he hops over the boards with Nash. I've been playing so shitty this game that Coach moved me off their line. We are the first line of forwards, the three of us together. Nash and Crew are in their own battle for the most face-off wins this season. I am their trusty winger. Coach loves to put me on right-wing because I'm a leftie and it fucks with the other team's defense. But I've made not one but two sloppy passes this game, which caused a turnover and I've taken two penalties—hooking and slashing. One of the penalties gave the Barons a goal to add to their four-two lead.

It's not just my worst game of the season, it's probably the worst game of my professional career. And tomorrow I have to leave for a road trip. The first since Dylan and Mallory showed up in my life five days ago. The adjustment to having a son is why I'm playing like garbage. He's doing this thing now called sleep regression and he's been waking up at all fucking hours.

Mallory is sharing a room with him, so she handles it, but it wakes me up. That boy has some serious lungs on him. Also, because I need to get used to this as a dad, I've been getting up and knocking on her door every time I hear him, so I can help. She's let me try twice and both times his screaming got worse, so now she tells me to just stay in bed. It's fine. But it isn't fine. I should be able to handle this without her. And one day soon I will have to.

And there's been endless trips to the grocery store and Target and my house is overflowing with kid shit now. I don't mind, but it's an adjustment. And now, I'm constantly worrying about leaving her and him alone in LA while I'm on this road trip. I keep thinking of things I need to tell her or show her before I go, things about the complex like where to toss the garbage or recycling or how to drive my car because I can't leave her without wheels.

All of these things have blown up my focus like a nuclear bomb. No one else knows that though because I haven't told a soul about what's going on. Well, except my lawyer. This guy my agent recommended when I told him I had a friend who just found out his girlfriend is pregnant and wants a legal custody arrangement. Yeah, I pulled the "I have a friend" routine, but my agent bought it hook, line, and sinker because everyone knows I've never had a girlfriend.

The guys on my new line for the rest of this game start to get up, as my old line starts to come off. A hand lands on my shoulder. "Piakoski you're in for Garrison this shift."

My veins flood with frustration and I look up at Coach Braddock. He's staring down at me. "Angry? Good. Channel it."

A couple shifts later he orders me to head out with Nash and Crew and I force everything out of my brain except hockey. It works. I set up Nash for a glorious goal. Unfortunately, four minutes later, the Barons score again and there's no time left to win it. The final buzzer goes and it's over. I feel like the entire loss is my fault and I hate myself. That's become a common new feeling that I'm not a fan of but it's all I seem to feel lately. Especially when I try to bond with Dylan.

The team is relatively silent as we march our way to the locker room. As soon as everyone is sitting, and before the media comes in, I clear my throat. "Sorry guys. I should have been better out there tonight."

"Yeah you should have," Nash replies firmly and he scrubs his sweaty face with a towel. "And I should have scored in the second not sent it wide."

"Twice," his twin notes. Nash nods as Crew adds, "And I shouldn't have been so fucking slow in the first. We all need to figure out where we personally went wrong and make sure not to do it again. No one person owns this loss. We all own it."

"Media time!" Adam announces as he walks into the room. Adam is the media director for the team. He's all business. He doesn't seem to even like hockey, but he loves public relations and media. He worked for a movie studio before he joined us at the start of the season. I know I'm going to have to loop him, and the coaching team and management, into this new development in my personal life. Because our lives as hockey players aren't always our own. Even here in Los Angeles, where the majority of people honestly don't give two fucks about hockey, players still manage to find their way into the gossip sites every now and then. Like when Crew's engagement ended abruptly last year.

Yeah, Adam and the team will want to set the tone and narrative around Dylan and my leap into single parenthood. I know that the media finding out before they do will be catastrophic to my tenure on this team and I *do* want it to be a tenure. The Quake drafted me when I was eighteen and made it clear then they hoped to make this a long-lasting relationship. I'd always taken that very seriously. I wanted to be a franchise player somewhere. The rare breed that starts and ends his career in the same place. This new development could ruin that if I don't handle it properly.

The media tonight, of course, starts with me. Everyone wants to know what's up. Why I was so subpar. This confirms, despite Crew's words, it's my performance that everyone noticed. I fed them the usual bullshit lines a player gives when they suck—it was an off night. These things happen. I will do better. I'm not worried this is the start of any kind of long-term downswing.

We shower and change, and eventually, the words between players go from grunts and muttering to full-blown conversations. Crew and Nash are debating where to go out and blow off the stench of the shitty game. Nash turns to me. "Feeling like some burritos at Casa Rosa? The crowds should have dispersed by now."

I love the Mexican restaurant by the arena. We rarely go to it on game nights because fans are usually milling about, but on nights we lose they dissipate fast. I could use one of their amazing chicken burritos or a few of their fish tacos but I know I have to get home to Mallory and Dylan. "Another time. I have something to do."

"What do you have to do?" Nash looks perplexed.

"Or is it a who?" Crew asks with a broad grin as he pulls a dress shirt on over his tattooed arms and torso. "You've been M.I.A from everything for a week. I think you've found a new playmate."

I huff. God, I wish it was that simple. I shake my head. "Nah. I've got a friend from home visiting and... I've just been busy is all."

I shrug into my blazer, tucking my tie in my pocket because I can't be bothered to put it on again. I shove my feet into my dress loafers, sock-less. The coach walks into the room and claps his hands to grab everyone's attention. The room falls silent. "Look, tonight was not great. It's gonna happen. Shake it off. But know that I expect to finish this season on a high note. And then we have playoffs. So, I'm locking us down right now, boys. We've got eight games left in the regular season but starting tonight we're in playoff mode. Curfews, extra strategy meetings, morning skates every day except travel days, no excuses."

No one complains. No one reacts at all, at least externally. Internally I am groaning, big-time. How the hell can I manage that and figure out a routine in this new home life of mine? Plus I have lawyer meetings and I have to get Dylan and me into a lab and do a DNA test for the courts. Mallory won't stay forever, and I'm not going to be able to get a nanny, get the legal paperwork in place, find a more kid-friendly home, and tell my family and team before playoffs start.

Coach turns and exits and then I feel a hand on my shoulder. Crew stares at me with confusion. "You need to talk about something? You look kind of stressed and you *never* looked stressed."

"Yeah, I've got some stuff to figure out," I tell him and before I can elaborate someone else is calling my name.

It's the security guard outside the locker room door. "You have a visitor."

"What?" I panic and march to the door. Is it Mallory? Did she come here? Is something wrong with Dylan?

I step into the hall and am confronted with an entirely different Echolls. Chance Echolls, Mallory's dad. He's the general manager for the Brooklyn Barons, so I guess he came with the team on the road trip. But why the fuck is he coming to *our* locker room to look for *me*? He isn't smiling, but I wouldn't expect him to. We aren't friends. In fact, he hates my dad with a burning passion and they came to blows when they were about my age—over my mom.

"Can I help you?" I ask, trying not to sound too rude.

"Yeah, maybe," he says and folds his arms over his chest. His suit crinkles and creases like the corners of his eyes as he frowns. "I know you used to be friendly with Diana Hutchens, my daughter's best friend."

"Yeah. A long time ago," I reply as Quake employees and teammates' friends and relatives walk by us, all of them doing a double-take. This is highly abnormal, having a person from the opposing team's management yakking with a Quake player in the hallway, or at all. "I haven't seen Diana in almost two years."

"She died."

"I heard," I stop myself from adding 'I'm sorry' because I would bet money that Mr. Echolls doesn't give a shit that his daughter's best friend died. "It's horrible news. She was a good person."

"Yeah. Well, I was never her biggest fan," Mr. Echolls replies without a hint of empathy. "But my daughter loved her like a sister, and I don't think she's taking the news well. But I don't know because she isn't really talking to me. I'm worried about her."

"Okay," I say because I don't know what else to say. I mean, I haven't even asked Mallory what she's told her parents. Do they know she's here? Did they know Diana had a kid? Where do they think Mallory is, currently?

"She said she wanted to stay in England until she was completely healed but... I think she's back in the States," Mr. Echolls tells me and the frown on his face falls and he looks worried. Like a dad should. "She answered her brother Beckett's FaceTime two days ago, and it would have been, like, eight at night in London but she was outdoors somewhere and it was daylight. Full sun."

"Okay." I think it's the only word in my vocabulary suddenly.

"I'm asking if you know where she is?" he snaps like I'm an idiot not getting the point of this conversation. "You and Di were the only people she stayed close to from home. I know she and Diana visited you here once. I wondered if she's talked to you since Diana died. Has she emailed or texted or anything?"

"I can tell her to contact you if I hear from her."

"Thanks," he grunts and turns to leave without another word.

And then something he said snags in my brain. "Wait! Mr. Echolls!"

He turns to glare at me over his shoulder. I clear my throat. "What did you mean she was staying in England until she was completely healed? Healed from what?"

He blinks and his face contorts with anguish for a flash before it falls back into its standard annoyed look. "Mallory was in the car with Diana when they had the accident. Thankfully her injuries were superficial. A few broken ribs, some cuts from the broken glass, and a mild concussion. My wife and I were all set to fly there immediately when we heard but Mallory didn't want us to."

He looks genuinely hurt when he shares that and I almost feel for him. But I know this guy isn't a great dad. I have been friends with Mallory long enough to know he failed her in a lot of ways, but he clearly loves her. "Oh. Well, like I said, I'll tell her to contact you if I hear from her."

"What's this about?" I hear Coach Braddock's no-nonsense voice behind me and turn around.

"Personal business." Mr. Echolls marches off, back toward the visiting team's section of the arena.

Braddock looks rightfully pissed as he glares at me. "Coach, he's from Silver Bay. My hometown. I'm friends with his daughter and..."

"Do not!" He raises his hand to quiet me as I approach him.

"Do not tell me you are dating the daughter of an opposing team's general manager and who we may have to face in the playoffs."

"No. I am definitely *not* dating his daughter." Finally, I can say something that isn't a lie. "She's a friend and she was living in London with.... my ex. And they were in a car accident."

His stern face softens and his blue eyes grow sympathetic. "Shit. I'm sorry. Is everyone okay?"

"No. My ex..." Calling Diana my ex is a stretch and she would laugh in my face if she heard it, but calling her anything else is messy. "My ex died and Mallory, his daughter, was injured and he was just... well, touching base with me. About all of it."

Coach Braddock nods and grips my shoulder, giving it a squeeze. "I didn't mean to jump on you. I had no idea. I just thought of the media speculation if you two were caught talking so close to playoffs."

"Fair," I say with a nod. "I didn't mean to make problems. I honestly didn't know he was going to want to talk to me about it. And don't worry. I'm loyal to the Quake. I know after tonight's performance, you might be wishing I wasn't on the team, let alone loyal."

"Shut up, kid," Coach chuckles. "We all have off days. I may have won back-to-back Cups and been a Conn Smythe and Art Ross trophy winner, more than once, but I shit the bed too on occasion, trust me. Like I said in the room, shake it off and do better."

"Intend to," I promise and with another squeeze of my shoulder he starts to leave. But he stops and turns back to me.

"You know we have a sports psychologist on staff right?" Braddock informs me and I nod. "If you need to talk out any feelings about your ex dying. It's tough to lose anyone you know, and we pay these guys to handle more than just on-ice issues for our team. Use Dr. Vance if you need to."

"Okay." I turn and head out to the parking lot. I wonder, briefly, if Dr. Vance could help me with my feelings about Diana's death, finding out I'm a dad, and how to deal with it all? I mean, I know my cousin Conner sees a shrink. And Grady. For hockey shit I assume. I mean I thought that's all these people dealt with.

I pull out of the underground parking and onto one of the downtown Los Angeles streets and tell my car. "Call Conner."

My cousin Conner is located in Maine. He was traded there last year from Brooklyn. Well, actually he wasn't traded, he was put on waivers, which is like getting dumped. It basically ruined his self-confidence and almost drove a rift between him and the entire family. He thought we were all judging him or that he wasn't worthy or some shit. Anyway, luckily Portland picked him up and he's doing great there.

"Hey Tater, since when do you use your phone for calling?" he questions immediately as he answers, instead of saying hello. "Aren't you the one with the voicemail that says 'I'm sorry but this phone is only for texts and video calls. Hang up and do one of those two things if you need to reach me?"

"I decided to go old school tonight," I reply tersely and dive right in. "You see a shrink still?"

"Hey, how are you Con? How's Mac? That hat trick you scored on the weekend was top-notch, buddy," Conner says, pretending to be a better version of me than the one I'm giving him. And then he answers for fake me. "Thanks, Tater Tot, that hat trick felt pretty damn good. How's the quest to crush Uncle J's record going? How's the weather in Cali?"

"No one calls it Cali except people not from California," I remind him. "Sorry. I had a shit game. I'm... a grump-ass."

I hop on the 10 freeway which is busy, as always. The only

part of LA that grates on my nerves is the traffic at weird hours, like ten at night on a Tuesday. Where the hell are all these people going?

"One shit game so you call me at one in the morning, my time, and you want to shrink your head?" Conner is laughing at me now, which does nothing to improve my mood. "A little dramatic, don't you think?"

"Sorry. I know you don't have a game tomorrow and you're a bit of a night owl. And it felt like an emergency. It's not about the one game." I sigh. "Look, forget it. I'll call Grady. He's way less judgey than you."

I'm about to punch the end button on the screen on my dash when Conner speaks again. "Hold up! Hold up! I'm sorry. I'm being a dick."

"You are."

"Sorry. Again. Honestly." Conner's voice loses its teasing tone. "To get back on track, yes. I see a sports psychologist. Ever since the waivers bullshit last year. And I highly recommend it, for on-ice issues and off."

"You have off-ice issues?" I ask, floored because Conner is the absolute most calm, cool, and collected Garrison... hell, human, I have ever known. I've always felt like the expression 'Golden Boy' was created for him. He's smart, talented, level-headed, and life just always seems effortlessly perfect for him.

"Dude, seriously?" He seems one part miffed and one part stunned that I'm questioning it. "I was about to become the first Garrison to fail at hockey. I'm the eldest of a generation that, sometimes, seems far more talented than my old ass. I was trying to woo a woman far out of my league when my confidence was in the toilet. Yeah. I had off-ice issues."

Hearing him talk like that blows my mind. We all knew he was still the best of the best, even if the Barons weren't willing to admit it. "The only thing that's true in that statement is that Mac is kind of out of your league."

"She is, and fuck you," Conner laughs. "So you gonna tell me what's up? If it isn't just an over-dramatic reaction to one shitty game?"

"I..." I want to tell him so badly, but I can't risk it. If my mother and father find out about their grandchild from him, or Mac because I know he shares everything with her, then I'll never forgive myself. So I keep the depths of my turmoil to myself. The surface stuff is enough. "Diana Hutchens died in a car crash in the UK and I'm kind of all over the place about it."

"What? Shit. Tate... that's horrible," Conner says and he, once again, sounds genuinely concerned for me. "You guys were close."

"Yeah. I mean, we were..." I pause. "It's just fucked. I didn't... I feel guilty that we weren't more, you know. Like I don't know... I just... I never thought I would never see her again."

"Did you want more with her?" He seems genuinely shocked, which is fair.

"No," I admit and I envision Dylan's cute little face as I exit the freeway and I feel like I'm drowning in grief again. "And I hate myself for that."

"Did she want more?" Conner asks gently. "I know some people, men or women, agree to the no-strings thing but really, they want strings. I can understand feeling guilty if Diana was like that and you weren't and you never got the chance to talk it out."

"No. I mean... she had the opportunity to try and..." I stop before I say too much. "No. She never pushed. Never wanted more. I just... I don't know. I'm messed up and need an ear. And no offense but not someone named Garrison."

"Fair enough," Conner says, his tone soothing and most

importantly understanding. Then I hear a muffled sound. "Sorry baby. I'm coming to bed now. Promise."

There are more muffled sounds and a distant female laugh. I know it's Mackenzie, his girlfriend. When he speaks to me again, it's crazy but I can hear the happiness in his voice. "I will text you my shrink's contact info ASAP."

"We don't like the term shrink!" I hear Mac call out and I cringe because she's now going to know I asked for a psychologist. But she's a full-fledged, practicing psychiatrist so she must not go blabbing about stuff like this, right? Doctor oath or some such crap.

"Sorry Princess," Conner calls out.

"I don't like Princess either!" she yells back but her voice is light and happy.

Their whole vibe is nice, cute even. Kind of delightful, but utterly foreign to me, and that doesn't bug me one bit. I don't mind not knowing what a committed relationship is like. I have other things to concentrate on, a lot of other things now. "Thanks, Con, and I don't need to ask you and Mac to keep this out of the family group chats. All of them."

"Yeah of course," Conner replies solemnly. "You don't need to ask. And Tater, if you do ever want to unload on a Garrison, I'm your man. Seriously. Day or night."

"I appreciate it cuz," I say and my shoulders relax a little as I say goodbye and turn onto Abbott Kinney. I have a bit of a plan. I mean, I have a start. Between the lawyer and the psychologist maybe I can make this work, in my head and real life.

Chapter 7

Tate

My street is bustling, almost as busy as the freeway. I wonder if the traffic is part of the problem for Dylan's sleep regression. It's loud on my street. Always.

I swipe my fob and the gate to my complex slides open. I see Tara, my neighbor who works for some silly celebrity website, getting out of her Porsche a few stalls over. We've been flirting for the last two months since she moved in, but I haven't made an official move. Yet. There was a yet there, but now... well hooking up is the last thing on my To Do list.

"Hi Tara," I say with a wave and she parts her perfectly painted lips in a broad smile.

"Mr. Hockey!" she calls back. "Coming home from a game or a night out with a lucky lady?"

"Game. We lost," I admit and frown.

"You'll get 'em next time," she replies easily. Typical response from someone who doesn't get that hockey players don't shrug off losses, ever. "Wanna go for a drink at the wine bar down the road? I always go there after a bad day, and mine wasn't great. They're open until one and have an amazing selection of Spanish reds."

Now, if this was happening two weeks ago, I'd say yes without hesitation. We'd get warm and fuzzy on wine, and I'd kiss her. She'd let me. And then I'd give her my number and walk away. Because I don't fuck drunk women. It's my only rule. I need sober consent. I call it the Mallory Rule now because I broke it with her and that was a huge mistake. Mallory never blamed what happened between us on the booze, but I did. I hate feeling like she only let me touch her because she was drunk.

So I would wait until Tara was sober again to make a real move, but the scene would be set and flirt-texting would happen next, while on my road trip, and then next time I was home I would invite her over and...

"You okay?" Tara's voice interrupts me. "I'm trying not to take you zoning out personally."

"Crap! Sorry!" I give her a sheepish smile. "I had a really shitty game. Also, I have house guests right now and just... a lot going on."

"That friend of yours and her kid still with you?" Tara asks and her blue eyes sparkle mischievously as she makes air quotes around the word 'friend'.

"She *is* a friend," I reply, not addressing Dylan's existence at all because it's definitely none of her business. "And yes, they're staying a while and I'm cool with it. But I just... We've been put on lockdown for the upcoming playoffs. Curfews and all that stuff. I should head to bed."

"So, like, do they not allow you *any* fun?" Tara asks, still smiling, now devilishly. She leans a little closer and whispers, "Do they really ban extracurricular activities?"

She's an attractive girl, but right now, in my current state of mind, I observe that fact passively. Because it doesn't matter to me right now. Attractive girls who are down for casual sex are not on my bingo card anymore. For now, anyway.

"Not technically." I give her a quick smile and then jerk my thumb toward my place. "Gotta go."

"Right. Your friend and her baby." I just nod. "Okay well, if when your houseguests leave and you need company while on your team lockdown... I'm three doors down."

"Noted," I reply and give her a wave as I turn to follow the short path to my unit. Hers is down the footpath on the other side of the entrance to the building, but she doesn't turn that way. She watches me walk all the way up my porch steps. Now I know what it feels like to be a woman walking by a construction site.

I try not to notice as I unlock the storm door. It's a hot night so Mallory had the big door open and just the storm door locked, which means she probably heard some of my exchange with Tara I realize as I step inside. Kicking off my dress shoes, I drop my keys on the console table and shrug out of my jacket as I walk into the living room. Mallory is sitting on one of my couches, arms crossed over a plain yellow T-shirt. Her long blonde hair is pulled back in a loose ponytail. Her face makeup-less.

I stare at her and she stares at me and for some reason, even though I have a lot to discuss with her, I can't even find the courage to say hello. It's the way she's looking at me. Mallory has a def con five resting bitch face right now. It's classic, old-school Mallory. She's quiet with her words but not with her expressions. I remember the first time I saw this type of look on her. We were at a high school party, one of my teammates was talking shit about a girl he just broke up with. Really disrespectful stuff and Mallory overheard and glared at him just like this. She never spoke but the dude saw her face and shut the fuck up.

Now, she gets up, also without a word, and walks away. I watch her as she climbs the stairs and doesn't even realize I'm fixated on her perky ass as it jiggles with every step in the boy short pajama bottoms she's wearing until my dick starts to twitch and grow in the front of my suit pants. Mallory Echolls is a smoke show. Who hates me. But my dick doesn't care about the semantics.

I pull off pieces of my suit while I make a BLT for a bedtime snack. There's no sound from upstairs. Mallory must have gone straight to bed. Or she's quietly making a voodoo doll with my name on it.

I sit at the dining room table and quietly eat my sandwich in nothing but my underwear. I don't even feel weird about it because I'm too grumpy and exhausted to care and I'd bet money, from that look on her face, that she would rather eat glass than be in the same room with me right now. And honestly, even if she did come down, whatever.

I finish my sandwich and my glass of water and leave the dishes on the table. I can't be bothered to clean anything. I grab my suit and carry it upstairs, stopping at the small cart in the dining room to grab a bottle of tequila and take a swig, hoping it will loosen the knot of tension between my shoulders. I'm a foot from the door to my room when the guest room door opens and Mallory steps into the hall. She stops abruptly and stares at me. It doesn't start as a classic Mal RBF, it actually starts with a soft, slightly shocked look because I'm just in my underwear, which is very snug.

"Jesus, Tate," she huffs and covers her eyes. "You forget I'm here?"

"No," I reply and shoot my balled-up suit from one hand to the other. "I just thought you were asleep."

Her fingers split a little in front of her eyes, but she doesn't look at me. She's looking past me. "Are you alone?"

I blink. "What? Yeah. Of course. Who the fuck else would be here?"

"The pretty woman you were talking to outside."

So she did hear me with Tara. Is she... jealous? I tilt my head and try to wrap my head around that, and why the thought turns me on. "Tara is a neighbor. Nothing else."

"Whatever." Mallory keeps her hand over her eyes, fingers still split, as she turns with her back to the guest room door and motions with her other hand for me to pass. "Please feel free to take yourself to bed."

I start to walk by her but I'm annoyed and, as anyone in my family will tell you, I love to push buttons when I'm pissed off. So as I pass, I slow down when I'm right in front of her. I step closer, so I walk sideways by her, making sure my bare chest brushes around her front. She drops her hand to give me that RBF again but her cheeks are flaming red, so I shoot her a cocky smirk and as our eyes lock I slide by even slower. Now I can feel her nipples harden through the thin fabric of her loose t-shirt and blood surges downward, and my plan instantly backfires.

I might be getting under her skin but she is also getting under mine. And it's making me hard. Quickly. I take the final step needed to slide by her and move my crumpled suit to cover my boxer briefs, even though I have my back to her now as I walk into my room. I'm figuring out how to close the door without looking like I'm covering a boner. But I hear a hard click look over my shoulder and realize Mallory closed the door for me.

Well, this is going well, I think to myself. I throw my crumpled suit in the bin in my open closet that's marked 'Dry'. My cleaning lady also takes everything in that bin to the dry cleaners for me and picks it up too. She also does all my laundry but I doubt she'll be happy about adding Dylan's laundry to the pile when Mallory leaves and I have to handle this on my own. Right now Mallory is doing her laundry and Dylan's. I guess I can ask the next nanny to do his laundry?

Shit. I don't like the idea of a next nanny. I don't like the idea of anyone with my son except Mallory. I know shit about child-rearing, but I watch her and it reminds me of my mom. She's been amazing with him. Patient and sweet and she smiles at him like he hung the moon.

And she makes my dick hard.

Okay well, I have business to take care of, I guess. I can't remember the last time I whacked off. I have an urge, I find a willing partner. That's my life and I'm proud of it. It's always mutual, and above board. If there was no Dylan or Mallory, I'd be at the bar with Tara. Or I'd call one of my three regulars—Christine, Allie, or Grace. But I can't do that for multiple, obvious reasons. The unobvious reason is that I would be thinking of Mallory the whole time. And I don't do that. I don't use a woman if I've got another one on my mind. I've never had to because no woman has stuck in my brain like Mallory is right now. So I flip off all the lights except the one on my bedside table, peel out of my underwear, and drop back on my bed. I open the drawer in the nightstand and pull out the small bottle of lube I keep in there since I tried anal with Grace a few months ago.

I squirt some onto the tip of my cock. I groan when my palm slips over the tip and down the shaft. My eyes roll back in my head and I let my mind wander. It doesn't go very far. Just right back to the memory of Mallory's perky ass in her pajama shorts swinging its way up the stairs earlier. I think I cupped her ass that night we fooled around, but I can't really remember. All I remember is how wet she was when I put my hands in her underwear and how tight she was when I slipped my fingers inside her. And the way her eyes flared with excitement when I put my fingers in my mouth...

"Fuck!"

My eyes fly open and I catch the back end of Mallory as she darts from the room. I bolt up off the bed, grabbing my underwear and holding it in front of my rapidly deflating cock. "Mallory!"

I hiss out her name in a stage whisper because I have the common sense not to scream and wake Dylan, but inside, I am not just screaming but roaring with rage. And humiliation. I grab a pair of sweats out of the open closet and yank them on. I march across the hall and fling open the door to the guest room.

Mallory is standing between the side of the queen-sized bed and the open bathroom door. Our eyes connect and she spins and darts for the bathroom. She's fast but I'm faster and manage to get there before she can close the door in my face. I push my way inside and close it behind me so she can't escape. "What the hell?" I hiss at her. "Are you unfamiliar with the concept of knocking?"

"Are you unfamiliar with the concept of cleaning up after yourself?" she snaps. She turned around when I pushed my way inside so she's facing the shower, not me. "I went downstairs to make tea and found your dirty dishes. I'm here for Dylan not to be your maid."

"Then don't touch the fucking dishes," I snap back and step closer to her. "You barged into my room to tell me that? Look, it's my house and if I want to clean up in the morning, after a shitty game, I'll do that. If you get up before me, then just ignore them. I'll deal with it. I'm dealing with every fucking thing."

"Are you pissed off you couldn't fuck your neighbor?" Mallory asks and finally turns to face me. Her resting bitch face has been elevated to animated bitch face. Eyes narrowed, jaw tense, shoulders up. She's like a feral cornered cat. And I'm like a pissed-off lion. "You haven't fucked a random person in a week. You must be frustrated. You want to bring your neighbor home, do it. I'm not here to cramp your style."

Is she fucking serious right now? "I didn't ask for your permission to fuck anyone and I don't intend to ask. I will do what I want to do when I think it's appropriate. I'm not so driven by my dick, Mallory, that I can't go five days without a warm, wet place to stick it."

She folds her arms over her chest and glares. I glare back. She arches one eyebrow. Oh right. I was jerking off. "I didn't say I could go without release. I said I didn't need someone else to do it. Sorry if you're like some kind of sexual camel and you can store up your desires for months or whatever. I enjoy sex. That doesn't make me an asshole or a deviant, Mal. But I can also take care of my own business if I have to. You should try it sometime. Maybe you'll stop being so fucking—"

I stop. I'm crossing every line. All the lines. I'm being cruel and saying shit that isn't even how I feel because I'm humiliated. The fury on her face is fading fast. Her eyes are a little wetter than when I walked in here. She unfolds her arms and bites her bottom lip for a second. "I was angry and didn't think. I should have knocked."

I take a deep breath and run a hand through my hair on the exhale, forcing myself to get my anger and ego in check. "I'm embarrassed. I'm sorry. But yeah, you really need to knock."

She gives me the faintest nod and then moves her hazel eyes to the floor. Her top teeth finally release her bottom lip. "I might stop being what? A frigid bitch? An uptight cow? A bitchy friend? What?"

"No. I don't know..." I sigh again. "It doesn't matter. I didn't mean it."

"What were you going to say?"

"I was going to say..." I pause. I really don't want to confess this. "I was going to say maybe you would stop being so fucking angry all the time if you made yourself come every now and then."

I hear her take a short, sharp breath at that but I don't dare look at her. I turn toward the door. "I'm sorry. It was mean and childish and I don't mean it. Just... let's go to sleep. I'll apologize again in the morning, I promise."

"I can't exactly play with myself when I have a tiny roommate who pops his head out of his sleeping pod whenever he wants," she says, stopping me in my tracks as I reach for the door handle. "I know exactly how to get myself off when I have the opportunity, Tate. Trust me. I know what I'm doing. It was my ex who didn't, remember?"

Oh yeah. I remember. I slowly turn back to face her. The tears that threatened to fall from her eyes are gone. Her shoulders are back and she looks defiant. Her cheeks are pink but not from anger anymore. She's embarrassed but she isn't backing down. "I tried relieving my own stress in the shower but..." She lifts the hem of her shirt, one hand holding the fabric close to her breasts, and turns and shows me the vicious-looking faded purple marks across her ribs. "This still throbs a lot and moving my arms and stuff... for too long doesn't feel great."

"Oh." That's the best I can come up with because my brain is melting faster than ice in August. Am I really having a conversation about the logistics of masturbating with my ex-friend and son's nanny?

She moves to drop the hem of her shirt but I cross the room in a flash and grab it before it can fall. I take a closer look at the bruises, even trace my fingertips over the marks. "You should probably have a follow-up with a doctor. Make sure everything is setting right."

"I don't have health insurance here anymore Tate," she whispers. "But it's fine. I'll figure that all out when I get back to Silver Bay. I think I can be put back on my parents if I live at home for a while. I'm under twenty-five."

"But I need you here for a while longer," I say, and I let the shirt drop but keep my fingers against her tender flesh under it. Her eyelashes flutter. "I'll get you in with the team doctor. It'll be free. Or else I'll absorb the cost."

"I can't ask you to do that."

"You didn't ask," I reply. "I need to know you're okay."

She doesn't say anything. My fingertips move, sliding slowly up her rib cage. She shudders but doesn't reach to stop me or move my hand away.

"Mallory?" I keep my eyes on her face and she finally looks back at me. "If you need some release... I'm right next door. And I know how to do it."

She blinks. My fingers ghost the underside of her bare breast. I glance down to see her hard nipples against the thin fabric and then catch her eye again. "I would scratch your itch and you can scratch mine."

My mouth is close to hers. So close. And I want to kiss her so bad I feel the urge in every nerve-ending in my entire body. It's a pulse. A beat like my heart, only stronger.

"What were you thinking about... while you fucked your hand?"

Mallory's crass words ratchet up the desire in my veins. "You."

She tips her head up and presses her mouth to mine. She grabs my shoulders, pulling me closer until her back is pressed to the wall and her front is flush with mine. And when she parts her lips and slips her tongue into my mouth my hand cups her perfect left tit and my fingers pinch that rock hard nipple. She moans into my mouth and I kiss the sound away.

And then Dylan wails.

We jump apart like someone drops a bucket of ice water on us. Mallory pushes past me and flings open the door to the bedroom. I count to ten and think of baseball to get my dick to deflate again. After the ten count, I'm ready to head out there.

Mallory is standing at the foot of the bed, rocking Dylan in her arms. He is screaming like he's been lit on fire. I stand there feeling useless. "I'd offer to take him but he just screams louder when I'm holding him," I mutter.

"He'll get over that," she promises. "Can you heat up some milk on the stove? Not too hot, just lukewarm. Put it in his bottle?"

I nod and head downstairs. When I return almost fifteen minutes later his wailing has dulled to gentle sobs. His face is beet red and his eyes heavy with exhaustion. I hand her the bottle but she shakes her head. "Sit."

I sit on the edge of her bed, near the headboard. She gently shifts Dylan in her arms, cooing sweet words to him as she does, and then she places him in my arms. He blinks up at me, stunned, and then his face starts to twist up like he's prepping to release one hell of a scream. "Give him the milk."

I softly shove the bottle toward him and both his fat hands grab it and he pulls it to his mouth. A few sips and his whole body relaxes in my lap. He wiggles a little, snuggling himself into the crook of my arm as I sit up against the headboard. He makes a few little almost-cry sounds but he settles. I stare at him in awe. My son.

Mallory walks around the bed and crawls up beside me. She sits there watching silently over my shoulder for a few minutes and then she slides down and lies on the bed next to me. I give her a quick smile and she returns it with a sleepy one.

I turn back to study Dylan. I think this is the first tranquil moment we've shared. He stares up at me with eyes that I swear he stole from my mom and wet cheeks and that dimple, like mine and my dad's, in his chin and the stubborn clench of his jaw, that reminds me of my sister. "You gotta work with me, Dylan. I promise I'll take care of you if you let me. Just relax and give me a chance lil bear. I've never been a daddy before but I'll do my best for you."

He keeps sucking on his bottle, eyes getting heavy, and I hope gives my words some consideration before he drops back off into sleep. I run a hand over his hair and just stare at him. I made this. This perfect little person. Without even knowing or trying. It scares the hell out of me, but I'm also so fucking amazed. And in love. I love this kid. How? Fucked if I know but I do.

"I love him," I tell Mallory. I look over for her reaction, but her eyes are closed her mouth is slightly open and she's drooling on the pillow beside me.

Dylan's eyes close before he can finish the milk, so I gently take it from his pudgy hands and put it on the night table. I sit there with him asleep, propped up on my lap, cradled in my arm for about half an hour. Then, when I'm sure he's sleeping well, I walk over and carefully lay him out in his sleeping pod. I cover him with a loose blanket and take his giraffe stuffie and place it near his left arm.

He doesn't blink or stir so I leave him and walk over to Mallory. She's also out cold. I walk to her closet and pull down a velour throw blanket with the Quake crest on it. They always give us random merch. I unfold it and lay it on top of Mallory because she fell asleep on top of the covers and I don't want her to wake up cold.

I force myself to walk out of the room and close the door behind me. As much as I want to pick up where we left off, the moment has passed. Maybe it's the universe stepping in and saving me from making a complicated situation even worse.

After all, Mallory is only here for Dylan. She's said it time and time again. And I can't give her the end-game she wants. I'm not ready for that.

So I go back to my room, drop into bed, and force myself into a restless, unsatisfied sleep.

Chapter 8

Mallory

I wake up as the sun rises at five-thirty in the morning, under a blanket I didn't recognize. The memories of the night before flood my brain and I spend an hour googling flights to Maine and almost booking one. Then finally I fall back into a humiliated sleep, tossing and turning. When my eyes flutter open again, the room is empty and bright. And the clock says nine-thirty and Dylan is not in his bed. But I can hear him screaming.

My heart rate takes off like a Red Bull car on an F1 track. My body does the same. I leap out of bed, fling open the door and rush down the stairs before my legs are actually aware I'm awake. I start to stumble, grab the railing, and bump into the wall and pain explodes in my side. "Ouch! Fuck!"

"Mallory?" Tate appears at the bottom of the stairs as I right myself, hand gripping my side, vision blurry with pain. "What happened?"

Dylan is in his arms, every inch of his skin that isn't covered in his onesie is blotchy red. He twists and reaches for me as soon as his watery eyes see me.

"I'm fine," I lie and lift my arms to the traumatized kiddo. "How long has he been awake?"

"About an hour," Tate says and lets me take him. "He's been fussy the whole damn time. Even while eating the spinach omelet you said he loves."

"He does love it." I hold Dylan's squirmy body up and sniff him mid-torso. "You just scooped him out of bed and fed him?"

"Yeah." Tate looks defensive. "I could hear him and you were dead asleep. I thought I needed to start handling this so no time like the present."

"You have to change him," I say bluntly and start back up the stairs. I hear Tate following behind me so I keep talking and try really hard not to sound annoyed, just informative. Tate's trying, in his own way. "As soon as he wakes up, always check the diaper. Nine times out of ten he needs a change."

"Oh." Tate sounds dejected and when I glance over my shoulder at the top of the stairs, he looks as sad as he sounds.

"I never told you that so you aren't expected to know."

"Yeah. But I mean, it sounds like common sense," Tate mutters and follows me into the bedroom.

"Grab me a towel please."

Tate scurries to the bathroom and grabs a fresh towel from the shelves there. They are all tightly rolled and fluffy like a hotel thanks to his cleaner, Josie, who I met the day before. He holds it out to me, but I don't take it. I give him instructions instead. "Lie it out on the bed, not too close to the edges. You should invest in a changing table. He's got a while longer in diapers."

Tate nods and lays out the towel. I drop Dylan onto his back in the middle of it. As I start unsnapping the onesie and changing Dylan, I give Tate step-by-step instructions. He's very quiet so I glance up as I toss the used baby wipe into the trash beside my nightstand. Tate is facing the wall, not me or the baby. "What the hell are you doing?"

"Giving Dylan some privacy."

A smile blooms on my lips. I can't control it. His answer is too ridiculous. "You are giving an infant privacy?"

"I mean, he doesn't need everyone looking at his junk."

"Tate Garrison, have you lost it entirely?" I'm trying to sound stern but a giggle bubbles up and finally, Tate looks over at me.

"Don't laugh at me. I feel weird seeing a kid naked," Tate mumbles, his cheeks tinging with the slightest bit of pink, and it's adorable.

"He is not just any kid, he's *yours*," I remind him and turn back to Dylan who is perfectly content, naked, and clean again. His chubby legs are in the air and he's reaching for his toes. "And do I have to remind you that you see, like, twenty men naked several times a week in locker rooms? This shouldn't freak you out."

"It's not like I'm looking at those dudes," Tate mutters. "And I mean, like, I've never cleaned a baby. I don't want to hurt him or put my hands in the wrong place."

"There is no wrong place," I reply, still smiling a little. "I once had to clean poop out from between his toes because something he ate gave him diarrhea and it leaked everywhere."

"That's so gross." Tate's handsome face twists into a look of revulsion.

"It was," I confirm and start to wrap a new diaper around Dylan. "But whatever, shit happens. Quite literally. He's a baby. He's helpless. He needs us to do the dirty work, Tate."

Once the diaper is on, I ask Tate to watch him and walk over to one of my still-not-really unpacked suitcases. I grab a clean shirt and elastic waist pants for Dylan. I make a note to add summer clothes to the ever-growing list of things Tate needs to buy for the baby. Diana didn't need an expansive warm weather wardrobe for him in England, but Los Angeles is a different story.

"He needs some lighter clothes," I say.

"I'll leave you one of my credit cards while I'm on the road trip," Tate offers. "And the car. Go get whatever you need. Food orders too. Just charge it all."

"I..." I stop myself from arguing because what choice do I have? "Fine. Thanks."

I walk over and dress Dylan. Tate isn't watching the kid, he's watching me. I confirm it with a glance, but I *felt* it before that. Suddenly my pajamas feel a little more revealing than they did before. The fabric is thin, the boy shorts are tight and, well, short. And I'm bent over. I think of last night and that psychotic break we both had that ended in a make-out session and his hands on my breasts. I feel a warmth spread through me and I straighten immediately, grab Dylan off the bed, and hand him to Tate.

Tate's eyes flare but he takes his son and tries to get Dylan to settle on his hip. But Dylan starts fussing immediately. "Try bouncing him."

Tate bounces. Dylan fusses more and reaches his little hands out toward me. I step out of reach grab a pair of sweatpants from my suitcase and pull them on over my pajama shorts, keeping my eyes averted from both Dylan and Tate. "He doesn't want me."

"He's uncertain," I reply and rake my hands through my bedhead. "Give him a minute."

"During this minute I'm giving him, should you and I discuss the tonsil hockey session in the bathroom?" I look up at that question and find his gorgeous eyes focused on me with trepidation. "Or are we going to pretend it didn't happen?"

"No," I lie. "Not pretend. Forget. We should forget it ever happened. Neither of us is in our right mind right now. And..."

I look up at him again. He's staring intently. Dylan is wiggling in his arms and Tate rubs his big palm across his back, which doesn't help ease Dylan at all. Now he's starting to voice his discontent with frustrated squeaks. "And...?"

Shit. "We owe it to Diana to keep our focus on Dylan."

As if emphasizing my point, Dylan's arms and legs kick and punch the air and he lets out an ear-piercing wail. Tate grimaces and lifts Dylan, holding him out to me. I sigh and take him and he immediately simmers down. "He hates me."

"He doesn't know you, yet," I argue. "And he's been through a lot."

"I'm not blaming him," Tate replies quickly as he runs a hand through his thick hair, somehow creating a beautiful chaos with his locks. "I just... I wish this was easier for me. Maybe that would make it easier for him."

"Probably not and you're doing fine," I assure him. Although I do wish he wouldn't give up on Dylan and hand him off to me so quickly. "When you get back from the road trip, you can handle morning duties again and it will go better because you'll know to change him."

"And there'll be a proper changing table here tomorrow because I'll order it ASAP," Tate replies and motions towards the door with a tilt of his head. "Coffee? Donuts?"

"Donuts?"

"I have to really crack down on the diet after today so I wanted to go out with a bang," he replies and a small smile quirks the corners of his lips. "I ordered Trejo's Donuts from Uber Eats and I have Roscoe's Chicken and Waffles on its way, too. I got you the Carol C Special."

My mouth starts watering immediately. "Amazing. Thank you."

We ate at Roscoe's when Diana and I visited. It was amazing and I have literally dreamt about those waffles with the perfect hint of nutmeg and that savory crispy-fried chicken breast. I wasn't expecting to eat it again, but am thrilled with the prospect. We leave the bedroom and start down the stairs and he keeps shooting me weird glances. "You okay?"

"Yeah." I shrug. "We got hormonal. I blame the intense emotions we're dealing with."

He smirks. "I meant your ribs, but you can keep making excuses for the kissing. I won't believe a word of it though."

His smirk deepens and there is the classic Tate Garrison twinkle in his eye as he changes the subject. "I asked the team doctor to swing by and take a look at you."

"What? No. I have no insurance."

"It's a favor," Tate says firmly. "And I won't take no for an answer. I have to leave the state and you're the only caregiver for Dylan so I need to know your own health is on track. What I saw last night looked pretty banged up."

I freeze at the bottom of the stairs. He was behind me and I feel his whole body slide by mine, his chiseled torso against my back, as he squeezes by and comes to stand in front of me. His eyes are kind. Concerned, even. "We played the Barons last night."

"So?" It's all I can manage to squeak out.

"Your dad traveled with the team," Tate replies. "And he sought me out after the game to ask about you."

I feel my heart seize in my chest. "He knows I'm with you?"

"No, but he knows you didn't stay in London," Tate replies. "I lied and said I didn't know where you were, but I don't know why. Why aren't you telling him?"

"Because if he knows I'm here, he'll know I'm with you," I explain as I start walking again, mostly to get away from Tate and his intense stare. "And we all know how much he loves you and your family. Plus, he knows Diana had a baby, and I was the nanny. He thinks the baby was Felix's, but... My dad is a lot of things. Stupid is not one of them. He will put this together quicker than a Mensa student with a child's puzzle."

"Oh. So you're lying to protect me?" Tate seems utterly stupefied at the concept.

"Yes. Just like I was lying in London to protect Diana. Well, actually I just ghosted you so I didn't have to lie," I reply as I settle Tate in the playpen Tate ordered for him. There's a bunch of cool new toys in there that he also picked, all on his own. Sure, one is a plastic hockey stick and puck, which Dylan chews on more than plays with, but the other toys are all fancy, eco-friendly learning toys. I was impressed when the order arrived. "All I do I lie to help everyone else. Anyway, I will tell him I am State-side today but not where."

"Okay." Tate swallows and a look of guilt washes over him again. I've seen it on his face daily since I turned up here and I feel bad. "And you'll let my doctor take a look at those ribs?"

"If you deduct his fee from my paycheck," I reply tersely.

"Fine." He rolls those pretty eyes of his. "He is supposed to be here around eleven. I know that's during Dylan's nap so hopefully, he doesn't see or hear the kid. If he does, will you..."

"I'll tell him he's mine, and I won't let him see Dylan. If he cries, I'll make the doc wait down here and go deal with it. More lies. My specialty." With Dylan happily entertained with his toys I right myself and move toward the kitchen. "I need donuts, caffeine, and that Carol C Special."

He pulls out his phone and glances at the screen. "It's four minutes away."

"Great." I walk into the kitchen. He leans on the door frame and I try not to stare.

He looks gorgeous, which is insane. He's just wearing a plain blue T-shirt with a small Quake logo on the breast and a pair of wrinkled charcoal-colored shorts. His hair isn't brushed but yet, still perfect. There's a dusting of stubble on his strong jaw. Some of the hairs hold more ginger in them than brown. He hates it because it's patchy and he thinks it looks like a Calico cat. He once said the ginger makes him embarrassed to grow a playoff beard. I think it looks hot as hell, but I've never told him that.

"I'm worried about you," Tate blurts out.

"I'm fine."

"You deserve to be more than fine, Mallory," Tate replies, which wasn't what I expected to hear come out of his mouth so I'm thrown.

"I was there when my best friend died, up close and personal," I confess, my voice soft and scratchy because it hurts to make this confession. "I was the only witness to her fiancé abandoning the perfect little boy he promised her he would look after no matter what. And then I was forced to fly that perfect little boy here to blow up your life. So yeah, I've had better days. But trust me, the broken ribs and concussion and this little cut are the least of my injuries."

He blinks. His eyes move from my hand, which is pointing to the little scab on my forehead where the stitches used to be before they dissolved. And then, before I can change the subject and reach for the coffee pot, my nose is buried in his pecs. His thick arms are wrapped around my shoulders and his neck is bent so his face is pressed into the top of my head. And it feels so fucking good I start to cry. And I hate him for it so I shove him away and wipe at my eyes. "Don't do that."

"Sorry," Tate whispers. "I just... you've been through so much and I wanted to comfort you."

"Thanks but don't, okay?" I choke out and take a deep shuddering breath to calm myself. "I'll deal with myself later. Just work on bonding with Dylan and figuring this out so I can walk away, okay?"

"I'm trying," he whispers.

I pour my coffee. He walks around the counter and grabs a mug from the ones hanging next to his fancy coffee maker and I pour him one too. He slides a box across the counter to me and I flip the lid and see a colorful delicious-looking assortment of donuts. I pluck up one covered in powdered sugar as the doorbell rings.

"Roscoe's," Tate winks at me and heads out of the room.

I take a deep breath... well, as deep as I can with my ribs. Every moment of every day that Tate and I are in the same space I feel heavy. There's so much weighing on us. The things we still have to talk about, the things we are talking about, and the stuff we will never talk about.

He arrives back in the kitchen with a bag that smells like heaven. "Oh my God, I should have asked you to order this the very first night."

Tate smiles. "I would have, but I was busy having my life turned upside down."

I glance at him and he shoots me a quirky little smile. I can't help but smile back. He opens the bag and quickly dishes up my breakfast and his. He got the same thing, only he ordered an extra chicken breast. We both devour the delicious waffles and chicken in a nearly comfortable silence. As I'm licking the last of the syrup off my fingers he tears into his second chicken breast and asks, "Can I ask you to interview your replacement while I'm on this road trip. I talked to a local agency and they've got four candidates they can send over this week."

I hate that he used the word replacement, even though it makes sense. I reach for what's left of my coffee, walk around the island, and peer into the living room. Dylan is happily chewing on a teething ring, on his back kicking his feet in the air. "Shouldn't you be the one who interviews them?"

"I will, as a second interview, if you think they deserve one,"

Tate replies. "But you're better suited to vet their actual skills. You know what Dylan needs more than I do, at the moment."

"Okay, I guess," I say with resignation because I hate the idea that someone else will be with Dylan. And Tate. I mean some strange woman will be living in that bedroom, right across the hall from him. "This is a live-in position?"

"Yeah, but not here," Tate replies and I turn to face him, stunned. "This place is too choppy for a kid. All the stairs and no grassy outdoor space. I mean if I don't move now, I'll end up moving next year anyway. I have a realtor looking into stuff for me. Also, a lawyer writing up an NDA for the nanny."

Wow. He has been handling more than I realized. Had I been getting frustrated with him for no reason? "Okay yeah, I will do the preliminary interviews."

"I'll set it up at the coffee shop around the corner," Tate says. "Safer there than having strangers here. Also, if you need help with Dylan while I'm away there's this married guy on the team, MacFarlane and he says his wife has a really good babysitter. I got her info."

"You told a guy on the team about Dylan?"

He shakes his head squashing the little bloom of hope in my chest. "I told them I had a friend visiting with a kid."

Oh. My heart sinks.

And then his phone rings and he makes everything worse. He grabs it off the counter and his eyes find mine. He looks mildly panicked. "It's my sister."

"Okay."

"If I don't answer, Tenley will go all Olivia Benson on my ass and hunt me down," Tate explains. "She may even show up here or something nuts. She once broke into my place at two in the morning because I ignored her calls and texts for two days and she thought I was dead or kidnapped or something."

"So answer it," I prompt and Dylan coos loudly from the

living room. He's sitting up now and getting bored, I can tell. He's also a little tired judging by the way his eyes are dropping.

Tate looks at me and then at Dylan. "Can you guys... give me some privacy."

"You haven't told her."

"Not yet."

I inhale deeply, swallowing down the disappointment and frustration I'm feeling toward him right now. "Tenley isn't going to rat you out to your parents. And she could help with him."

His shoulders stiffen defensively. "It's not exactly an easy conversation, okay? I'll tell them all, at the same time, when it's right and that's not now. So can you please give me some privacy?"

I turn and march out of the kitchen. Grabbing Dylan I gently plop him on my hip and grab the baby Bjorn from the fancy hook on the hall stand by the door. "Where are you going?"

I shove my feet into my slip-on Sketchers and grab the extra set of keys he gave me off the console table. "Out. So you can have your privacy."

"You don't have to leave," Tate argues. "I just meant—"

The door closes behind me, cutting off whatever else he was going to say. I walk out of the complex with Dylan strapped to my chest, wandering down Abbott Kinney toward the beach a few blocks away. Tate is not the man I thought he was. I think eventually he will be the father Dylan deserves. Hopefully, before the kid is old enough to know the difference.

When I get back to the house, Tate is gone. What's left of my Roscoe's meal and the remaining donuts are wrapped up on a plate on the counter. There's a post-it on the cling wrap that says *Dr. Carter. 11. And I'm sorry it has to be this way.*

"And that's why I'm annoyed, Tate. It doesn't have to be this way," I mutter. Dylan is already nodding off so I take him upstairs, make sure he doesn't need a diaper change, and put him down for a nap.

There's a knock on the door not long after I finish my chicken and waffles. With trepidation, I answer it to see a middle-aged man with a gentle smile. Dr. Carter is actually great. He does a quick, relatively painless exam and determines I seem to be healing well. I don't even need X-rays, he can feel the ribs are in place. But he tells me not to rush things, especially with the concussion and if my headaches persist for another week or two, he wants to see me again.

When he leaves I decide it's a good time to deal with my dad. I look around Tate's place to find an innocuous backdrop for the video call I have to make. Our family are video people. If I simply call him on the phone, he'll know I'm hiding something.

There's one wall in the kitchen without a painting or picture. So I go stand with my back against it and video chat my dad. He answers quickly and his face is awash with concern when it fills my screen. "Where are you?"

"I'm in the US," I say simply.

"Where?"

"The United States."

"Mallory Lisa Echolls, stop being obstinate and answer your father!" The phone shifts and now my mother's face is filling it. She looks pissed off.

"Hannah give me the fucking phone," Dad snaps in the background. "She called me, not you."

"Where are you, Mallory?" Mom snaps.

"I'm in Oregon," I lie because at this point, what's one more?

"Why the hell are you in Oregon?" Dad barks. "Hannah, give me the phone!"

More jostling, I get a quick glimpse of the ceiling in my dad's study at their apartment in New York and then the fabric of my mom's lavender sweater, and then my dad's face fills the screen again. His crow's feet look deeper than ever. His silver hair is whiter. "What, or who is in Oregon?"

"A yoga retreat." More lies. "I needed to decompress. I've been through a lot."

"Which is why you should be with us," he argues.

"Dad New York isn't my home," I remind him. "And I don't need to be dodging a billion strangers on every sidewalk with broken ribs."

"How are you feeling?" Mom's voice floats through the phone and I think I see her chin just behind Dad's left shoulder as she tries to get in on the call again.

The two of them have never been a team. Not one day of my life. At least, not the type of team you think of when you picture the perfect marriage. I have wondered more than once why they got together and why they stay together. Everything about them seems difficult. "I'm fine. I just... I wasn't ready to see anyone."

"You'll be at Beckett's wedding, though, right?" Mom asks. All I can see is her chin and the blunt edges of her wavy silver-blonde bob. "You're in the wedding party, you know. Now that you're not in London there's no reason not to attend."

She's right. I didn't want to attend because I didn't like his fiancée, who is his old high school sweetheart. They rekindled their romance while he was dating, and living with, someone else, which I also didn't like. But Beckett said the same thing my mom is saying. I'm a bridesmaid. His fiancée insisted and now that I don't have to leave a job or fly across the ocean, I can't say no. "It's not until the end of June, Mom. I don't know what I'm doing next week let alone three months from now."

"You can't bail on your brother's wedding," Dad barks. "The local paper is covering it and if the Barons win the Cup, which is a distinct possibility, I'm going to have ESPN and Sports

Center cover it too. Because I'll make sure my day with the Cup is the same day."

"The General Manager gets a day with the Cup?" It's a tradition where each player gets twenty-four hours in the off-season at home with the trophy after they win, but I've never heard of the management getting the same honor.

"It's not called that. I mean, we don't get it specifically," Dad backtracks. "But if I win the team the Cup, I'm having it at your brother's wedding."

My brother who doesn't play hockey. Who is a doctor who was made to feel like that was a subpar accomplishment because it wasn't hockey. That brother is going to have the Cup at his wedding. Beckett will be thrilled. *Not.*

"I'll be at the wedding." I sigh in defeat. "I'll likely be home well before that anyway."

"Just go home now, Mallory," Mom chides. "Yoga isn't going to help you. It's all hogwash, new-aged crap. Your brother is a doctor. You can stay with him and he and Heather can heal you while you help her plan her wedding. That will be exciting."

"Nope. I'll stay where I am for now. I'll let you know when that changes," I reply firmly.

"Since when did you become the stubborn child?" Dad grumbles. "I saw that Garrison kid you hang out with, by the way."

I furrow my brow like I have no idea who he's talking about for a millisecond and then act confused. "You saw Tate?"

"Yeah. I went on the west coast trip with the team," he says, adding, "We beat his team."

"Good for you Dad," I say with no cheer whatsoever.

"Kid played like shit. I don't know how he ever got close to his dad's record," Dad laments.

"Because his dad's record isn't that great." There goes Mom, always willing and able to jump on the Garrison-Haters bandwagon.

"Well, if you play him in the playoffs, tell him hi," I say and an alert pings on my phone telling me there's motion in Dylan's crib. If he's waking up and I don't get up there, he'll wail and they'll hear him. "I have to go. I have a Vinyasa class to get to."

"What's that?"

"Yoga, Dad." I sigh. "I'll reach out again, but don't worry about me. I'm okay."

"We love you, Mallory!" Mom insists, and I know they do. In their own way.

"Love you both. Talk soon."

I hit end at the same moment Dylan lets out a cry. Tucking my phone into my pocket I head upstairs. I can't believe how many lies I'm telling lately. I can't blame Tate for all of them, but we better sort out Dylan's custody fast so I can just get the hell out of here. Because the biggest lie of all is the one I have to keep telling myself while I'm living under Tate Garrison's roof. And that's the lie that I don't want to pick up where we left off in that bathroom last night.

Chapter 9

Tate

No one sits next to me on the flight to Seattle, and I don't blame them. By the time I left for the arena, for the eleven a.m. skate, Mallory hadn't come back from her walk. And when I got home after the skate to grab my luggage, she and Dylan were in her bedroom with the door shut so I never even got to smooth things over with her or say goodbye to him. Now I was angry at her too.

I wanted to say goodbye to Dylan. He would probably screech at me but I still wanted to see him before I left for four days. He was mine. My brain was finally starting to wrap itself around that fact, and every day I saw him I started to feel more and more for him. It was nuts. The fear and confusion I felt when I looked at him has faded and now it's being replaced with a warm, tight feeling in my chest. Love? Awe? Pride? Probably all of that.

The plane taxis to the gate and most of the guys are already out of their seats grabbing their carry-on stuff. I unclip my seat belt and take my phone out of the seat pocket in front of me. I turn it on and feel a pinch of disappointment that there isn't a text from Mallory. Dylan would be having dinner now. I would love an update. A picture. She said she'd send them while I was on road trips.

"She's being unfair," I growl to myself but a head pops up over the seat in front of me. It's Nash.

"Who is being what?"

"This woman... I'm..." Oh shit. What do I say? "I'm involved with is being unfair. About something. We're fighting. It's a long story."

Nash smiles. "Gee, Garrison you seem like you're great at communication. I have no idea why this woman would have a problem with you."

"Ha. Ha." I roll my eyes as his brother pops up next to Nash, and rests his thick, inked forearms on the back of his seat.

"Do not tell me you're in a *relationship*," Crew says, the disgust in his expression is matched only by the disgust in his tone. "You promised me you'd be here for my single era. All of it."

"I *am* here for it," I promise and rise myself, slipping into the aisle and yanking my Tumi leather travel bag from the overhead. "Bachelor for life, amigo. This is just... someone I'm involved with for, like business reasons. And she's being unreasonable and I'm pissed off. But yeah, single for life bro. Or at least until this career is over."

"Well, thankfully you had your shit together at morning skate so the career isn't on the chopping block just yet," Crew jokes, and Nash snickers.

"You two are fucking comedians," I mutter as we all start to file off the plane.

I'm hit with a gust of frigid air, which reminds me that it's barely spring. It's hard to keep track of seasons in LA because they don't have any. March feels like January or November. It's not any different. Although Tenley jokes that they do have seasons in Los Angeles. They have drought and fire instead of summer and winter.

My phone buzzes in my pocket and I yank it out hoping to see Mallory's name. But it's not. It's Tenley. I swear she's a witch and she knows when her name is thought or uttered anywhere in the world.

> Hope you landed safely so that you can read this text and know I still think you're a dick.

> I said I'd rent you any listing on Air BnB as a replacement. I'm trying Ten. Fuck.

I had forgotten I promised to let my sister and her friends use my apartment while I was away on this road trip. Tenley is in her final year of year of Film and Television at UCLA and she and her classmates wanted to shoot a big chunk of their final project at my place. It didn't seem like a big deal two months ago when I agreed, but I hadn't anticipated having a baby hiding out there.

So when she called today to confirm, I had to lie and tell her a teammate's house had a pipe burst and I'd agreed to let his wife and kids stay at mine while we were away. I had no idea how good I was at lying and I'm kind of bummed I know now. Lies suck. Liars suck and I'm one of them. And I've made Mallory one of them too.

"You haven't stopped scowling for more than three seconds the entire flight and now you're doing it again," Duke Hendrix tells me. He's our backup goalie and one of the guys I'm closest to on the team besides Nash and Crew.

"Yeah. Not a great day." I growl and the lighthearted look on his face grows serious. "I'll be fine."

"Have you met with the sports psychologist yet?" Duke's question almost makes me stumble. "I'm related to the coach, remember? It was my aunt Winnie's birthday last week and they're in town from Maine so we all went to dinner and Jude... Coach Braddock mentioned it. Before you get all pissy, know that I've been seeing a sports psychologist since I was sixteen, and a regular therapist since I was six. I had a deadbeat dad and a mom who grew up with some serious emotional trauma. She was pro-active and it was the best thing ever."

"I've lined up a private one. Not the team's shrink," I tell him because even though I think they have some oath where they can't share my personal info, I don't trust this guy on the Quake's payroll to keep my baby news to himself. "Gonna talk to the one my cousins use. Can we keep this between us, though?"

"Yeah. Sure." Duke shrugs as we walk through the small private jet terminal. "You still hung up on that bullshit stereotype the world feeds us that men can't have emotions or get help for them?"

I glare at him but that just makes him smile. "I'm not some kind of caveman. I'm cool with feelings and mental health. My cousin Conner is basically living with a psychiatrist, remember? She's family even if they aren't married yet. I just... don't want a bunch of questions from the guys. Or my family. I know you're friends with Grady but can you maybe not mention me or this to him if you guys hang this trip?"

"Dude, you don't have to ask. I don't talk teammates with Grady," Duke replies. "We don't talk hockey at all."

Grady and Duke were on the Winterhawks together last year, but then Duke got traded here. It was great for Grady because my cousin got moved up from backup goalie to the starter, but Duke, who is older and on the backend of his career became our backup, which isn't so great for him but also not unexpected since he's pushing thirty-four.

We all get on the private bus that will take us to our hotel in downtown Seattle. Duke sits next to me and is blissfully quiet. I lean my head against the window and start checking my emails. There's a notification from Amazon and I click on it. Someone has gifted me a book. I recognized Mallory's email as the sender. She's had the same one since high school.

The e-book she sent me is called *Conscious Parenting; Creating Positive Bonds and Raising Emotionally Secure Children* by Laurel Rody. No note. No explanation, but one isn't needed. I need help and she may be mad at me but she's still trying to help me. I really need to fix things with her before she takes off. I've let my friendship with Mallory be fucked for many reasons for far too long. And yeah, I am still wildly attracted to her, but she's right. We have to restrain ourselves because getting naked together won't do anything to improve our friendship. And in the end, that's the most I can ever be to her. For her. At least for the foreseeable future.

* * *

Forty minutes after we get to the hotel, I'm flat on my back on my bed in team sweats reading the book Mallory gifted me. I'm two chapters in and so overwhelmed I'm making notes on the hotel stationery. I had no idea all the intellectual and emotional thought involved in raising a child. I know that sounds insane, and now I have a new respect for all parents—especially mine. They did all of this without me even realizing it.

I decide to call my mom. I would normally just text her if I had something to say or video call her. As Conner pointed out I'm the Garrison who uses his phone for everything but calls. Right now, though, I need to hear her voice and I also know if she sees my face, she'll know something *big* is up. So a good old-fashioned voice call is the only option. Sitting up with my back against the headboard I hit her personal cell on my list of contacts. When she answers she sounds pleasantly surprised.

"Hi Tater Tot!" Her calm, melodious voice instantly relaxes me. "What a surprise. I was just talking to Auntie Callie about you."

"Oh. You're with Auntie C?" I say, and immediately want to hang up. My aunt Callie, my mom's middle sister, is also married to my dad's older brother. She's an aunt twice over to me, technically, and I love her dearly, but she's intense and couldn't spell the word boundaries with a dictionary in her hand. She is like a drug-sniffing dog at an airport when it comes to problems and secrets. She finds them without even trying. So I have to be guarded on this call. "Well, I just wanted to say hi. So hi. I'll let you get back to whatever it is you're doing."

"We're just having donuts after the gym," Mom says with a small, guilty giggle.

"It's all about balance, Tater. You could use some donuts!" my aunt calls out, and Mom shushes her.

I smile. I do love my family. And that's why this situation is even harder. I care what they think more than anything. If I see looks of disappointment on their faces when they find out about Dylan, I will literally wither and die inside.

"What's up with my favorite son?" Mom asks lightly. I'm her only son, by the way, so it's not a hard title to earn.

"I just... wanted to say thanks," I say and feel a knot in my throat. "You and Dad are awesome."

"We are," she agrees but then her voice drops an octave. "Why are you finally noticing?"

I laugh but the sound comes out like a choked gargle. "I've always noticed, I just never bothered telling you."

"Good to know we're appreciated," she says. "I don't need to hear it, but thank you. I love you. Now what's going on?"

"I've just been..." I close my eyes. I can't tell her. Not over the phone with Aunt Callie right there and not Dad. I should tell them together. In person. "Under a lot of pressure recently and it's got me thinking deep thoughts. Not a big deal, I promise. I mean nothing I can't handle but I've been thinking a lot about you and Dad and my childhood and how lucky I was without even knowing it."

"Tate," she says my name softly. I can picture her auburn eyebrows pinching together and her wide mouth falling flat with concern.

"Is he okay?" Callie's voice, also heavy with concern, filters through the phone.

"A minute," Mom says to her sister and then. "Seriously Cal. Give me a second."

"Mom, don't be freaking out. Don't let Auntie C freak out. This is not some kind of crisis." I open my eyes and stare at the cream-colored ceiling. I realize Dylan must stare at the ceilings a lot. It's just plain old white in the guest room. I should change that. "Can't a guy just have an adult moment of clarity without everyone freaking out?"

"I'm outside the donut shop now. Alone," Mom tells me. "Did you know we got another foot of snow yesterday? It's all white and pretty but it's way too cold. I could use some warmth and vitamin D. I think maybe your dad and I should come to LA."

"No!" I say it so loud and forcefully that even I realize it's a red flag. Fuck. "I mean, I'm not even there, Mom. Road trip. And with playoffs looming Coach already has us on lockdown so I can't do much outside of workout, play, and sleep."

"Ah yeah, lockdown." She lets out a small sigh. "I don't miss the slog of the playoffs, being a player's wife. It was like being a single parent who lived with a grumpy, distracted polar bear."

"So Dad wasn't exactly a hands-on parent when he was a player?" I mean, I sort of remember. My dad retired when I was twelve. But his last few years his team didn't make the playoffs and before that, well, I was too busy being a kid to notice who was tucking me in at night or reading me a story. I remember Dad doing things, though, but maybe they stick out in my head because it was so rare.

"He was there for the big stuff," Mom replies. "He even blew off a practice the morning of a Game 7 when Tenley spiked a fever and needed to go to the emergency room. The coach was not sympathetic because it was just an ear infection, and we kind of guessed it at the time too, but Tenley was just inconsolable and I had you to handle too. You used to cry when she cried, over anything. It was the cutest thing. It was like you were trying to back her up or had sympathy pains or something."

I bite back a smile at that. It's hard to believe I ever felt that close to Tenley. I mean, I love my sister, but we are so different and tend to bicker a lot now. Mom keeps reminiscing. "He got benched for two whole periods for that, but he never bitched to me or the coach. But yeah, for the most part, in playoffs your dad kept his own schedule. Slept in the guest room so he wasn't disturbed by me or you guys. If they went deep into the playoffs the coach put the team in a hotel, like every day was a road trip, to keep them in the right mindset. That pissed me off, but even when he was home he ate his own meals because his diet got so strict. He kept his own hours. You kids would see him maybe two hours a day. Sometimes I took you to the practices with the other wives and kids just so you could have a glimpse of him. It was tough, but I knew what I signed on for when I married him and I regret none of it."

"But how do single parents handle it?"

"You know any single dads in the league?" she asks.

"Mmm... I don't know any single parent players personally but there're divorced players who have a kid or two."

"And I would bet it all that they aren't the primary custodian," Mom replies. "Which means the ex does all the heavy lifting when they're on the road or in playoffs or whatever. Ask your ex-Aunt Ashleigh. She divorced your Uncle Devin but she couldn't divorce the lifestyle. Even after Devin married Callie, Ashleigh had to stay in New York because of the shared custody agreement. Before Devin married Callie, Ashleigh took Conner every road trip. You can leave the player but not the lifestyle. Not if there's a baby involved."

"Right," I sigh. "So you basically just can't be a single dad and a professional hockey player. At all. It's impossible."

"I mean, you can. You can do anything but..." Mom pauses and it sends the fear of God into me. She's thinking about what I'm saying and trying to figure out why I'm saying it. "Why are we talking about single dads and hockey?"

"A guy on my team might be..." Oh God, here we go with the lies again. "Might be having a kid with someone who... he thinks won't stick around so he'd have to do it on his own."

"As a hockey player?" Mom sounds skeptical. "Then he needs to get himself a very good nanny because, for nine months of the year, his kid is going to be raised by one, sadly. Unless he has family close by."

He doesn't. Except a sister even younger than him. But he does have a great nanny, for now.

"Is this fellow player young like you?" Mom asks and I hear wind rustling into the phone mic. I know Silver Bay wind in spring can be bitingly cold. "I don't envy a young single parent. Babies are not for the faint of heart. Now, why did you call? For real. Be honest. I am starting to freak out a little with this conversation."

"I'm fine," I lie and try to sound bright and chipper, which is probably another red flag because I'm not a bright chipper person. I'm more of an even-toned, snarky person. "I just really want to break Dad's record and I haven't been playing my best lately so it might not happen. And we have playoffs coming and we could actually win the Cup and I'm..."

"Upset about Diana Hutchens?"

"What?"

"I heard she was in an accident in London and died," Mom informs me. "I know you must know. And I don't know how close you two really were, but I do know you spent enough time together that this should be a little upsetting, to say the least."

"Yeah. It is," I admit. "More than I care to admit."

"Did you have deeper feelings for her than you thought, Tater?"

"Not like... nothing heavy or anything," I admit and that wave of guilt washes over me again. Because I wish I had been madly in love with her, for Dylan's sake. "But I liked her as a person. We were friends above all else. I just... it shouldn't have happened."

"I know. That's why they call it an accident," Mom replies and then I hear Aunt C again.

"Get your butt in here before you freeze!"

Right. My mom is outside in the cold in Silver Bay, Maine. "Mom, thanks for the talk, but go inside and get warm. I'll be fine."

"You call me anytime, for any reason Tate," she says and the worry in her voice is amplified by the fact she said my real name and not my nickname.

"I always do, Mom."

"You can tell me anything, honey," she says and oh how I wish that were true at the moment, but it isn't. I need to settle his custody and make him like me before I announce this to my parents. I need them to see I have it handled. It's going to be okay.

"Love you and love to Dad and Auntie C." I hang up the phone, toss it across the bed, and stare at the ceiling again.

Eventually, I continue reading the book Mallory sent, adding notes to the hotel stationery. I finally break down, reach for my cell again, and text her.

> Hope he settled okay tonight. Thanks for the book. Already started it.

I can tell she's read the message almost instantly but all I get as a response is a thumbs up. So I text again.

> I hate fighting with you.

It's not eloquent but it's honest.

She texts me a picture of Dylan. He's asleep, sucking his thumb.

> I miss him. And you. Have a good night.

I really do miss him, which is crazy because a few weeks ago I didn't know he existed. I need to get my shit together. For him. This is my new reality and I need to adapt to it as fast and as well as possible. I scroll through my contacts to the number Conner sent me and I call the sports psychologist.

Chapter 10

Mallory

Of all the things that have gone wrong in my life, especially recently, I've never once felt targeted, like the universe was conspiring against me. Like I was doomed or jinxed or cursed. But as I push the stroller through the gates to Tate's complex and see his front door wide open, I can't help but wonder if maybe there *is* some kind of cosmic vendetta with my name on it.

I know Los Angeles has its share of crime, and I've been careful since I got here to lock the door, even when I'm home. Park Tate's fancy car near the entrances to the stores I go to so the walk isn't long. Be vigilant when I'm on strolls with Dylan, like the one I just returned from. To find the house being robbed? I mean, what else could it be? Tate is still on his road trip. He doesn't get back until tomorrow morning. His cleaner came yesterday. Maybe she forgot something and came back?

I move myself and the stroller so I'm blocked from the open door by a large palm. And then I dig into the belt bag I have on. I have the house keys and my cell in there but not the car keys. Shit. I was hoping to maybe get in the car and drive to a police station. Instead, I pick up my phone and start to dial 9-1-1.

Tate is going to be so mad, but like, what else can I do?

Before I can hit send, I accidentally drop the phone. It hits the pavement with a clatter that sounds like fireworks going off in my brain. So loud! But was it really? Dylan coos, unaware of the precariousness of the situation. I bend to pick up the phone and glance around, hoping another tenant is out and I can call to them for help.

And then I see her.

Tenley Garrison, walking up to the front door of Tate's townhouse, carrying a giant light... the kind used on movie sets. I start to back up, pulling the stroller and myself toward the front gates. But of course, she sees me. Our eyes literally lock and I look away and spin the stroller around quickly, Dylan squeals happily, like he's on an amusement park ride or something.

"Mallory? Mallory Echolls?"

Oh no.

I keep walking. Fast.

But being Tenley, she doesn't stop. And she gets louder. "Hey! You!"

I make it to the sidewalk, which is amazing because the automatic door beside the gate for pedestrians opens super slow. But Tenley is bogged down with that light she's holding so she can't exactly run after me. Except that she must have put it down because I hear fast approaching footsteps and then suddenly there she is, directly in front of me. I immediately drop the sunshield over the front of the stroller so she can't see Dylan.

"Mallory," she says with a warm but confused grin on her face. "I knew it was you! Didn't you hear me call?"

"No. I... S-Sorry," I stutter. "Hi, Tenley."

Tenley is the only Garrison that intimidates the hell out of me. Out of probably everyone. She's this... *force*. She's just so unabashedly sure of who she is and has been like that since we were in high school. It doesn't hurt that she's drop-dead gorgeous too. Even now with her hair in a ponytail under a UCLA Extension baseball cap and no discernible makeup on her face, she's stunning.

"What are you doing here?" she asks, still smiling. "Did you know Tate lives here? This is crazy. I thought you were in England."

"I was. I'm here now." I try to smile back at her but I'm in full-blown panic mode. "And I have to get somewhere. I have a meeting."

"A meeting?" Tenley blinks those big blue eyes of hers. "So, wait, you live here now? In Venice? And you, what? Babysit for someone in Tate's complex?"

"Yeah. I babysit one of his neighbor's kids," I hate lying about Dylan, or at all, but I have no choice. Tate made it clear he doesn't want his family to know yet.

Tenley reaches for the sun cover to lift it and I gently push her hand away. Our eyes meet again and I smile more effectively than last time. "I forgot to put sunblock on him so I'm keeping him covered."

"So you and Tate must be hanging out again," Tenley states and she seems to have no intention of unblocking my path so I have no escape at the moment.

"I have run into him."

"Yeah, I mean must be hard to avoid him. What with your bedroom directly across the hall from his," Tenley notes and her arms fold across her chest. She's not smiling. Her big blue eyes are narrowed. "His house is filled with baby stuff, Mallory."

"Oh." That's my admission of guilt and she knows it.

Tenley looks so proud of herself. I heard she was minoring in criminology and I guess she's acing it judging by her deduction skills. "He said I could use his place for filming and then he canceled saying he had a teammate's family staying with him. The Quake are renowned for having a relatively young roster. There are only two players with kids on the whole team, and I've met them both volunteering at Quake events and going to games with Tate's family pass. I called them both and neither of them were staying at Tate's so I used my spare key."

"He's going to be pissed you found out this way," I whisper to her. "And things with him and I are already strained."

"It can't be that bad if he's letting you and your baby stay with him," Tenley says, still not getting the entire picture. Probably because it's a plot twist even too big for her detective brain. "I mean Tate is not a kid person or a guest person. Women never even spend the night in his bachelor casa. Even after they take a ride on his hockey stick."

"Ten, you should just talk to Tate about this," I suggest. "In the meantime, you can finish filming whatever you're filming and I'll take Dylan to a coffee shop and come back in, like, an hour. Does that work?"

"We need three hours," Tenley says, and her expression gentles. "You and... Dylan, did you call him? You two can be there. It's a quiet scene between a mom and a daughter. We just need the kitchen and the patio."

"Okay." I nod. "He needs a nap anyway so I'll stay upstairs until you're done."

Tenley nods and we walk side-by-side back into the complex. There're a couple other people in the house, I can see them through the front window as Tenley helps me lift the stroller up the stairs to the front stoop. "So when did you have a baby? While you were in England?"

"Yeah. He was born in England," I answer and my brain does backflips trying to figure out how I'm going to get Dylan out of the stroller without Tenley getting a good look at him. If

Tenley gets a good look at him, I'm sure she will figure out he's Tate's son.

We're face-to-face on the small front porch with Dylan's stroller between us. He makes an agitated noise and his little legs kick. He wants to be out of the stroller and I don't blame him. "Can we shift positions so I can get him out? The entrance is too small to manage the stroller in there. I usually take him out and collapse it before bringing it in."

"Sure," Tenley says and we shimmy past each other. I squat and stick my head under the cover instead of lifting it. I reach to unfasten Dylan and he claps his hands and grins at me.

"I know Dyllie Bear. I'll free you and we can grab a snack and take a nap while... my friend does her thing, okay?" I say to him and he gurgles and grins and babbles what sounds like "babees" on repeat, which I think is his way of saying berry. I usually give him blueberries and raspberries as his after-stroll snack.

"How old is he?"

"Almost ten months," I reply and scoop him out, holding him to my chest so his head is on my shoulder, facing away from his unknowing aunt. Then I gently cup the back of his head to keep him there.

The screen door is held open by a big black box with wires hanging from it. I think it's a speaker or something. She motions for me to enter the house, but I don't move and nod toward the door, suggesting she goes first. Neither of us move.

"So his birthday is..."

"July," I reply. "Why do you care, Tenley?"

I probably sound rude, but I'm freaking out about her line of questioning. I can literally see her brain taking every piece of information I give her and putting it together like she's solving a puzzle.

"Because you and Diana were visiting Tate last fall," Tenley says, filling my heart with dread. She tilts her head, the ends of her long blonde ponytail grazing her tiny bare shoulder covered only by a tank top strap. "Let's see your little bundle."

"He's tired. And shy."

"Mallory. I'm not going anywhere until you let me see the little guy," Tenley replies quietly, her voice so calm it's terrifying. Like she already knows the answer to the question she isn't asking.

So I take Dylan and turn him around in my arms. I keep my eyes glued to Tenley's face as she looks at Dylan. She smiles and bends forward and gives him a little wave. And he gives her a little wave back, which is really just opening and closing his little chubby fingers.

And then, Tenley reaches for him and I let her take him out of my arms, lifting him over the stroller and into her arms. He doesn't cry or fuss. He blinks up at her with a goofy semi-grin on his tired face and reaches for the end strands of her ponytail that are sitting on her shoulder.

"Hi little man," she says sweetly as he stares at her. "Dylan, I'm your Auntie Tenley."

And there it is. She knows.

When her eyes look up at me, I stare back without a word. No lies. No argument. I've lied and lied and lied again and I'm just too emotionally exhausted to do it again. And she's too smart to fall for it anyway. Tenley nods at me as if accepting my silence as the answer and her eyes well with tears. But she smiles and turns and carries Dylan into the house.

I feed Dylan a snack in the living room, with Tenley's help, while the other people she brought set up the camera equipment and lighting and two actors do their own makeup in the dining room. When I bring him upstairs for his nap, Tenley comes with me and once he's settled she heads downstairs to finish prepping for her shoot. I stay upstairs, sit on the bed, and contemplate calling Tate. He needs to know what happened but I don't want him to yell at me. This isn't my fault. And I also don't want him to get so upset it throws him off his game. They play Vancouver tonight and then get on a flight home first thing in the morning.

We haven't really talked since our fight before he left. I interviewed four nanny candidates yesterday at a coffee shop around the corner. Two were good matches. I sent him their names and my notes via email. He texted back that he would set up second interviews. And other than sending him shots of Dylan, we don't speak.

I start to text him now, but then erase it and then text again and then erase it, and then... there's a soft knock on the door. Tenley pokes her head in. She shoots me a smile. "Have you told him I know yet?"

"No," I admit.

"Well, it can wait. Come watch the action downstairs." Tenley motions for me to get up and out of the room. "Ever seen a film being shot? It's fun. Plus I'm the director on this so you can watch me boss people around."

Her grin gets wider and I laugh a little and head downstairs with Tenley.

Chapter 11

Mallory

As soon as we get downstairs she starts commanding everyone, giving orders and directions and everyone listens and scurries around quickly. She's not rude about it or anything. She's just authoritative.

She tells me to sit in the dining room and watch. A guy walks by me, holding a camera. He's a big, hulking guy with dark wavy hair and sparkling blue eyes. He's hot. So hot I'm not sure why he's behind a camera instead of in front of one. As he brushes by me again he gives me a smile and I smile back. It feels awkward but if he notices, he doesn't react.

The scene in the kitchen is about a mom confronting a daughter about having lied about something. I'm half-paying attention, half lost in my thoughts. But it is interesting to see the behind-the-scenes view of this. Tenley is incredible too. She's an entirely different person than the girl I knew growing up. She's so professional and focused. No hint of the party girl who loved to throw social grenades around like confetti, starting trouble and walking away with a smile.

The shoot is done before Dylan even wakes from his nap and Tenley announces she's staying the night here, so everyone else has to take the equipment back to the school for her, in their cars. The handsome camera dude groans. "Ten, you promised us all beers at the Saddle Ranch after this."

"Yeah, well, rain check," Tenley says, reaching up to pat his broad shoulder. "I need to bond with my brother's baby mama."

"That's not me," I announce and now every eye in the place is locked on me. I stand up, the dining chair making a squeak as it slides back. "I'm Dylan's nanny, Ten. Not his mom."

"But... well, where the hell is the..." And then it hits her. She must have heard about Diana's death. She still has ties to Silver Bay and I've seen mention of Di's death popping up on local friend's social media in the last couple of weeks as the news spread.

Tenley's eyes widen and fill with tears. "Diana?"

I nod.

The hot guy, whose name I still don't know looks between the two of us. Trying to figure out what the hell is going on, I'm sure. Tenley takes a shuddering breath and her hands lift to her mouth. "Oh my God, that poor boy."

She walks out of the room and out the front door, probably to collect her thoughts and emotions. I get it. I just dropped one hell of a bomb. Hot guy is collecting cables, and the actors are grabbing their things to leave. The sound woman is also gathering her things and the light guy is already on his way out the door.

The silence makes my stress levels escalate. I close my eyes and take a deep breath. And then I hear someone speak. The voice is deep and close. "Well, I have no idea what drama we've just stepped into but I, for one, am happy you aren't the mother to Ten's brother's baby. Because now I can ask for your number and not get punched by Tenley."

My head spins and I find him looking at me with a friendly

but sheepish grin. The man has a toothpaste commercial smile. "You're joking right?"

"No. You're cute," he tells me flatly. "And this seems like a hell of an interesting meet cute, so why not?"

"You know the term meet cute?"

"I'm studying film, so yeah," he says and extends his hand. "I'm Fisher by the way. Fisher Adamson."

"Mallory. Echolls."

"My favorite hockey player growing up was Beau Echolls."

"My uncle."

"Of course." He grins. "Any friend of Tenley's is always hockey or hockey adjacent."

I smile. I can't believe it because of everything going on, but I smile. He grins back. "So...? Digits?"

"I... I mean..." I can't give this guy my number. "I'm probably not staying in California much longer."

Probably? Why did that word leave my mouth? I am *not*. One hundred percent not staying in California.

"Okay well, then we'll have to go on a date sooner rather than later," he replies and walks over to the refrigerator in the kitchen. There's a magnetic whiteboard on the side. It's got a dry-erase pen hanging on a string. Tate uses it to leave notes for the cleaner. Fisher grabs the pen and scrawls a number on it. "Now you have my number so you can think about it. Text or call if you want to take me up on it."

And then he grabs his camera, a bag, and some cords and walks out the front door. I sit there staring at the number and watching everyone pack up and go until I get an alert on my phone Dylan is moving in his crib.

I quickly rush upstairs. When I get back down the crew of film students is gone and it's just Tenley texting madly on her phone. I freeze with Dylan on my hip. "Please say you aren't telling anyone about this."

"No," Tenley says and her blue eyes lift off her screen briefly. "I think Tate's in enough of a clusterfuck. I don't need to add to it by outing this situation to the rest of the fam. Especially not my parents."

"How do you think they'll take it?" I ask because I'm curious and I've never had the courage to ask Tate. And he's not offering his opinions or predictions to me.

Tenley sighs and drops her phone on the couch beside her. I place Dylan on the floor in front of her with his blocks, which he immediately grabs. Tenley leans down and cups the back of his little head. He looks up at her with a slobbery smile. "He's teething right now, so he's slobbering worse than a Saint Bernard."

I toss Tenley one of the facecloths I keep handy and she wipes his face. He gurgles and goes back to his blocks. Watching Tenley watch Dylan is surreal. Her pretty face is awash with emotion. She looks both in awe and in fear. "Tate is not on anyone's bingo card as the first offspring to produce offspring, you know? If you polled every single member of the family, they'd probably have him tied for last with me. So, obviously, my parents will be a bit shocked. But they'll just melt when they meet Dylan. It'll be instant love. And joy."

"I don't think Tate believes that," I tell her, sitting at the other end of the sofa. "I think that's why he's so reluctant to tell anyone."

"I'll try to reassure him," Tenley tells me and leans back. Grabbing a pillow and hugging it to herself, she sighs. "How are you holding up?"

"I'm..." My eyes prick with tears. "I'll deal with me later."

"That's not a healthy attitude," Tenley says softly. "She was your best friend for years."

"Since third grade."

Tenley reaches over, takes my hand, and squeezes it. "I can't imagine how devastating it must be."

"I was... I was with her. In the car. When we crashed," I tell Tenley and I wish I could shut up, but suddenly I need to spill all of this onto someone and she's the only one here. "It was horrible weather, but Diana was managing. We'd come from a bridal fitting. She was engaged you know."

Tenley shakes her head. "I didn't know."

"She was engaged to this guy named Felix. He was rich and charming and she thought she'd won the jackpot. She didn't want to miss the fitting or cancel it because of rain." I shake my head. "Felix agreed to stay with Dylan so I could go with her. Anyway, the accident wasn't her fault. We were driving along on the freeway... they call them motorways, and then suddenly some car a few cars in front of us slammed on their brakes, and that caused the car in front of us to slam into him and we just didn't have enough time to stop. She slammed on the brakes. I remember that, but we slid, I guess."

I take a shuddering breath. "I don't remember much except waking up, upside down, hanging from my seat belt. My head was crushed against the passenger window that was covered in mud. I couldn't move my head so I couldn't see her.

"I think that's probably for the best," Tenley whispered. "Rumors at home say it was ugly."

"I could hear her." I sniffle and that's when I realize tears are sliding down my cheeks. I take my hand out of Tenley's and wipe at my cheeks. "Her chest had been crushed and she was choking on her own blood. And all she kept saying was 'Dylan'. And 'Help'. She wanted me to help him. It was her only thought as she died."

"Oh my God, Mallory."

The next thing I know Tenley is right beside me, almost on top of me, and I'm in a bear hug. Luckily her arms are across the top of my shoulders and neck, so she isn't squishing my ribs. I close my eyes and cry. Sob. And cling to her the way Dylan does me when he has a meltdown.

"I'm sorry," I whisper through the hiccups and tears.

"Don't be. Jesus, Mal, you haven't told anyone about this, have you?" Tenley rubs my back gently.

"No. I mean, I haven't seen anyone but your brother and Diana's ex-fiancé," I swallow and sniff. My head is pounding now, with all the emotion I've just expunged. "Felix didn't want to know anything. I thought he was in shock. Maybe he was. All he cared about was getting me and Dylan on the first plane out. And Tate... I mean he has enough to deal with. He doesn't need to add my sob story to his list of emotional trauma and he would take it on. He's that guy."

"I know," Tenley agrees. "Our parents think he's aloof and avoids commitment like the plague because he's in his selfish era. I think he thinks that too. But I know it's because when he has feelings, he only has big ones. And he is terrified of them. A kid... well he has no choice but to feel all the big feels. It must be fucking with him so bad. That explains why his game has struggled."

"He's trying harder than I give him credit for, I think" I pull out of her hug and see Tenley nod as she takes off her baseball hat and drops it on the couch beside her. Dylan automatically reaches for it and she lets him have it. "I wish Di had told him sooner. I wish I didn't have to come here and ruin his season."

She waves a hand dismissively. "Forget about that. Tate will figure it out on the ice. He's a Garrison. Let's focus on the important stuff, which is you and this perfect new Garrison. How can I help?"

"I have to meet Tate at a medical clinic tomorrow morning," I explain. "He's going straight there from the airport when the team lands. It's in downtown Los Angeles and I'm stressing about taking a freeway there. I've only done short runs to Target or the grocery store in his fancy car. Lord knows we don't have five-lane freeways in Silver Bay and after the accident..."

"Say no more. I will gladly drive my brother's car and take you to the appointment," Tenley agrees and squeezes my hand again.

"So I guess I should text him and give him a heads up." I sigh. I am not looking forward to telling Tate his secret is out.

"Nah. No need to stress him out now." Tenley pats my hand and gives me a reassuring grin. "Besides, over text or the phone, he won't believe I have his back. Little shit will think I'm going to stab him in the back and blab in the family group chat or something. Better he sees with his own eyes I'm on Team Dylan and not going to make this worse."

That makes sense. And besides, I don't want to throw him further off his game. Tenley reaches down and takes her hat from Dylan's hands then lifts it up and drops it on his head, making a goofy face while she does it. Dylan giggles with delight. She giggles back. I didn't realize how similar Tate and Tenley's features were until now, because I see her in Dylan too.

"I don't want to speak ill of the dead, but fuck Diana for not telling Tate." Tenley sounds furious and I can't blame her.

"You said it yourself," I reply. "He's not willing to give anyone anything of substance and Diana knew it. She accepted it. And then she found Felix."

"Felix was good to her? And Dylan??"

I nod and picture the guy who turned from Jekyll to Hyde the second Diana's death certificate was signed. "Felix was older than us. Thirty-two and wealthy and settled in a good career and he *was* very good to her. He agreed, without hesitation, to help her raise Dylan and was set to adopt him after they got married."

Tenley's big eyes get even bigger. "So Tate was going to lose all rights without even knowing it?"

I pick at the fringe on one of Tate's throw pillows. His style in this place doesn't really feel like him. It feels like he hired someone to decorate how a rich guy's place should look. "For the record, I intended to tell Tate myself if and when she tried to go through with the adoption. I knew she would disown me as a friend, and of course, fire me as a nanny, but I knew it was the right thing to do. But then we had the accident and I never got the chance."

"And now here you are."

"Here we are," I confirm.

Tenley shifts her blue eyes down to Dylan who is happily playing with her hat again, waving it like it's a flag and he's at the finish line of the Daytona 500. The late afternoon light sliced into the living room, showering him in golden hues. Angelic is the only word for him at the moment. Tenley tears up but ignores it, wiping calmly at her tears. "He's going to be so loved by everyone," she says with a soft smile. "As soon as I get my brother's head out of his ass and make him tell the fam."

I stare at her and try not to worry. Tenley is a bit of a bull in a china shop and Tate is fragile right now. She might just break him.

Chapter 12

Tate

"You really don't want to join us for wings?" Nash asks again as we make our way through the small, private parking lot at LAX for the charter planes.

I shake my head. "Nah. I'm exhausted and I have stuff to do at home."

"Are you finally banging that hot neighbor?" Crew asks crassly. "That would explain why you never come out anymore and what you have to *do* at home that's more important than an afternoon with us."

I smile at him because a couple of weeks ago, he would have been right with that guess. But the truth is I haven't thought about Tara at all. Or any of my current hookups, like Christine one of our communications team members. She and I hooked up after the Quake Christmas party and again on a road trip a couple months ago. She texted me her room number because she came on this road trip too, but I didn't do anything with the information. She's sent me a couple of texts since and I've ignored them.

It's not that I don't need to fuck, because, Jesus, do I ever. It would likely help immensely with all the stress I'm carrying. But my mind doesn't wander much from thinking of Dylan, and what's best for him, and keeping things with Mallory on a good note. I don't think bringing a strange woman over to fuck would help anything right now. And honestly, the only person I want to have sex with is Mallory.

I want it so bad I'm starting to have sex dreams about her. I mean, it's not weird. Mallory's gorgeous and we just had a brief but super-intense make-out session recently. Plus, that night we had together, as messed up as it was, was also hot.

Anyway, I don't correct Crew's assumption. It's just easier if he thinks I'm involved with someone. Then he and everyone else will stop questioning me about my absence from things. "Remember the curfew boys. Have some extra spicy wings for me."

I walk to my waiting Uber, which also confuses Crew and Nash because I always drive to the airport myself. Why wouldn't I? "Leant the car to Ten this week."

"I thought she was banned from driving your baby."

Baby. Yeah, I have a new definition of that word and it doesn't involve a vehicle. I shrug. "She wore me down."

"You'll be lucky to get it back in one piece," Nash jokes. He and my sister aren't exactly the best of friends. He thinks she's a loose cannon and she thinks he's a wet blanket. Neither is wrong.

I laugh at his comment and get in the back of the Uber. I reconfirm he's got the address of the clinic. It's supposed to be this high-security place that the lawyer says all of Hollywood goes to for their really top-secret medical stuff. He swears no one will ever know I'm getting a DNA test done there.

I'm being ridiculous about the secrecy of this, but the fact is, when the news of Dylan's existence breaks, I want to control the narrative. I haven't exactly figured out what the back story will be but I feel like 'Tate Garrison only takes responsibility for son after the mother dies' shouldn't be a part of the public history. No one will believe I didn't know about him, but if they did that just makes Diana look bad. Headlines like 'Woman tried to hide baby from pro athlete after one-night stand' aren't what I want the world to know either. Shit lives on the internet forever, and one day Dylan will be old enough to Google.

The DNA test is required to get my name on the birth certificate but no one needs to know about this. Once I'm legally named Dylan's dad, I'm going to hire my own PR person, who will work in tandem with the team's PR and we'll spin it that I knew about Dylan but agreed to have him raised in London. This tragedy changed the plan and I gladly stepped in. Because that part is true. I am gladly taking responsibility for Dylan. Even if he still hates hanging out with me. I am never letting him go.

There's not a ton of traffic, which is a miracle in L.A., and I feel a surge of excited anticipation as I get out of the Uber. The sun is shining, the sky is cloudless, and because we won both games on the road trip Coach says we don't have practice until tomorrow afternoon. So my mind is on how I can bond with Dylan in my extra free time.

I'm thinking of maybe taking him to the park, with Mallory of course, and maybe we can all go out to dinner. If Mallory is still ticked off at me, then maybe she can have the day off and I can take Dylan. She can go explore L.A. or whatever she wants.

All these ideas are running through my brain and I'm feeling optimistic as I round the side of the building, where the private parking lot is located. I had texted Mal and asked her to meet me there, so we could walk in together. I didn't want her to have to go in there and fill out the forms alone.

I turn the corner and see her standing by the passenger door of my Mercedes. She's got three takeaway coffee cups from Coffee Bean and Tea Leaf in her hands.

But leaning against the driver's side door, holding the car keys and my son, is my sister.

"Morning bro!" Tenley calls out like she's Mary Freakin' Poppins about to break into song or something. "Good to have you back home with your son. My nephew."

It feels like the ground underneath my feet has turned to liquid. My blood pressure spikes. Tenley motions for me to keep walking because I've stopped. "Put your luggage in the trunk and we'll have a chat as we head into the clinic."

"Did you tell anyone?"

"Of course not," she replies and my heart starts to beat in a normal rhythm again. "Now hurry up or you'll be late."

I start walking toward them again. My eyes slide over to Mallory. She holds out a coffee cup. "I didn't tell her. I was ambushed."

"I don't know why I'm surprised," I mutter and drop my bags in the trunk as it opens. I hit the button for it to close on its own, ignoring the coffee Mallory is still holding out to me, and reach for my kid.

Tenley doesn't look like she wants to give him up, but she does. I hold him up, high above my head. "Hey! How's my boy?"

He wiggles his arms and legs and gurgles. Did he... smile? Maybe? A little. I think he smiled! I bring him back down and try plopping him onto my hip but he twists his chunky little torso and reaches for Tenley. Fucking Tenley! She's known him, what? A day? Two?

I don't let her take him. I just turn and start walking toward the medical building with him. Mallory drops into step on one side of me and Tenley starts to walk with us too, but I turn and say, "You don't need to be here."

"But yet, here I am." Tenley shoots me that smile she's had since she was born, the smug, I-give-zero-shits smile. ARGH.

Dylan continues to wiggle and pout. I stop walking and turn to Mallory. "Trade you coffee for kid?"

She nods, hands me the cup I ignored earlier, and a second one I pass off to Tenley, and then takes Dylan from me. I ignore Tenley as she follows behind us into the building. I walk up to reception. "I have an appointment with Bedard Labs."

The woman types on a computer. "Identification please."

I put my coffee down on the counter between us and pull my license from my wallet. Mallory is digging in her bag and pulls out her passport. The receptionist's eyes move to Tenley. "She's waiting down here."

Tenley slaps her license on the counter next to mine and gives the woman a sugary smile. "I'll be going up. I'm his emotional support animal."

Mallory smiles. It's small like she's trying to hold it back.

"Don't encourage her."

"Sorry." She bites back the smile even more.

"I'm going with you Tater Tot so stop wasting time arguing," Tenley replies.

The woman behind the desk has already chosen to ignore us. She's back typing on her keyboard and then there's a buzzing sound and she starts handing us passes. "Fifteenth floor."

I grab my coffee and pass and turn toward the bank of elevators. Tenley falls in step beside me, bumping her shoulder against mine. "Fifteen. Lucky number. This is a good omen."

"Fifteen, like your jersey number," Mallory says and I nod.

"He loves the number fifteen."

"Why?" Mallory asks my sister, instead of me, as I punch the elevator button and the third one from the end opens with a ping.

"Because he needs to score fourteen short-handed goals to tie my dad but fifteen to beat him," Tenley explains.

We all step into the elevator and I notice Mallory's mouth

has fallen open. "But you've had number fifteen on your jersey since you were in high school."

"Since I was seven years old, actually," I replied and hit the button for floor fifteen. "That's when I realized my dad had the record. And that's when I told myself I would beat it."

"I had no idea that's why it was your number," Mallory whispers thoughtfully.

"Dyllie Bear is your number going to be sixteen?" Tenley asks Dylan and she tickles his belly through his little navy hoodie with white polar bears on it. He giggles and squeals and babbles something I think he thinks are words.

"He's going to play hockey?" Mallory asks.

"Of course," Tenley and I say in unison, in the exact same confident tone.

Mallory smiles. "I don't know why I even asked."

The elevator doors swish open and Tenley steps off before all of us. I quickly step off and block her from walking ahead of us. "Can you please just take a back seat? You shouldn't even be here."

"It's a good thing I am here," Tenley replies as we walk down the hall. "Otherwise you were going to force a woman who just had a serious car accident onto the shitshow that is L.A. freeways."

Oh. I hadn't even thought of that when I asked Mallory to meet us here. Fuck. I'm a total shithead. I glance over at her but she looks away and fusses over Dylan. I turn back to my sister. "How did you find out?"

"I decided to use your house for my shoot despite you saying no."

"Tenley, why can't you, for once, stop trying to control everything?" I reply my voice hard.

"Stop being an asshole," Tenley barks back. "I'm not controlling this. I'm just here for *you*. Whatever you need."

"I needed you to mind your own business and not break into my house and find out about him before I was ready to tell you," I hiss at her and then turn a corner and find yet another reception desk. This one is unmanned and just has a little sign that says to take a number from the dispenser on the counter and wait for it to pop up on the screen in the waiting room.

I yank off a number and move to the plastic seats across the hall in the glassed-in waiting room. There's a little play area in one corner and I walk to the seats closest to it. Mallory immediately sits Dylan on the plush gray playmat in front of the toys.

"Okay then." Tenley's glare gets steely. "Then I'm here for Mallory. She's been through it, Tate, and someone needs to watch out for her. This arrangement of yours isn't making her life easier."

Oh my God is Tenley really trying to pretend she gives a fuck about Mallory? She doesn't even know her. Not really. Not like I do. She's *my*... friend.

"Mallory loves Dylan like he's her own and she's here of her own free will," I reply tersely and shift in my small, almost too small, plastic seat to glare at Tenley. "And in case you forgot, her last name is Echolls. You think that the family will be thrilled to know she's the one who technically has custody at the moment? Or that *her* family will be thrilled she's shacked up with me? No. That would make this whole situation more complicated so keeping Dylan on the down low right now isn't just about me. It's about her too."

The room is silent when I finish my little rant. Mallory is watching me from her seat on the other side of Tenley with a look I can't fully understand. She seems... shocked and maybe a little hurt. Fuck. Did I hurt her feelings again? Why am I such an idiot without even knowing it?

Before I can rectify the situation, the electronic board above our heads beeps, and our ticket number and a room number appear on the board. I get up. Mallory gets up and picks up Dylan. Tenley gets up and I put my hand on her bony shoulder and gently but firmly push her back down into her seat. "You wait here."

She twists her face up in this ugly, pouty frown. "Hold that pose. Forever. Then maybe my teammates will stop hitting on you."

I turn and walk to the door, holding it open for Mallory who is carrying Dylan.

Chapter 13

Tate

The testing is simple, a swab of the inside of my cheek and Dylan's as well as a little clip of both our hair. I was super worried that he wouldn't like the swab in his mouth but he barely fusses at all. The nurse assured me that all his teething slobber made it easy to get a good sample. She assured us that the results would be ninety-eight percent conclusive and that I should have them in seven to ten business days. They are checked three times, by three different labs which is why it takes longer than other places.

The nurse leaves the room, and Mallory and I both get up to leave too, but she turns to me with a curious look in her caramel-colored eyes. "Are you worried about the results?"

"No. I know he's mine," I say simply. "I'm only doing this test for legal proof."

She nods and as soon as we get into the waiting room, Tenley springs out of her seat and reaches for Dylan. He goes to her happily and I have never been so jealous in my life. It must show on my face, because in the elevator on the way back down to the lobby Tenley shoots a sympathetic smile. "Don't get all butt hurt. He's a ladies' man, just like his daddy. He prefers hanging out with girls."

Mallory giggles. I roll my eyes. As we cross the parking lot I tell Tenley, "I'm going to call you an Uber."

"Nonsense. I'll drive you guys home. My car is at your place anyway."

She hands Dylan to Mallory pulls the keys from the front pocket of her jeans and punches the unlock button. Mallory heads to the passenger door to get Dylan into his car seat. I snatch the keys from Tenley's hand. "You have to Uber or pretzel yourself into the back seat with my son."

"Pretzel." She sighs and walks toward the car. "You know this car is not meant for a man with a baby."

"I know. I've already bought a G-Class but the dealer needed to order it because I wanted the model with all the extras, not just some. And in blue, which they didn't have at the dealership."

"You ordered a new car?" Mallory balks.

I nod and open the driver's side door, pushing my seat forward so Tenley can get in. "Yeah. Obviously, I need one that Dylan fits in. Also, it makes sense to have two cars. One for each of us."

Tenley twists even farther as she climbs in the back so that she can stare up at me with this what the fuck expression. I shoot her one back before pulling my gaze up to look at Mallory over the roof of the car. "You mean one for you and one for your nanny."

Actually, I mean Mallory. I even ordered it in blue because I know it's her favorite color. But I can't say that right now. Tenley will think it means something and Mallory will get all weird about it. So I just nod. "Yeah. The nanny car. Whatever."

I slide into the driver's seat as Tenley whines that her knees are at her ears and I need to move my seat up. Instead, I push it back a little bit more.

When we get to my townhouse, Mallory immediately grabs Dylan and rushes for the front door, mumbling something about checking his diaper, and then I'm stuck alone with Tenley in the parking lot.

"We need to talk," my sister says.

"I don't want to talk to you." I know I sound like a belligerent teenager. I kind of feel like one, and it's making me even more mad. "I should just go meet up with the guys."

"It's not even noon," Tenley replies. "Where the fuck are the guys going?"

"Our local spot opens early when they know we're home from a road trip. Nash, Crew, Collingwood, and a few others, including me, always want hot wings," I reply. "It's like a tradition."

She laughs at that. "Nash Westwood? Only spicy thing about that dude is his taste buds, I guess."

"He usually gets teriyaki."

"That tracks." Tenley rolls her eyes. I start toward the house but she blocks my path with her skinny, lanky body. "Just let me say what I have to say, okay?"

I sigh and stare at the gray cloud cover above us. "Fine."

"Why have you been keeping this from us?"

When I finally bring my head down to lock eyes with her Tenley looks soft. No fight in her eyes, no stubborn set to her jaw. She just looks gentle, which is a bit unnerving. We stare at each other for a long moment and all you can hear is the rustle of palm fronds in the light breeze and the cars on Abbott Kinney. Her eyes, which are exact replicas of our dad's, get a little teary. "No one is going to be disappointed about this, Tate. Shocked. Confused. Worried. But no one is going to look at that perfect little boy and be disappointed he exists. Your lack of faith in our family is astounding, Tater Tot. Especially considering you're the Golden Boy."

Her words are comforting but I laugh them off because of that last comment. "Conner is the Golden Boy. I'm just Tater Tot."

"Shut up," Tenley gives my shoulder a rough shove as I start walking towards my front door and she falls into step beside me. "You have always been the Golden Boy. Conner is special because he's the firstborn, and he lived through some shit when his parents divorced. But you... you are the firstborn of the favorites. You can do no wrong. They'll love Dylan without hesitation just the way they love you."

"Favorites?"

"Oh please, you don't see it? Gran and Gramps love Dad best," Tenley announces. "And Gran adores Mom because she's the one who kept her sisters safe and sound when our great-grandmother abandoned them. Gran was best friends with Mom's mom, remember?"

"Right." Of course I don't remember all that crap. It happened well before I was born. Our mother's mom died before our mom was a teenager and our great-grandmother who was supposed to raise them but didn't really, died when our mom was my age. Her funeral is the reason our parents found each other again. That part I remember. "But I'm still not the Golden Boy. And... Ten, it isn't just the fam. It's the team and the media. I have to make sure the legal stuff is in place and that I have Dylan well looked after before the world turns its judgy eyes on him."

"He seems well looked after with Mallory," she states as I hold open the storm door for her. Something down the pathway catches my eye and I see Tara dressed in running clothes with her headphones in. She smiles and waves and I return the friendly gesture before stepping inside and getting slammed with an annoyed look my Tenley.

I lock the door behind us and nod. "Mallory is the best with Dylan. I wish I could keep her as his nanny forever. But she wants to go back to Silver Bay."

"Does she?" Tenley asks, her left eyebrow raised. I just nod. "Well, maybe she'll change her mind after her first date with Fisher."

My brain stumbles over the words they have to absorb. Tenley walks through the house and into the kitchen. The back door to the patio is open and I assume Mallory went out with Dylan. I can hear him babble-talking out there. "Her what with who?"

Tenley smiles around the refrigerator door she just opened. I rake a hand through my hair again. "She met some of my crew —fellow students—when we were filming here. My hot camera guy asked her on a date."

I'm still in my suit and I'm wildly uncomfortable suddenly so I start undoing some buttons on my shirt. Thankfully I didn't wear a tie home. "And Mallory said yes?"

Tenley pulls out one of my expensive juices from Pressed Juicery and cracks the lid before I can protest. Then she shrugs at me and closes the door with her hip. "Not sure. But that's his number on your fridge."

She points to the phone number scrawled across the wipe board where I leave notes for the house cleaner. I stare at it like I'm trying to make it catch fire.

"Weird. You have this look on your face I don't recognize..." Tenley notes and pauses to gulp back some of my expensive beet, spinach, carrot, and apple blend before narrowing her eyes on my face. "Is that... jealousy? Yeah. It is. Like how you looked at me when Dyllie Bear happily let me snuggle him earlier. You worried about who is going to snuggle Mallory, Tater Tot?"

"His name is Dylan, not Dyllie Bear," I growl. "And she's my *friend*. I don't want her dating one of your douchey film friends."

"He isn't douchy."

"You have terrible taste in men."

"You have great taste in women," Tenley mutters back. "You just don't know it yet."

"What?"

She ignores me and walks out onto the back patio. I follow. Mallory is on the floor, crossed-legged, playing with Dylan and smiling so brightly at him that it makes my heart feel warm and gooey in my chest. I love her for loving him.

"Mal, why don't you go grab a shower?" Tenley suggests and sits down next to her on the patio tiles. "I know you didn't have a chance to grab one before we left for the lab. I can watch him."

"I can watch him too!" I sound like a jealous boyfriend.

Mallory glances up at me and then at Tenley. "That would be epic, thanks."

"And grab one of the fancy juices. They're delicious." I kick Tenley lightly in the back as Mallory heads upstairs.

I drop down on the couch and tip right over as I watch Tenley and Dylan play on the floor in front of me. I'm exhausted. My muscles ache from the road trip games. I'm also growing more and more hungry by the minute. But all I want to do is watch Tenley and my son. They seem so... comfortable and easy with each other, nothing like how he is with me. I study them like I'll be able to unearth some kind of secret code.

"He feels your hesitation," Tenley announces like she's reading my mind. Because I swear she's a freaking witch. "He knows you're freaked out by him."

"I'm... not anymore. I mean, I just... what the fuck do I know about being a dad?" I rake my hands into my hair and stare at the palm fronds hanging over my privacy fence.

"The same thing every first-time father knows," Tenley laughs. "Absolutely sweet fuck all."

"But at least other dads got a chance to prep. They saw it coming."

"Mostly. Probably. Yeah." She shoots me a small grin. "I know this throws a wrench in your carefully mapped out life plan, Tate, and you've never done anything by accident, but well, you just need to get over it."

She's not wrong, but I somehow still hate that she's right.

Tenley stares at me for a long moment and then she grabs my hands in hers and squeezes them. "You've got this. All of this. You just have to be honest with yourself, take it one day at a time, and not just accept help but ask for it."

"I've got Mallory for help. For now."

"You two need to talk," Tenley replies letting go of my hands and standing up. "Mallory cares about that little boy more than anything. If he needs her, she'll be there. And she'll also be there for *you* if you let her. If you can just stop protecting your fucking heart like it's Fort Knox."

"Excuse me?"

"You're a lone wolf, Tate," Tenley announces her hands on her hips and her eyes fierce. "The Garrisons are a pack but you've always been the lone wolf. You never really let anyone in. Even your friends, which is why now that you need help you don't think there's anyone you're close enough with to ask for it. Because you don't ever let anyone really, truly, *in*. So let her in. As a friend if nothing else."

I try to think of an argument to throw back at Tenley but I don't have one. She's right. I am a lone wolf and I've always loved how I could handle anything on my own. But this situation is impossible to handle alone. I need help. I need Mallory.

"Well, can you help me convince her to stay and help me?" I

ask and that gets me one of Tenley's trademarked sarcastic laughs.

"Oh hell no." She pats my shoulder. "But what I will do is take Dylan for a stroll to the beach so you two can have the conversation uninterrupted."

She plucks Dylan off his playmat and walks into the house and I follow. "I don't know if you should be alone with him, in public."

"I'm not going to do anything that would risk my nephew," Tenley replies, and the casual way she says nephew causes a lump to instantly appear in my throat. I really love hearing her say that. She walks to the bottom of the stairs. "Mal! I'm gonna take Dyllie Bear for a stroll."

"Alone?" Mallory's voice floats down the stairs. It's distant but the angst in it is clear.

"Yeah. Tater needs to stay here and have a talk with you!" Tenley calls up the stairs and I shove her, lightly because she's holding my baby. She shoves me back, not so lightly.

"Right now?" Mallory calls back.

"No! Just shower. I'll talk to you after! No rush!" I turn to Tenley and whisper heatedly. "Don't say another word. I don't want her to hurry. She deserves alone time. She hardly ever gets it."

Tenley pats my head like I'm a puppy who followed a command. I swat her hand away and grab the folded stroller. I pull it out onto the front porch where I open it and watch carefully to make sure Tenley straps him in right. "I need to see if there are any dudes who think single moms are hot."

"Excuse me?"

"What?" Tenley grins. "Babies are chick magnets for men. Let's see if they're men magnets for chicks."

"I'm about to veto this idea," I warn.

"Shut up," Tenley replies. "We'll only be gone like half an hour so get it done with Mallory."

I watch Tenley until she and the stroller are through the gate and out of view. Then I go back inside, lock the door, and take the stairs two at a time. I need to change and think of what I can say to make Mallory stay with me indefinitely. For Dylan's sake.

Chapter 14

Mallory

I rush through my shower, my brain listing all the possible reasons for this serious conversation I'm about to have with Tate. I decide it must just be about the nannies I interviewed. I focus on the candidates and the meetings I had with them as I get out of the shower, towel off, and throw on a long sundress. I haven't worn much besides shorts and sweats since I landed in L.A. and it's time I started making more of an effort. My ribs aren't sore anymore either. Well, not as sore, so I'm starting to feel more like myself.

I review the candidates mentally as I brush my hair. I think about the candidates I already shortlisted and sent to Tate, and then I think about one of the ones I didn't put on the list. The one who was twenty-two, size zero, and with shampoo commercial hair.

Yep. I did that. Nixed a perfectly valid candidate because she was gorgeous. And it's been bugging me ever since so I know when we talk nannies I have to tell him about her too. So what if she's young and hot and probably his type. If he ends up fucking her, why do I care? It's not like he's going to date me if I don't tell him about her. Tate doesn't date. I stare at myself in the bathroom mirror as I rub in some tinted moisturizer and a little liquid blush on my pale cheeks.

He does fuck, though, and he'd fuck me. He said it. Offered it up like an... arrangement. But I don't want him to *want* to fuck me. Okay, maybe I do want him to fuck me. Nope. I don't. Well, I shouldn't. And regardless, I'm leaving once he hires someone else, so I should just stop cock blocking something that hasn't even happened and add the competent and pretty nanny to the shortlist.

I'm still having this insane internal monologue with myself when I walk into the kitchen and find Tate there. In nothing but sweats riding low on his tapered hips and dear God, yeah I would like to have a man who looks like that naked on top of me just once in my very vanilla little life.

"Hey," he says like he isn't standing there emoting sex appeal. He runs a hand through his damp hair and I try not to remember how thick and amazing it feels. "You look great."

I smooth my hands over the front of my dress. "Surprise! I own more than just sweats and shorts."

"I don't," Tate jokes back and flashes me a grin. "Except suits."

I smile and he tips his head toward the patio we were on earlier. "Back outside to enjoy some sunshine? It finally popped through the haze."

I nod and follow him. He's got two fresh mugs of coffee and he hands one to me before I sit down. I thank him and settle into one of the sofas, pulling my phone out of one of the side pockets on my dress. "So I have one more candidate to add to your list of potential nannies. Are you ready to hear why I say yay or nay to them?"

"No."

I sip my coffee. He made it just how I like it with extra cream and just a pinch of sugar. "I know the road trip was grueling. Did you not get a chance to review the notes I sent you? One of them was a nanny for J Lo. How crazy is that?"

"No, I read everything. I'm just not ready to replace you," Tate says and I freeze with the coffee cup halfway to my mouth. He leans forward, aquamarine eyes reaching over me and landing on my face. His tongue slips across his bottom lip for a second. "I want you to stay."

"Why?" I don't know why I ask the question. The answer will never be what I truly want to hear.

He leans forward and puts his mug on the coffee table. With his elbows on his knees and his fingers twisted together he clears his throat and responds. And I was right, it's not the answer I wanted to hear. "I've been talking to a sports psychologist, because this has a huge impact on my career as well as my life. Forever. Anyway, he pointed out to me that in unexpected life-altering events like this, there are changes I can't control and changes I can. He meant like, I cannot let this affect my on-ice performance. But it applies to more than the game. There are off-ice changes I can control too. I don't have to find a new nanny. I have the best one already."

"I see." Every fiber of my being is disappointed, which is ridiculous. "So you're asking me to stay because it's one less hassle to deal with. For how long?"

"I'm asking you to stay because my son loves you, and..." Tate pauses. Our eyes meet and then he looks at his coffee mug. "I consider you one of my best friends and I like having you here. For how long? Well, for Dylan's sake, until he gets drafted. For my sake... until he gets drafted."

I can't help but smile, and it only grows bigger when he flashes me one back. "Seriously though, I don't know for how long. Can we start with a six-month contract?"

Six months living with Tate. In his sweatpants and nothing

else. Well, except for the thick silky hair, piercing aquamarine eyes, and casual masturbation conversations.

"Contract is such a shitty word," Tate backtracks, assuming my silence is a sign of annoyance, I guess. He looks contrite and slightly panicked. "Agreement? Arrangement? Pact? Call it whatever works for you and I'll agree."

Tate looks away, at something on the tiled patio floor. His mouth opens like he's going to say something else but he doesn't. He closes his eyes and when he opens them he looks at me with a pleading stare. "I know it's a lot to ask. I know you've gone above and beyond for him, and me, already. I won't hate you if you have to say no."

"I don't have to say no," I reply softly. Because I *don't* have to say no. Yes, my family is waiting for me, but nothing else is. No job. No prospects. No boyfriend. No best friend. I have no reason to say no, but at the same time, for my own sake, maybe I should. "I will do anything to make this easier on Dylan. None of this is his fault."

"Thank you, Mallory," Tate replies, and before I realize what he's doing he's off his couch and on mine. Right beside me circling me with his strong arms and pulling me into him.

His hugs are always so damn comforting. My whole body relaxes into him and I rest my chin on his shoulder and close my eyes, inhaling the smell of his soap and shampoo and savoring the way the damp ends of his hair brush my cheek. He's got a wide palm flat against the center of my back between my shoulder blades.

"I lied to you," he whispers so low and soft against my ear that I almost don't hear it. I want to pull back, to look at him, but that palm of his is holding me in place. "I need you to stay for more than Dylan. I need you to stay for me."

I hold my breath. My heart trips over itself in my chest. That hand on my back moves up, under the ends of my hair, towards my neck. His voice gets softer and raspier, like velvet sandpaper. "I spend every day lost in a sea of emotions and you are my only anchor, Mallory."

His palm is now against the back of my neck and his fingers curl around it gently but possessively. I inhale sharply, almost a gasp. "Tate..." I pull back just enough so we can look at each other. His features are a blur, and I can feel his breath against my lips.

"I know I ruined our friendship, and I'm sorry," he confesses. "I know you are still hurt and angry about the night in the hotel room."

"I'm mad at myself about that," I whisper hoarsely. "Not at you. I knew how I'd feel right afterward but I didn't stop it. I didn't have an ounce of self-restraint, or preservation, and that's my fault, not yours. You gave me ample opportunity that night to opt-out."

"Well, if it makes you feel any better, I wanted you so badly, and still do, if I had the chance to do it again knowing it would make you run to another country and cut me out of your life, I probably still wouldn't be able to stop myself from touching you."

What the hell do you say to that? What does he want me to respond with? I say nothing. And that's when I feel his lips brush my cheek. And we both move our heads like this is some grand, thought-out plan. The next logical step.

When his lips touch mine it feels as right and comforting as his embrace, and I lean into it just like I did the hug. Unlike the other times we've made this glorious mistake, this time he doesn't taste like tequila and isn't fueled by sexual frustration. This may be another bad decision, but it isn't rash. That hand of his at the back of my neck slides into my hair as my mouth opens slightly in invitation and his tongue finds mine and every molecule in my body reacts. I grip his shoulders and am basically crawling into his lap when—

The front door slams and Tenley's panicked voice calls out, "We have an emergency! Help!"

We both break apart and leap off the couch. My heart is in my throat until I see Tenley holding a perfectly healthy-looking Dylan out in front of her like he's a ticking bomb. "His ass exploded!"

Oh. He's a bomb that already went off.

Tate reaches him first and pulls Dylan close only to immediately hold him at arm's length like Tenley had. Tate's face scrunches up and he chokes back a gag. "Oh my God, something is desperately wrong."

"Nope," I inform them calmly, trying not to smile. "Just regular baby shit. Literally."

Tate turns, holding Dylan out toward me, but I take a step toward the stairs and shake my head. "Oh no, Daddy. This is your chance to bond with your son."

"I feel like he'd be happier if you handled this," Tate replies but he follows me up the stairs, Tenley behind me and Dylan still dangling from his hands.

"He seems just fine, for once," I note and glance over my shoulder. Dylan is swinging his feet. There's a yucky dark brown stain seeping bigger and bigger in the front of his pants. One of his white socks is also tinged brown. Kid let a good one go.

"Oh God, it smells so bad. Are you sure we shouldn't call a doctor?" Tate asks me as he follows me into the bedroom. "Does he have a baby norovirus or something?"

"We'll monitor it but I think it's just breakfast didn't agree with him," I reply and point to the bathroom. "Ten, can you run a lukewarm bath. Just a quarter full please."

Tenley happily leaves the room, which is filling up with the scent of Dylan's mess. Tate gags again. I bite my cheek to keep from laughing as I walk over to the changing table I put together two days ago after Amazon delivered it. I motion for Tate to bring him over and he does and lays him down on his back.

I hand him some rubber medical gloves I ordered for occasions just like this. "Put these on." I reach into the first drawer pull out laundry clips and hand him one. "And put this on your nose."

Tate's eyes flare to the size of dinner plates. "Seriously?"

"You'll thank me later," I promise him. "Even if you get baby poop out from under your nails it still smells after, no matter how much soap you use or how much you scrub. I think it's psychological. Anyway, the gloves prevent it."

"I have a set of protective goggles in the storage locker," Tate says as serious as a heart attack. "Should I grab them too?"

I giggle. It bubbles out of me and there isn't a damn thing I can do about it. Tate looks mortified.

"I'm sorry. Valid question." Dylan makes a noise that is a coo on the verge of a cry and his poop-covered sock juts up in the air. Tate jumps back like someone has just pointed a gun at him and I giggle again, which makes him blush. Blush! So freaking adorable. "Sorry again. Okay, no time for goggles let's just get to work. Start undoing his clothes."

Tate follows each and every one of my instructions and by the time Tenley comes to tell us the bath is ready, we've got Dylan down to his birthday suit and wiped up as best as possible. Tate is still holding him, dangling at arms-length, as we walk into the bathroom. I test the water and the temp is perfect so I tell Tate to lower Dylan in and he does.

"Stay by the tub at all times," I warn him. "Keep your eyes on him always. Babies can drown in an inch of water."

I slide his bath seat into the water and Tate instinctively lifts him into it and reaches for the baby soap on the side of the tub.

Tenley and I lean against the counter and watch Tate and Dylan bond. It's actually finally happening! Dylan loves baths and he happily lets Tate clean him as he splashes. And once the washing up is done Tate grabs one of the bath toys and continues to play with Dylan.

"I can't believe I'm saying this, but this is the cutest thing ever," Tenley whispers to me in awe. "I never thought Tate would be good at this, honestly."

"I knew he would be. Eventually," I whisper back, my eyes never leaving the father and son.

Eventually, I coax Tate into getting Dylan out of the water before it gets cold. Of course, Dylan whines about it because he loves water and now he's also overtired. When he starts to cry Tate's face falls and he looks at me with desperation. "It's not you, it's him. Just dry him off and get him into a onesie and we'll put him down for a nap."

In the bedroom, I hand Tate a pale blue onesie and Tenley jumps in to help him dress the little guy, not because he needs help but because she wants to be involved. A few minutes later, Dylan's dead to the world and we're all sneaking back downstairs. Tenley announces she's going to head back to West Hollywood. "Gotta beat the rush hour traffic."

"It's only two," I note.

"Rush hour in Los Angeles starts at three and goes until eight," Tate explains, shocking me. "Ten, do I have to beg you again to keep this to yourself. Don't even tell Liv."

Liv is their cousin and she also attends UCLA and is one of Tenley's roommates. Tenley gives her brother an annoyed stare. "I am a vault, Tater Tot. Stop worrying. Besides I hardly ever see Liv during the school year. She's always studying. The nerd."

I smile as Tenley rolls her eyes. She hugs me and then she hugs her brother. "You are doing great, bro. When it's time to tell

Mom and Dad and everyone, I will be there for you. Hopefully, Mallory will be too."

With that, she disappears out the front door and Tate and I are left alone to stare at each other and come to terms with what happened before Dylan's poop explosion.

The feeling of his lips against mine, the need and the desire with which he explored my mouth, come flooding back to me. I take in a sharp breath and look away. "Tate, I think we need ground rules."

"Okay," Tate replies easily and steps closer. I can see his left foot next to the plank of hardwood I'm laser-focused on instead of looking at him. "How about you stay and nanny Dylan for six months. I'll pay you whatever Diana paid you plus twenty-five percent because L.A. isn't cheap. Also, we'll move. So both you and Dylan can have your own rooms."

Now I have to look up. Is he serious about giving up this place? When Tate bought this place he was so proud he sent Diana and me a video tour of it. He loves this townhouse. But there's no flicker of humor or hesitation as he speaks. "Even if I don't have a live-in nanny one day, Dylan needs a proper, safe yard and a quieter, larger space than this."

He's right and I love that he figured that out on his own. That he's putting his son's needs above his own wants without being asked. "You're a good dad."

"I'm working on it," he replies and then he steps closer still. Now we're chest to chest, almost touching. I stare at the small space between our feet until his left hand comes up and he presses his thumb to the underside of my chin and tilts my head up, forcing my eyes to land on his. "Now let's talk about the fun ground rules."

"Fun rules?" I repeat. He smiles. It's deep and intimate and it warms me in ways I know is dangerous. "What are fun rules?"

"Fun rules are things like what happened on the patio earlier," Tate replies and his thumb under my chin slides lightly against my jaw. "It's letting it happen again if we want it. It's letting more happen if we want to. If we need it. Do you need it, Mal?"

"Need to kiss you?" I whisper.

His smile deepens. "Need to kiss someone. Need to touch someone. Need to be touched by someone. Need to orgasm. All of those things. Why don't we make a rule that we help each other out that way too?"

Is he serious? I stare at him in complete shock. "That kiss was a slip-up. Our emotions were running high."

"Like that last time?" Tate counters and I nod. "But what about the first time?"

"Alcohol."

"So right now," Tate says as he pins me with those smoldering eyes of his, "I'm calm, you're calm. Light-hearted even after that poop escapade. I haven't had a drop of alcohol in over a week. Are you tipsy right now? Drunk?"

"Stone cold sober," I admit.

His hand has moved from my chin and jaw to the back of my neck. He cups it gently but also possessively and I like it. A lot. Tate tilts his head so our foreheads touch. "So right now then, completely sober and void of big emotion, you don't want me to kiss you?"

I open my mouth and say absolutely nothing. Because I just can't bring myself to lie. He smiles again. I feel a tremor of desire and a shiver of need ripple through me. Also, though, there's a rattle of fear. "If we give into this, aren't we just inviting trouble into an already troublesome situation?"

"Maybe we're just giving each other a break from the trouble," he replies, and Tate sounds so confident that I almost believe him.

I reach up and wrap a hand around his forearm, gathering

the courage to step away from him and pull out of this grip he has on me, physically. Emotionally I don't know if I'll ever break free. I've spent what feels like half my lifetime enamored with Tate Garrison. "Don't you have regrets? After that first time."

"Yeah," he admits after a long moment of just staring at each other. "My biggest regret though, the one that keeps me up some nights, is not going further with you. Taking everything I wanted."

Once again my breath catches in my throat, like the air has been sucked from the room and I can't expand my lungs. It doesn't get easier as he tilts his head and his lips brush mine. "I lay awake sometimes and think about how you tasted on my fingers and how badly I want that taste on my tongue."

My lips find his. I have no resistance left. No rational thought. Only selfish needs and wants. I *want* Tate. I *need* him to touch me. Right or wrong I've needed it for years so I kiss him and he kisses me back. Long and hard. And the deeper the kiss gets the more we start pawing at each other.

Tate is twisting his fingers in my hair with one hand and cupping my ass with the other. I'm basically doing the same with my hands. He feels so good against me, so I lift my leg and wrap it around his hip. He ruts himself between my legs with a growl, like we're cave people, just figuring out what nature intended.

I feel that primal. I am radiating with a desire to touch him, be touched by him. I let my hand slide down his back and under the waistband of his sweats. His ass is round, hard, and bare as I palm it. He isn't wearing underwear. He pulls back, my leg falls to the floor, and he yanks me to him. He pauses, cupping my cheek. "I'm sorry. I know I have to be gentle because of your ribs. It's just... I'm usually not."

He wraps his arms around my back and kisses me again, walking us both over to the living room couch. He gently pushes me down onto it and lowers himself on top of me. We kiss and grind and let our fingers roam. My dress is being hiked up by his left hand as it slides up my outer thigh. "I love you in dresses. I remember my hands under the last dress I saw you in."

"I think about that a lot too," I confess as I shove his sweats lower, over his ass, and down his thighs. "I think about it every time I touch myself."

I am going to blush profusely when I look back on the fact I said that out loud, but right now the only thing heating my blood is lust. Tate has my dress bunched up at my hips and his fingers are skirting my panties. "Before you ask, don't stop."

I feel his lips, against mine, parting in a triumphant smile. "Tell me I can lick your pussy." Oh God. This may not be dirty speak for some women, but for me, it's downright lewd. I have never talked with a sexual partner like this, so boldly, so blunt. So hot. "Tell me to put my mouth on you."

"Do it."

"Mallory. Say the words."

I heave in my breaths like an Olympic runner at the end of a marathon. Heavy, hard breaths. I close my eyes and move my hands from his bare ass, over the tight muscles in his back, up into his hair. I feel his fingers slip between my folds and he sighs like he's content. Like he's at peace. Like he's home. "Tate. Put your mouth on me. Lick my pussy, I am begging you."

"You don't have to beg." He kisses me roughly and then slides down my body, one hand pulling my underwear lower and lower down my legs. When he slips them off one ankle, he shoves one of my legs off the couch and throws the other over his shoulder, and with one last heated look on my face, he dips down between my legs, and all I feel is the confident swipe of his tongue across my sex. I arch my back and whimper. "How do you taste even better than the first time?"

I don't answer with words. Instead, my hips twist and my

butt lifts and I'm essentially fucking his face. I'm not even trying to be timid about it, I keep rocking into him and he meets me with his warm, wet talented tongue every time. Inching me closer to a black abyss of white-hot pleasure. He keeps licking, exploring, tasting and the inching is more like shoving now. Every time that tongue dances over my clit I stumble closer to that prize.

"Tate, I'm going to…"

"Come all over me baby girl. Don't hold back. Use me."

I fist his hair in my hands and swallow my moan because Dylan can't hear this, and if I let go, the way I want to, not only will Dylan hear me, the entire state of California will. He crawls up my body, kissing my knee, my thigh, my hip, my forearm, my collarbone, my neck. And I get more and more lucid with every touch. More and more aware that I not only need to, I want to, return the feeling he just flooded me with. I reach down and wrap my hand around his hard cock as soon as he's got his lips on my neck. "Mal, you don't—"

"Tell me you don't want me to suck your cock?"

He blinks and flashes me a grin. "I will not be saying that. Ever."

"Then lie back and enjoy yourself." I slide lower down his body, between his legs, as he takes my place on the couch. Without giving myself time to freak out I press my lips to his leaking tip and slide him into my mouth.

My pace is slow, and kind of tentative at first. I'm not shy or unsure of myself, I'm just taking a minute to enjoy the moment. How his cock makes my mouth feel overwhelmingly full. The salty, thick taste of his pre-cum. How he whispers curses at the ceiling and tangles his fingers in my hair. "You are killing me."

"Mmm…" I hum against his shaft and he quakes. And then his fingers twist as I move at a faster, steadier pace and he punches his hips, softly at first and then harder and faster and he is fucking my wet waiting mouth with abandon.

And then his pace stumbles. "I'm going to shoot."

I grab his hips, holding on, pressing my fingers into his skin, letting him know I'm not letting go. He grunts out each syllable of my name. "Mal-lor-y."

And then he curses again and I feel a quick pulse of come explode into my mouth followed by another and another and... I almost choke there's so much, but I manage to swallow before that happens. I don't have time to wipe my mouth or do anything because he's hauling me up and pulling me into him and pressing breathy kisses to the shell of my ear. "See? Fun rules. We're really good at this... together."

"We make a pretty good team." I smile and as he pushes his fingers through my messy hair I nuzzle his neck and drift off on the spicy scent that is all Tate.

Chapter 15

Mallory

I wake up to find myself alone on the couch in the living room. The house is silent. The sun is low in the sky and when I grab my phone off an end table I realize it's almost dinner time. How come Dylan hasn't woken up? Where is Tate? Oh, and also, what the hell did I just do?

I sit bolt upright and push the heels of my palms into my eyes, hoping to rub out the sleep and temporary insanity. I grab my phone again and realize I have a text alert from Tate. I open it and find a slightly blurry selfie of him with Dylan strapped to his chest. Dylan looks... confused and apprehensive. Tate is grinning proudly. The photo tugs at my heartstrings.

The text that follows does too, even though it's simple.

> Took my son out for a walk so you could rest.

The next text he sent a couple minutes later has me blushing.

> I'm picking up dinner too so just relax. You'll need your energy later. For round two.

Round two? We can't! *I* can't. But I know, without a shadow of a doubt that not only *can* I fool around with Tate again, I will. Because I am completely crushing on him and he somehow handles my body better than he handles a puck, which is nuts.

I get up off the couch and smooth out my wrinkled sundress and then I decide that since Tate is handling dinner, I will handle dessert. It's also an excuse to do something other than obsess about what we did. I bought some berries and peaches at the local farmer's market a couple days ago and they need to get eaten. I dig around the pantry and see what supplies I can add to this to make it a tasty dessert but also not mess too much with Tate's strict diet.

I make fruit parfaits with protein granola and Greek yogurt. I'm humming to myself in the kitchen, trying hard to concentrate on what I'm doing and not let my mind wander to what I've done. Tate. I had his cock in my mouth. Oh my God... And he went down on me and made me come harder than I have in my life. Oh, my double God.

I let out a little scream. Tiny but shrill because how is this my life? I am screwed. And yet, I'm happy? Yeah, that's happiness bouncing around inside me like a balloon in a windstorm. Oh my foolish heart, I hope I'm wrong and I don't regret this one day.

I hear the metal storm door open as I'm putting the homemade parfaits in the fridge and call out. "How was the walk? Did Dyllie Bear behave? He looked a little—"

I close the fridge, my head turns to the entry hall, and I lose my ability to speak. The man standing there isn't Tate, and for a split second I don't know who it is and fear floods me. "Hey! Sorry! I'm not Tate or... Dyllie Bear? Did Tate get a dog?"

As soon as he speaks and shoots me a smile my brain finally kicks in and I realize it's one of Tate's teammates. A Westwood brother, if memory serves me correctly. The tattooed one, I note as I take in the intricate ink sleeves on both of his exposed arms. I met both brothers briefly on the trip with Diana. They came out after the Quake home game we attended for wings and beers at a bar on the beach. I wipe my hands on a nearby dishtowel and nod. "Hi. Umm... Tate isn't home at the moment. How did you get in?"

He pulls a key from the front pocket of his pants. "I have his key in case of emergency and he has mine."

"Oh. Okay." It seems everyone and their brother has a key to Tate's house. Good to know. I walk out of the kitchen and through the living room to the entry. The Westwood brother just stands there, clearly not in the mood to leave, so I repeat myself. "Tate's out. I don't know when he'll be back."

"Okay I can wait," he says like that's an option. "You're... shit. I forget your name but we've met before, right? You're from his hometown."

I nod slowly. "Yeah. Mallory."

"Right! Mallory Echolls. Your dad is Chance Echolls," he says. "My dad played at the same time as yours."

"Yup," I reply and I know I sound curt and unfriendly so I add a small smile. "I can tell Tate you stopped by. No need to waste your time. Or is there an actual emergency?"

"Oh... no. Not really an emergency." He gets it. I don't want him here. I hate that I seem so unfriendly but I don't want to see the panic on Tate's face when he walks in with Dylan and his teammate is standing there. And I do not want to hear what new lie comes out of his mouth to cover everything up yet again. "He's been avoiding time with the guys and I was coming over here to find out why, but I think I know now."

Our eyes lock and he smiles again, deeply, knowingly. I look away. "Sorry, are you Nate or Crash?"

He laughs. "I'm *Crew*. My brother is *Nash*."

"Oops. Sorry. I promise I'm not usually this big of an ass." I laugh now too because this whole thing is just... well, hysterically uncomfortable. "I'll tell him you came by, Crew."

And then, through the screen of the storm door behind Crew, I hear a cry I know like it's my own. Tate appears on the other side with a wailing Dylan still strapped to his chest. Crew spins around and I watch his whole body tense up at the shock of seeing his commitment-phobic teammate with a baby strapped to his chest.

Tate's eyes get wide with panic. Crew lets out a "Holy shit." And I push past him to unclip Dylan and lift him out of the Baby Bjorn.

"I don't think he had another catastrophic crap," Tate says to me as I plop Dylan onto my hip. "I forgot to bring water or snacks so maybe he's hungry or something."

"Maybe," I say and rush him toward the kitchen.

"Or maybe he just hates me," Tate adds as he follows me, and Crew follows him.

"He doesn't hate you," I promise even though Dylan stopped crying as soon as I held him. I place him on his chair at the dining room table and grab a package of rice puffs. "Can you fill a bottle with milk please?"

Tate walks by me and to the fridge, plucking a bottle off the drying rack by the sink. Crew is watching us in confusion. We get Dylan settled with snacks and juice and Tate finally looks at his teammate.

"So ummm... how's life, Tate?" Crew asks. "I feel like you got news you might want to share."

"I..." Tate swallows.

"I'm moving to Los Angeles with my son and Tate has been kind enough to let me crash here while I sort out my life," I blurt out.

Crew looks at me, then his eyes drift to Dylan and slowly up to Tate. I know from the small smirk on his face, that he doesn't believe me. Not totally. He has working eyeballs. He can see Dylan is Tate's mini-me. I feel Tate's hand, his palm smooth and gentle against the small of my back. He looks right at Crew. "This is my son, Dylan. Mallory is his nanny and she brought him here a couple weeks ago, after his mother, her best friend Diana, died."

Crew's face loses all color. His mouth, which seems to be set in a perma-smirk, falls flat. He looks at Dylan again then at me and then at Tate. "What can I do to help?"

Not at all what I expected from this burly hockey player but I've been shocked non-stop today. Tate sighs. "Dude, I will take anything you got. Like a lead on a decent realtor. We have to move. ASAP. This place is too small and not baby-friendly."

"Okay." Crew nods and walks right up to the dining room table. "You can move into mine. I'll move into this one. At least until after playoffs."

"What?" Tate and I say in unison.

"I have a three-bedroom house with a decent, private garden on the canal remember?" Crew says, looking at Tate. "I don't need all that space and I never even wanted the house. It would be perfect for you guys, at least for now. And I can easily live here. Especially if that hot reporter girl is still a few doors down."

"She is," I remark.

Crew lifts his eyebrows in an uh-oh moment. Tate chuckles uncomfortably. "Crew, are you sure?"

"Yeah dude, no worries." He looks at me. "You'll love it, Mallory. It's not a bachelor pad like this place."

I don't ask why a hot single hockey player has a non-bachelor pad. I just nod and thank him and when Dylan is done eating I scoop him up. Tate touches his cheek and Dylan grins, which we both know is progress so we high-five. "See, no hate. He was just hangry."

Tate looks so relieved it's adorable. "I'm gonna go back out and get food. I didn't get a chance to pick it up. I just wanted to get him home so he would stop freaking out."

"You don't have to, I can whip up something," I reply.

"Are you sure?" He looks sheepish.

"Yeah. No worries." I nod. "Why don't you and Crew go chat on the patio and I'll get cooking. Dyllie Bear will be fine playing with his blocks."

"Or I could take him onto the patio," Tate suggests. "He likes his jumpy thing out there."

I immediately hand Dylan over to him and thankfully the kid doesn't complain. Seeing Tate with his boy on his hip makes my ovaries dance a jig. He grins down at his son. "Let's go have our first boys night, Dylan."

He walks into the kitchen, Crew behind him, and grabs two beers out of the fridge before exiting through the sliding doors onto the back patio. I close the door behind them to give them privacy.

I can't believe he told his teammate the truth. Next, he'll tell his parents and then his team, and eventually this will be out in the open. And then... he won't need me anymore. But... maybe he'll still want me.

Chapter 16

Tate

Crew is staring at me like I'm an alien with seven heads who just explained my people copulate by bumping armpits. His hazel eyes are wide. His mouth open. His skin, hell even his tattoos, have paled.

"I know. This is a lot," I tell him as I glance at Dylan who is jumping in his swing thing and grinning a slobbery grin. "I am still reeling too most days."

"I just don't know why you didn't tell me right away," Crew replies and furrows his brow. "I could have helped you."

"How? You know less about babies than I do."

Crew blinks and then laughs. "Yeah. Okay. But I could have been supportive. I mean, this is... it's crazy. And you need someone to talk to, I'm sure."

"I have Mal," I say and a very inappropriate image of her with her dress up to her tits and her pussy inches from my mouth flashes through my brain. "She's been amazing."

Crew stares at me. I don't even bother to act innocent because he knows me too well to believe that bullshit. He grins slowly, but it's reluctant and cautious. "She looks like she would be amazing. But didn't you say she's your ex's best friend? And she's your baby's nanny? I'm no expert but that seems like adding problems to an already complicated situation."

I don't like the points Crew is making but that doesn't make them inaccurate. Well, mostly. I sip my beer. It's light beer because of our impending playoff run. "First of all Diana could never be classified as an ex. She was a bed buddy. Friends with benefits. We were both on the exact same page with that. And the fact that she never told me about Dylan means she wasn't interested in even co-parenting with me let alone dating me. And Mallory's not a complication, she's a lifesaver. She's not just his nanny but his legal guardian until I can get all the paper-work to get my name on his birth certificate."

"Can't you get one of your family to be his guardian?" Crew asks, concern still furrowing his brow. "I mean, if she's also your bed buddy then that makes this more complicated, Tate. I'm not trying to rain on your parade. Just speaking the truth."

"No one in my family knows about him," I admit and Crew looks downright flummoxed again. "Well, Tenley just found out. And I think we can both agree she's not an ideal guardian candidate."

"Why haven't you told your parents? Or one of your cousins? Someone?" Crew asks. "I have a really small family, and you know my dad..."

"The patron saint of hockey," I interject because he always calls his dad that, and he's not wrong. Avery Westwood was the poster child for the sport his entire career.

"Yeah, the patron saint of hockey would lose his mind if I knocked a girl up out of wedlock. He shit a brick when I divorced, because star players don't do that," Crew smiles bitterly then shakes it off. "But in the end, he'd be there for me. He'd support me and I know your parents would be the same. Come on, with that enormous family of yours, someone would be able to fly down here and help."

"I don't want their help," I admit what I haven't said out loud to anyone yet. "I'm the Golden Child, according to Tenley. I'm perfect."

"And humble." Crew rolls his eyes.

"Shut up, I'm telling you what they say, not what I believe," I grumble and pause to sip my beer. "They all also love to say that the way I stay golden is I avoid all responsibility and commitment like it's the plague. And they aren't wrong."

Crew thinks about my words and gives me a small nod. "You don't date seriously, you lease your car, you could challenge me and Nash the Quake captaincy, but you didn't even try. Yeah, I can see why that's what they think. Do you even own this place?"

I stare up at the townhouse. "Yeah but only because there are no rentals in this building. But I... I bought it in Tenley's name. I wanted her to have it in case I got traded or whatever. Just easier."

"Easier if you aren't attached or committed to anything." Crew smiles. "Jesus you are a textbook commitment-phobe. And now you're a daddy. Biggest commitment in the world."

It feels so surreal to hear someone else say it. But also, there's this flicker of pride in my chest that beats anything I've ever felt before. I nod. "Yeah. I'm a dad and it's not a commitment I want to shrug off. And it feels like, if I ask them all for help, it would be like shrugging it off. Or give them and everyone else an excuse to say Tate Garrison couldn't handle it on his own."

"Fatherhood is not a house plant or a puppy, Garrison," Crew warns. "Not many people can handle it on their own and I'm not sure they should if they can help it. So if I were you, I would reach out sooner rather than later. Also, eventually, you're going to have to tell Coach and the media team, because this will get out and you do *not* want to blindside them."

"I know," I say almost too sharply. I hate being reminded of what I've been ignoring. I look up at the cloudless blue sky. Dylan makes another happy gurgling sound at my feet and I glance down and see him bouncing and clapping his pudgy hands. "I just wanted to get through the regular season and then I was going to tell them in the week before we start playoffs. Because I want Dylan and Mallory to be able to come to playoffs, especially if we win."

"Yeah." Crew smiles and tips his beer bottle toward me. "You mean *when* we win."

I grin. "Yeah. *When.*"

We clink bottles and both down what's left in them. He plops his on the outdoor table and leans down toward Dylan. "So little dude, you gonna be a hockey player like your pops? Pretty sure it's in your DNA."

Dylan claps and grins and then lets out a happy squeal. I am smiling so broadly my cheeks ache. Shit. I love this kid. Even if he's still not sure how he feels about me. I fucking love him. "He'll get a pair of skates soon. But if he doesn't like it, so be it. Personally, hockey was all I ever wanted but my parents always made it clear it wasn't expected and I intend to do the same."

"Yeah, my parents were the same but I remember watching my dad in his last few seasons and thinking I *have* to do that," Crew replies with a soft smile. "It looks like the best thing in the world."

"Yeah," I agree and then my eyes fall to Dylan. I honestly don't care if he plays or not. I just hope that by the time he's old enough to pick a profession he likes me at least half as much as I like him.

Crew stands up and I stand too. We give each other a quick bro-hug. "So I was serious. I want you to take my place. I'll even line up the movers for both of us. We have two home games coming up so how about we move Friday? And we can have

Saturday to settle into our new places before our next game on Sunday."

"If you're serious, that would be amazing."

"I have wanted out of the place since Anne-Marie left me," Crew says flatly as he shoves his hands into his pockets. I'm shocked he uttered her name. He hasn't mentioned his ex by her actual name since the day he was served divorce papers at the arena last year. "She picked the place, not me."

"Okay well, it would work great for us until I can sort something else out in the off-season," I admit, and feel like one of the many heavyweights has been lifted from my shoulders. "Thanks, Crew."

"No worries." He gives me a crooked smile. "And before you bother to say it, I swear I won't tell anyone. Not even Nash."

"Thanks," I sigh. "I'll clear this up and be honest about it as soon as I can."

"I still say you should tell your folks or a cousin or something."

"Eventually," I promise.

I grab Dylan out of his jumper and he miraculously doesn't cry. Although he is still staring at me uncertainly. We go back into the house and we're greeted with a delicious smell coming from the stove where Mallory is standing. Crew declines her invitation to join us, says goodbye, and heads out.

Dylan starts squirming and lets out a frustrated grunt as he reaches for Mallory. "Just put him in the living room with his toys. Maybe play with him a bit while I finish dinner."

"Okay." I'm skeptical that he will want to play with me and not just keep fussing and whining for Mallory but I'm willing to try.

I sit on the floor with him and grab some of his toys. There's a precarious moment where he ignores me and his head stays turned to the kitchen. But then, he turns to me and I hold up his favorite giraffe stuffie and he happily wraps his chubby hands around it, pulls it to him, and bites the head. I pick up the hippo stuffie and make it dance on the carpet in front of him and he giggles. Wildly. I made my son giggle and not cry and I might as well have scored a game-winning Stanley Cup goal because I feel *that* elated.

I don't know how much time passes, but suddenly I hear Mallory say, "Dinner is served."

I look up and see her watching Dylan and me and the look on her face hits me like a hammer to the chest. It's so soft and sweet and her smile could power the freaking hockey rink it's so bright. God, she's gorgeous. "You look beautiful right now."

There. I said it. And the weird part is I said it without expecting anything. Usually, I compliment women in the throes of it. Like we're half naked already or well on our way to naked. I have an objective in mind and it's selfish. But tonight I said it only because I wanted Mallory to know how I felt.

She blushes and it makes her even more beautiful. "Get up here and eat," she mutters, still smiling. "And bring your son."

"Come on, son," I say and lift Dylan. This time he squirms and lets out a squeak of protest. "I'm going to tell myself it's just because you were really into the hippo dance moves and not take it personally."

Mallory lets out a laugh. I put Dylan in his chair, which still freaks me out a little because it's just bars on the table holding him up. I need to get him a real highchair, even though Mallory swears these things are safe. I sit down across from Dylan and Mallory sits beside him and places some cut-up veggies and meat on a plate in front of him with a bottle of water.

We eat together, sitting down properly, for the first time since they got here and it feels really nice. Great, even. Mallory asks me what I like about living in Los Angeles and I go on and on about the weather the people the beaches and the way the town makes me feel, which is something I haven't told anyone. "There's this vibe in Los Angeles," I explain between mouthfuls of the best couscous I've ever eaten. "The whole town is buzzing with hopes and dreams, you know? And everyone who comes here wakes up every morning thinking their world could change at any second."

"Because they might be discovered and become the next superstar or because an earthquake could shake us right into the ocean?" Mallory asks me and she's dead serious.

"Both. But mostly the first thing." I grin and then stop to drink some water. "The first earthquake is terrifying, not going to lie, but somehow you get used to them."

"I don't think I will."

I smile. "I said the same thing and now, three years of occasional tremors and I don't even blink."

She doesn't look convinced so I reach across the table and lay my hand over hers. "If there's a quake, I'll protect you. And Dyllie Bear, obviously."

Her eyes light up. "You've started calling him Dyllie Bear too."

"I'm not a huge fan of nicknames," I admit with a sheepish grin. "Tater Tot still haunts me, but he does look like a little bear. And he certainly shits like a bear."

She laughs and Dylan slaps the table like he thinks it's funny too I grin, and for the first time in a long time, it's not forced or tinged with trepidation. In this little moment, I feel like maybe I've got this.

The rest of the night we clean up together bathe Dylan together and get him ready for bed. Then I ask Mallory if she wants to watch some Netflix with me and she, thankfully, says yes. While I pull it up on the TV she is in the kitchen and comes out with the most amazing-looking parfaits. "The dessert I promised. And I made them as health-conscious as possible."

She slips onto the couch beside me, and since it's the one we fooled around on earlier I slide right over when I take the parfait from her so we're touching. She doesn't seem to mind. We both changed after Dylan went down. She's in a lacy cotton tank top and some matching capri pajama bottoms. She looks sweet yet sultry all at the same time. I'm in my pajama bottoms and an old wrinkled concert T-shirt Tenley got me for Christmas as a joke. She always gets me bands or artists I would never go see because it makes her laugh. This one is a vintage Spice Girls European Tour shirt from nineteen ninety-nine.

I take one bite of the dessert and groan. "This is amazing. How can this be healthy?"

"Well, healthy might be a stretch, but it's got lots of protein and is as fat-free as possible," Mallory tells me. I watch her lift the spoon to her lips and into her mouth and I think about how my dick was her last treat. Her eyes flutter closed for a moment too, like they did when she was giving me head.

"What do you want to watch on Netflix?" I ask, and my voice is deeper than normal. I clear my throat and shovel more parfait into my mouth to distract myself from the hormones pinging around my insides like a ball in a pinball machine.

"Umm... I like rom-coms," she confesses and I roll my eyes. "And that's the exact reaction I expected. You pick it, tough guy. Something with no emotions and a lot of explosions I'm guessing."

"Sounds right," I admit and scroll down to the action list. "How about this one with The Rock."

"I actually don't mind The Rock," Mallory says as she puts her empty parfait dish on the coffee table. Then her eyes read the title and she slaps my chest with the flat of her hand. "No way! Tate Garrison, you are a jerk!"

"What?" I blink at her feigning innocence. "We can call it research."

"I am not watching an earthquake action movie set in Los Angeles," she barks and hits me again, only this time I grab her hand. "It's tempting fate!"

"Well, then if you don't want to watch the movie, we'll have to do something else," I say. Her hand still in mine, I move it to rest on my thigh. Her hazel eyes flicker with heat and then they leave my face and land on my shirt.

"If you were a Spice Girl you'd be Scary," she whispers. "Because you scare me to death sometimes, Tate."

I lean in, ghosting my lips against the side of her neck before pulling back and smiling at her. "You'd be Dream Spice. Because every time I watch you come it's like a dream I don't want to wake up from."

"There is no Dream Spice," she tells me and takes a shaky breath. Her hand is moving up my thigh on its own, her want and her effort not mine. So I move my own hand to the strap of her tank and after I skim the lace with my fingertips, I pull it down slowly.

"Do you want to continue talking about nineties girl bands or do you finally want to let me bury my cock inside of you?" I ask, tired of waiting. Tired of games. Tired of pretending.

My bluntness has her shivering, but then she stands up, grabs my chin in her hand, and pulls me up by it. I tower over her, a few tiny inches apart, my breathing heavy and almost labored with the desire I'm holding back. She tips her head up, looks me straight in the eye, and speaks without an ounce of hesitation. "I'll take your cock. Every time."

My mouth crashes down on hers and I wrap my arm around her waist and lift her off her feet, carrying her to the stairs and my bedroom.

Chapter 17

Mallory

I'm naked in Tate Garrison's bed. He's kneeling between my brazenly open legs, concentrating on rolling the condom down his very hard cock. The duvet and blankets are bunched up behind him, the light in the bathroom is on and bathes us in a dim glow, highlighting all his hard muscles and smooth curves. His head is tipped down, hair dangling in front of his forehead and he isn't looking at me so I take the time to soak in the image in front of me. Odds are this isn't a big deal to him, but it is to me and I don't want to forget it, ever.

Once the condom is on he looks at me again, shoving his hair back out of his eyes with one hand and grazing the other down my body. It starts at my neck and pauses on my left nipple, which is still damp from his mouth.

We burst our way into his room and immediately pulled off each other's clothes and then he threw me down on his bed and climbed on top of me and licked and sucked his way across my body. I was seconds from climaxing again from his tongue on my clit but he pulled away and went to the bathroom, returning with the condom.

His fingers dance over my belly button and stop at my

neatly trimmed pubic hair. His eyes move down and then back to my face. "Are you sure, Mallory?"

"Yes."

His fingers slip lower, sliding between my damp folds, and he slips two into me and I arch my back. "I am not going to hold back, baby girl. I have wanted this longer than I think I even realized so if I get to fuck you I'm going to give it my all."

"I'd expect and want, nothing less," I promise, and the next thing I know his body is hovering over me as his fingers fuck me at a steady, hard pace. I grip his shoulders and push my head back into the pillow. "Where's that cock you promised?"

"Impatient girl," he chuckles against my neck. And then I feel the mood shift. All the energy between us intensifies as he removes his hand and I feel the tip of his long, thick cock against my entrance.

I feel one of his hands grab one of my thighs and then he cups my head with the other and somehow, some way, he manages to tilt us both so we're on our sides facing each other. He moves his hand to the back of my knee and hooks my leg over his hip. And then he tilts his hips and starts to slide into me. It's a crazy angle and not at all easy to get traction, but he has his feet against the footboard of the bed and uses it as leverage to push up into me over and over, gently, until I've managed to take all of him.

He stops moving, and kisses me deep, his tongue sliding over mine possessively. I pull back, panting. "I should be on top."

"You will be, eventually." He slides out of me slightly, and back in. It feels good, but not good enough.

"I won't be able to come like this."

His grin is feral. "Challenge accepted, baby girl."

And his hands grab my ass as he holds me close and pivots his hips again. And again. And he's grinding right against me with every swing of his cock inside me and it starts to feel not just good but absolutely magical. I wrap my arms around his broad shoulders and he kisses my head and my lips and my ear and whispers, "Your pussy is so perfect, baby girl. You feel so good on my dick. I want to lick you again once you come, taste you again. I can't get enough."

"Tate, oh God..." I arch into him.

The sheets twist and pull under us, I tug on his hair, and he holds my ass so tight I swear he's going to leave handprints. Although rationally I know he has no intention of stopping, I find myself begging him not to. The bed is rocking, the headboard tapping the wall with every thrust of Tate's hips and we'll probably wake up Dylan but I can't bring myself to stop. I'm *so close*.

"Come baby girl," he grunts. "Come all over my dick and kiss me while you do it."

His mouth covers mine, which is perfect timing because the orgasm ripping through me would have me screaming if he wasn't kissing me and would most definitely wake up Dylan. And everyone in Venice. As I finally start to come down, he flips me over onto my stomach, pulls me up onto wobbling knees, and slips back into me. I arch my back and he grunts approval and tugs on my hair and then with a smack to my left butt cheek, Tate comes. *Hard.* Collapsing onto my back and moaning into my shoulder.

My knees give out and we collapse onto the bed together. He gently rolls off of me, and out of me, and I feel his strong hands at my hips flipping me over again so I'm on my back this time and then before I can fully comprehend what's happening, his hands are pushing my thighs apart and his head is between my legs.

"Tate, wait. I..." I don't finish that sentence because his tongue is dragging slowly across my clit. I'm literally still quivering from my orgasm but he doesn't care. In fact, as he groans against my sensitive flesh and slowly licks my folds I realize he fucking loves it.

I sigh and sift my fingers into his hair spread my legs more and enjoy every pass of his talented tongue. Then the impossible happens. I come again. This one is crazy soft yet intense, rolling through me like a wave with a shocking hidden riptide.

I swear I almost pass out but then I feel his lips on my belly and he grumbles, "Shh... Dylan is going to wake up."

"Sor... sorry," I pant back and he kisses the curve of my left breast, my shoulder, the column of my neck, and finally my cheek as he settles in beside me.

"So... what were you saying about having trouble coming?" Tate asks, his tone mockingly serious.

I stare at him. He grins so damn proud of himself, and winks. I laugh and shove him. He grabs me and pulls me in for a scorching kiss before he rolls himself off the bed. He points to the condom still around his cock. "Gotta take care of business."

I nod and watch him disappear into the bathroom, closing the door behind him and leaving me with nothing but the faint street light breaking through a gap in the curtains. His bed is warm and so damn soft. Just as soft as that bed at the Beverly Wilshire from that night I refuse to think about. And now I don't have to think about it. I have new, better, wilder memories of Tate to replay in my mind whenever I want.

I reach for my pajamas and wiggle into them without really getting up and then I burrow under the blankets again and inhale the scent of him—of us—on the sheets. I smile as my lids grow heavy. This can't be wrong. We can't be making a terrible mistake here. Maybe this is the start of something right. Something good and genuine and meant to be. I deserve that. So does Tate and especially Dylan.

That's my last coherent thought as sleep pulls me under.

When I wake up, it's to the sound of a seagull mewing

outside the half-opened window and Dylan whining. I stretch. The opposite side of the bed feels awfully cold and Dylan's whines are awfully close. My eyes open slowly and with everything I see my heart sinks. Because it's my night table beside me. My light gray sheets, not Tate's charcoal ones. At the foot of the bed is Dylan's sleeping pod, not the old steamer trunk Tate has at the foot of his bed. The bed I fell asleep in.

He must have moved me back into my bed when he came out of the bathroom. Or I sleep-walked here, which is highly unlikely. I don't think I've ever sleep-walked a day in my life but maybe there's a first time for everything? I sit up, pull back the covers, and walk over to get Dylan out of his crib.

The door swings open slowly and Tate's head pops in. He's got the cutest bed head and it makes me smile. "Morning, baby girl."

That makes me smile bigger. "Morning."

"I heard him stirring," Tate says as I pull Dylan out of his crib. "Thought I would grab him so you could sleep more if you want. You were pretty exhausted. Didn't even wake when I carried you to your bed."

"Yeah, I was a bit confused when I woke up," I regret saying it as soon as I do because I already know the answer. I've watched his M.O. with Diana, up close and personal.

On that trip where Dylan was conceived, Diana and I were sharing this very room. When we were done for the night, they would slink off into his room, or she would sneak off to his room as I got ready for bed, and I would fall asleep alone. But every morning when I woke up she was back in the bed with me.

I asked about it once and she explained it with one phrase and a shrug. "He doesn't do sleepovers."

I'm not special or different. He never said I was. This is the same as all his other hookups.

"Mal? You cool?"

He's looking at me curiously. I nod and smile.

"Yep." I hand him Dylan, who immediately starts to whimper. "Don't take it personally, he is not a morning person."

Tate looks slightly crestfallen but he nods. I motion to the door. "Go downstairs and put him in his pack-n-play while you make him a smoothie with pineapple, mango, and the sugar-free vanilla oat milk. I'll be down in a sec."

"Okay," Tate says and disappears out the door, closing it behind him. I head to the bathroom and take a quick shower. When I get out I wipe the steam off the mirror and stare at myself in it.

Tate has never been anything but Tate. I knew that but deep inside me, I hoped that this... that *I*... was different. I'm not.

So far... my heart whispers.

I glare at my own reflection, but I know it's useless. As wrong as it is, as stupid and reckless as it is, and even if I'm dooming myself to heartbreak—the heartbreak I've purposely avoided my whole life by keeping Tate firmly in the friends zone —I'm going to keep being with him. For as long as he wants me. Because I want him and I'm going to hope against hope that somehow he starts to see me as more than just a bed buddy.

Yeah. I'm an idiot. But at least I'm honest with myself about it.

Chapter 18

Tate

"**G**arrison!" Coach Braddock bellows my name into the conditioning room.

We didn't have on-ice practice this morning because we have a game tonight, but we have conditioning practice and mandatory video review sessions for strategy. But he is bellowing like I missed a pass or cost us a goal in a game or something. My whole body freezes, the dumbbells hanging from my hands. "Yes, Coach?"

"My office for a minute. Now."

Every single one of my teammates' eyebrows shoot up but no one says anything. I walk over to the rack put the weights down, grab my water bottle, and head straight to the coach's office. Coach Braddock is already sitting behind his desk stirring a cup of steaming liquid. It's not coffee, I don't think. "Ever had chai?"

"I don't think so."

I slowly close the door behind me but he waves at me to stop. Okay, that's good, right? It's not some super-secret conversation. He leans forward in his chair and sniffs the contents of his cup and makes a face. "I think it tastes like dirt and weeds but the wife insists this will make me live longer. And my kid has left me high and dry. Declan, my eldest turned her onto it. He's a trainer. For the Winterhawks. Did you know that? Just started mid-season."

I shake my head because I didn't know. I should know because Grady plays for them and he could have said something. Although I haven't been communicating much with anyone in my family since I found out about Dylan, and I've muted all the group chats so... maybe he did say it somewhere. "And Liam is a goalie with Portland, right?"

"As of this season, yeah." Coach nods. "I left him a message to call me and weigh in on this chai debate but he hasn't called me back. He's the worst with communication."

I nod, wondering why he's telling me all this when Coach adds, "Kind of like how you've been lately."

My eyes dart to his and I grip my water bottle tighter in my right hand. Coach sips his chai and makes the most comical face ever. He curses under his breath and moves the steaming cup to the edge of his desk. "Sir? Did you call me and I didn't answer?"

"No." Braddock leans back in his chair, his hands linking behind his sandy blond hair which is cut short and laced with silver. "But Adam had to come to me today and tell me that you haven't returned one of Christine's messages or phone calls. About the ceremony they want to do for the short-hand goal record."

"I haven't beaten the record yet," I reply and my shoulders loosen. I mean, I'm still tense about the coach being called in to chastise me by PR, but this isn't about my on-ice performance and that's all that counts. "They want to make this a big deal, get my family involved, and it hasn't happened and might not happen. We only have three games left and I have to score two shorties to beat my dad. Two normal goals, at the end of the season when everyone is pushing to make playoffs and beat our asses, is hard enough. But two shorties? Nearly impossible. And if I just tie his record, it's not really worth throwing a big celebration. Tying isn't a big deal."

Coach frowns, drops his hands, and leans on his desk. He's in a team track suit and he's still in good enough shape that he looks like he could be a player, except for the gray hairs and crow's feet around his blue eyes. "Is this a superstition thing? Or is there something going on with your family?"

Both, I want to reply, but I can't. I scramble to figure out what I can say but Coach doesn't give me a chance before he elaborates with more personal stories. "I grew up with three younger sisters who made it their job to make sure I had little to no ego. It was all fun and games but sometimes... I needed space. Are you on a relative sabbatical? Because if you are, hate to break it to ya kid, but your timing doesn't work for the team."

"No sabbatical. I mean, not officially," I reply. "I don't want to have my dad here, and all the media see him in the stands and crap, and then I don't score. You know? It's bad enough that happens to players when they make it to game seven and don't win. It feels ridiculous to add this pressure to a short-handed goal record. I mean, let's just concentrate on playoffs."

"We can and will do both," Coach replies in a tone that leaves no room for debate.

"My parents... my family can't come to Los Angeles right now," I blurt out, the desperation in my voice is clear and shocking, to both the coach and to me. But I think I'm on the edge of a panic attack. Not that I know specifically what they feel like, but my heart is racing and my hands are so sweaty my water bottle is hard to hold. "Things are... I'm dealing with some personal stuff I don't want them involved in."

Coach Braddock looks deathly serious now, but also compassionate. There's a softness in his stare I don't think I've ever seen.

"I have to ask…" Coach pauses and gets up out of his chair. Walking around his desk he closes the door he told me to leave open earlier. I twist in my chair to follow him with my eyes. He looks down at me with even more compassion in his eyes. "Do not hesitate when you answer this next question and know that your contract, your career, your future in hockey is secure as long as you answer honestly. Do you need the player's assistance program?"

"No," I reply quickly and firmly. "This is not about any kind of substance abuse. It's… I'm fine. I promise you."

"Okay…" Coach doesn't actually seem like he means that word. He walks back to his desk with his arms folded over his chest but this time he leans the front of it instead of sitting behind it. "Well, please stop avoiding Christine. Go to her now. You can join us in video review when you're done. Use us as an excuse to keep the meeting with her brief. But Tate, sorry, we're gonna have to give PR something. They love the family dynamic of a player with your heritage. The fans love it too. You're from a legend and you're becoming one yourself. The PR bullshit comes with it part and parcel. Sorry, but I think you know what you signed up for, right?"

I nod. And when I think about it, once everything is settled with Dylan my parents will be my first call. But I don't think that's going to happen before I beat this record. Unless I just don't try to beat the record. I stand up and walk to the door. "Thanks, Coach. I'll handle it."

"And you know you can tell me anything," Coach adds as I start to open the door. "And you kind of have to. The Quake can win the Cup this year and I need to know if something is going to get in the way of you helping us get there."

"Nothing will stop me from getting us there, Coach."

"And you *can* beat this record."

"I can." I nod and I walk out of the office.

"I won't though," I whisper to myself as I head for the elevators to go up to the offices where the marketing and PR departments are located.

Christine is great. She's also a former bed buddy. Former I guess isn't the best word for it as we never had an official start or stop date. I mean, start and end dates are something that people in relationships do. Bed buddies are a less structured thing. But that is currently biting me in the ass because Christine is flirting, hard.

"I really have to go back to the team," I say for the second time since I got to her office twenty minutes ago. "We have videos to watch."

"Speaking of videos, you never responded to the one I sent last week," she replies and smiles.

I didn't know she sent a video. I saw two texts about inviting my dad to come and watch the last game of the season, and asking me to do an interview with ESPN and that was it. I saw a third message later that week but I ignored it.

"I haven't even opened your messages," I say, trying to make it sound like I was ghosting more than just her. "I'm trying to focus on ending this season on top of the division."

She sighs. "You are now officially a tease, Tate Garrison. And that's no fun for my work or my personal life."

She takes the clip she pulled out of her hair when I got to her office and grabs it off her desk. As she sits back down in her chair she twists her blonde hair back up the way it was. "So no Dad at the last game?"

"I mean, if I score a shorty in the next one, yeah. You can have him fly down and plan something. But that still doesn't mean I will break the record in the last game," I warn her. "And tying it means nothing."

"God you athletes are this toxic blend of narcissism and

insecurity." She rolls her eyes. "Tying a record no one has come close to for almost two decades *is* a big deal, Tate."

"Not to me." I sigh. "How about we reassess after the next game."

"What if you score both goals in the next game?" Christine asks and arches one of her pale eyebrows. "I won't have time to organize anything."

"Then you can kick my ass for ruining this media wet dream, and I will let you," I retort. "You clearly don't get how impossible that is."

"We'll talk after we beat San Diego," she says firmly and shoos me out of her office with a wave of her hand. "Watch that video I sent, jerk. And stop ignoring my work texts."

"Okay. Sorry."

I take off and power walk it back to the video room. No one frowns or balks when I walk in late. Coach must have mentioned I had a meeting. I slip in and take a seat in the middle row next to Crew. He leans in when the goalie coach is highlighting a play for our goalie and whispers, "Movers texted and said they're done. Both houses are swapped and it went smoothly."

At least something is going great.

A couple seconds later, he also whispers, "And the guy said the lady of the house was very sweet and offered them lemonade."

"That's my Mallory," I say before I can catch myself.

Dude, you're a bit crazy, I chastise myself. I've only been sleeping with her for three days. Nights, actually. Three absolutely fantastic nights. Last night was my favorite. Doggie style on the couch. She initiated it too. And fuck me if I didn't come so hard I saw stars. Mallory is bolder than I thought she would be. And comfortable with her sexuality. I thought that night in the hotel, the way she let go of her inhibitions was a fluke, but it's the norm.

Mallory was always a topic of conversation between me and the hometown guys. She was undeniably pretty and smart. But most everyone blew her off because for some of them, she was too smart and they were intimidated. For others, she just seemed too reserved and shy. She was marriage material and nobody wants that... yet. That's what excuse *I* told myself for not going for her when we were younger. I wanted a wild girl.

If I'd known she'd be comfortable being spread eagle on my bed, begging for my cock in her mouth, and letting me smack her ass while we fucked, and then trot off to her own room for the night, bare ass swinging like she doesn't have a care in the world, I would have definitely made a play for her years ago.

"*Your* Mallory?" Crew echoes his deep baritone melancholy.

"No. Not like that." I shake my head. "I mean... like that, but not."

"You are such a cliché." Crew covers his wide mouth with his tattooed hand to stifle his laughter. "You're banging your nanny."

I frown at him. And then Coach calls his name. "Westwood! You paying attention to this? Because if the co-captain isn't listening then why should anyone else."

"Yes sir," Crew says, immediately focused and serious. "I'm listening."

We both shut up until after the meeting. But then he's back on me. "She's a very pretty girl, but she also seems like marriage material not, like... your type."

Ouch. That sounds mildly insulting even though he's right. "We are both in a place where this works. She needs someone, and I definitely need someone, and it's not like I can call on my regulars and say 'Hey, just ignore the baby and let's bone.'"

Crew laughs freely now since we're not in a meeting. "No, I

guess you can't say that. But are you sure that she doesn't have... other ideas? That this isn't more than just a mutual friendly arrangement for her?"

"I'm sure."

I am so *not* sure. But Mallory willingly leaves my room every night, even on the nights when I'm cuddly after the sex and I foolishly entertain the idea of asking her to stay and maybe just doze off with me. So I'm fairly confident we're on the same page.

"What are you two talking about that's so important you catch shit in a meeting?" Nash asks, coming up beside his twin. He looks angry, which is rare for Nash who is always serious but rarely publicly annoyed.

"My move. His move," Crew replies, ignoring his brother's energy. "Today is the day we swapped places."

"I still don't get why that's a thing that had to happen," Nash gripes, still in a salty mood. "If you wanted to live somewhere new, sell your place and buy something else. Same with you, Tate. And why did it have to be done right now? We've got big stuff to focus on. Move in the off-season."

"Are you fucking done being a Karen?" Crew snaps at his brother.

These two are rarely this aggressive with each other. They are definitely polar opposites and rarely see eye-to-eye, and they bicker, but they don't fight. This is a fight. Nash is glaring at Crew now. His eyes, which are a slightly lighter shade than his brother's, are narrowed and his mouth is set in a hard, flat line. He looks a lot like his dad, the world-famous Avery Westwood, right now. In general, he looks more like his dad than his fraternal twin, but that's likely the attitude. My dad played with Avery and told me once Avery was more serious than a heart attack, all the time.

"If you're going to be a co-captain then—"

Crew stops abruptly and spins to face his brother. They're toe-to-toe and both look more ornery than a wet cat. Crew is almost growling his words they're so low and venomous. "In case you forgot, my wife, who picked out that fucking house, also cheated on me in it, in my fucking bed. So, if you can't get why maybe I need a change of scenery then fuck you, brother. I've done fine at my job and I'll continue to do fine."

Crew storms off and I'm left standing there with Nash, who isn't as shaken by that face-off as I am, even though it was directed at him. The rest of the team has already disappeared from the long curving concrete hallway so nobody else witnessed that. I kind of wish someone had so I wouldn't feel so awkward. Nash sighs, turns, and drops his back against the wall. The anger has left his face and he looks kind of remorseful. Tenley and I bicker and we've had an occasional full-blown fight and I've always felt like Nash looks right now.

"I didn't realize that's what went down between Crew and Anne-Marie," I say and scratch the back of my head. "That's fucked up."

"It is. She is." Nash shakes his head and stares at his feet like he's never seen running shoes before. "And so is he. What you also don't know is after she left he dragged that bed out into the driveway and lit it on fire."

"What?"

"My dad's media machine made sure no one found out," Nash admits. "I mean, coach knows but he gave Crew a pass. His only pass. So he better get his shit in line. I'm so over his recklessness and so is everyone else."

He stomps off before I can think of what to say to that. It was harsh. And shocking. Crew never told me the mattress story and I'm a little uncomfortable that Nash did without consent. I don't have time to dissect the Westwood family dynamic though. I have to get home, have my pre-game nap, and eat a decent pre-game meal before heading back here. And I also have to make sure everything is cool with Dylan and Mallory at the new place.

Crew and I exchanged keys first thing this morning when we walked into practice so I head straight to my car and drive to Crew's House. Which is now my house. This is going to take some getting used to. Crew's house... my house... is a beige, three-story Tuscan-Spanish creation with dark wood balconies on every floor and a decent gated patio garden area overlooking the canal. Like every house in this area, it's long and narrow and the only thing on the first floor that's facing the street is the garage.

Above the garage is a door with a Juliet balcony, which was a room Crew called 'the office'. Anne-Marie had been a lawyer and she worked from home a lot. I park in the short drive and walk along the left side of the house toward the front door, which is kind of in the middle of that side. I unlock it and step into the front hall, which almost immediately opens up to the left into the open-concept living-dining-kitchen area that over-looks the canal.

The floors are rich wood, the walls are white with a plaster finish, and there are ceiling beams that match the floors. I walk toward the living room, which has an incredible stone fireplace I can't ever imagine needing in Southern California, and see all my furniture is perfectly placed. But also, there isn't nearly enough of it. It looks ridiculously empty in this enormous room. My dining room table would be particularly teeny in such a cavernous space, but it's not there. Crew's giant farmhouse table with a resin and wood top is still here.

Mallory is at the kitchen island digging in a box on the coun-tertop. She's wearing cut-off jean shorts and a white tank top. Her hair is pulled up in a messy bun on top of her head. She's barefoot, makeup-less, and so damn pretty I can't help but stare.

"All good?" I ask, trying to fight the smile just seeing her brings to my lips.

"I have never had movers pack and unpack for me. It's glorious," Mallory announces. She holds up a plate from the box in front of her. "I asked them to let me do the pots and pans myself because I wanted to make sure they're in the right place for the space."

"There's a feng shui to pots and pans?' I smirk.

She levels me with a deadly serious stare. "There is nothing worse than being in the middle of cooking and having to ruin the buzz by hunting down a pot."

"I don't cook all that much or anything too complicated so..." And then it hits me. She's doing it because of her, not me. She will be cooking here. This is really going to be her kitchen. "You do whatever works for you. I want you to be totally Zen or in the zone or buzzed or whatever when you cook. Even if it's just popcorn."

I walk up behind her and circle her waist with my arms, pulling her into my chest and kissing the back of her neck. She lets out a little sound like a gasp and arches her back, but then slips out of my arms. "Your sister is here. Well, she's in Venice. She took Dylan for a walk."

"Brave considering the results the last time she tried that."

Mallory smiles. "Tenley isn't known for being easily scared off."

"You're not wrong," I reply and walk over to her. She holds the plate she's carrying out in front of her like a shield.

"She could come bursting in here at any second," Mallory tells me. "I figure you don't want her to know about... this."

"I don't want her to know I exist on most days, let alone who I am existing with and how," I joke, kind of. Mallory shoots me another smile before turning to stare at the cupboards and drawers, which are all open.

"Do *you* want her to know?"

I don't know why I asked the question. Mallory inhales sharply but doesn't exhale for a long beat. "It's your life, Tate. You make the decisions. Just like with this kitchen."

"Nope. The kitchen is most definitely your decision," I reply firmly and move so I'm standing beside her. I wrap an arm around her shoulders and hold her there when she tries to step away again. This is relatively harmless. If Tenley walked in right now, it would look friendly. "You will be cooking for Dylan and yourself a lot. I'm on pre-made chef-delivered meals for playoffs. And I want you to be as comfortable here as possible."

"I guess your permanent nanny can reorganize when that time comes," Mallory muses as she pivots on her tiny bare feet and puts the plate in a drawer in the island. "But you would have to be insane not to want the dishes next to the dishwasher. Super easy. Also love that Crew has... well, now *you* have... quiet closing doors and drawers. Felix used to slam the cupboards sometimes when Dylan was napping and he'd wake him up. Diana would get so pissed off."

Mallory hasn't talked much about this guy who was about to pretend to be my son's father. I have this very odd, slow-burning rage for the dude. It simmers deep inside my chest when I think about him. Not only because he was willing to steal my son, but because he just as easily was willing to abandon him. "Was he a total asshole?"

Mallory pauses, five more dinner plates in her hands. Her eyes find mine. The amber in them is really popping today. I think it's all the natural sunshine that fills this place doing the trick. "No. Honestly, Felix was great for Diana, and to Diana. He was also amazing with Dylan."

Mallory places the plates on top of the other one she put in the drawer and then walks back over to the box. Her motions as she gathers more things out of the box—drinking glasses this time—are slower. She bites her bottom lip. "I owe you an apology for not telling you about Dylan. I could have reached out and don't think that I wasn't torn about the whole thing. But by the time I showed back up in Diana's life, she was engaged and almost to term and she didn't even confirm it was yours until she was literally writhing in pain and he was crowning."

"What?" I blink and try to push the image out of my head. Thinking about Diana is still equal parts sad and upsetting. Thinking of my child's birth, which I was given no choice but to miss also sucks. "Where were you while she was pregnant? You both went to England together, I thought."

"We didn't." Mallory shakes her head and walks past me to put the drinking glasses in a cabinet by the farmhouse sink. "I left for England on an Au Pair visa. She followed two weeks later, but I didn't ask her to. I wasn't even talking to her. It had been our plan to do it together but after that weekend with you, here... I stopped talking to her."

She glances over her shoulder and our eyes lock. She's searching for something in my face. Understanding? Like I would ever forget that weekend. God, it bugs me she talks about it like we committed murder or something else unspeakable.

Mallory walks back over to the box. She carries two large pots I didn't know I owned to the cabinets by the huge stove. It has six burners and a griddle. I have never owned something like this, but it's similar to my parents' stove. I own a parental stove now. Wild. "It had been her idea to move to England because her sister was there, but I decided to go ahead and apply for au pair jobs without her and I got one right away. She followed but didn't contact me for months and then, out of nowhere, her sister Stephanie called and said Diana was in a hospital in London and wanted to see me. I ran."

"Of course you did."

She turns and stares at me. "Because I'm a pushover and a lap dog of a friend who just does whatever people want?"

"What? No." I step directly in front of her, brushing a tendril of hair hanging at the side of her temple back toward the messy bun. "Because you're an incredibly kind, compassionate, understanding, and empathetic human being. One of the best people I've ever known and you don't abandon or punish people, even when they hurt you."

Her expression softens but she ignores the compliment. "I thought she was sick but when I got there I found out it was bed rest. She had a preeclampsia."

I stare blankly. Mallory almost smiles. "High blood pressure, which complicates a pregnancy and can cause an early birth. And Dyllie Bear was early, but luckily only by a couple of weeks."

"And you were there when he was born."

"I quit my nanny job and stayed by her side pretty much from the day I went to see her in that hospital so yeah. I was there." Mallory nods and again moves away from me to put more dishes away. "I met Felix who was madly in love with her, coming to the hospital every hour he could, skipping work when it was possible. At first, I thought that Dylan was his. God rest her soul, but she might have slept with you and him within a short enough time frame to make it possible. It's not judgment, just fact."

I shrug. "If I was a woman and could get pregnant, there would be months where the father could have been nine different guys so, no judging here."

She takes a second to absorb what I just said. I don't know how she feels about it, but I'm confident she isn't judging me. I've never hidden who I was from Mallory and she's always been my friend.

"Is this one of the months where, if you were a woman and

found out you were pregnant tomorrow, the potential father could be a multiple choice questionnaire?" she asks me, her eyes on the spatula and potato masher in her hand.

She's asking if I'm still sleeping around in her cute, indirect way. I walk over to her, stand directly in front of her, and then lean in and cover her mouth with my own. She kisses me back without hesitation. When I pull back her cheeks are flushed. I'm breathing just as heavy as she is as her eyes flutter open and, still holding her head in my hands, I open my mouth to answer her silly question when—

"No poop this time!"

Tenley. Of course.

Mallory leaps away from me like I've suddenly caught fire, dropping a spatula on the ground at the same time. I spin as Tenley enters the living room, Dylan on her hip, and turns to the kitchen. "Where's Mal?"

"Dropped a spatula," Mallory announces and pops back up from the floor where she had been bent over.

"Oh. Cool," Tenley murmurs breezily, but she's watching us intently. Studying us. Assessing us.

I round the kitchen island and walk over to take Dylan from her. He's extra drooly, his teething is in high gear. "I have to go for my pre-game nap so let me say hello to my lil dude first."

He doesn't seem to want to come to me but he does, and there's only a little grunt of hesitation. Dylan then settles against my hip. He looks up at me, blinking those big green eyes. "Hey, Dylan. I have to take my nap, and then go to work but I wanted to get a hug from you. For luck."

"Your dad here might beat a record your gramps set."

"I won't. Not today," I tell Tenley and she immediately lifts an eyebrow.

"Is that humility? Some superstitious thing? Are you under the weather?" Tenley quips and tilts her blonde head.

I ignore her and give Dylan a squeeze. He reaches for my hair and tugs it. Hard. I wince loudly and he giggles and tugs again. I gently grab his chubby forearm and pull my hair free. "I need my hair so let's get you something else to yank on."

"I've got a frozen teething ring," Mallory says. Opening the freezer part of the fridge she pulls it out and tosses it across the dining room right to me in the living room and smiles proudly as I catch it with my free hand. I wink at her.

As I settle Dylan on a playmat next to the brand-new indoor/outdoor play set I ordered this morning with an exorbitant same-day delivery fee, my phone starts buzzing in my back pocket. I miss the call because getting Dylan settled is much more important. The number is Christine's. Shit. Well, she's not going to appreciate going to voicemail.

Before I can excuse myself from my family and call her back, she texts.

ESPN Interview tonight before the game so show up half an hour early.

Wear your best suit.

And next time, PICK UP YOUR PHONE!

I type back quickly.

K. Sorry. Will be there.

I'm not thrilled with this because it will cut into my already dwindling pre-game nap and meal but it is what it is. I don't want to piss off the coach or the communications department any more than I already have.

And then, as Dylan chomps on his teething ring at my feet, I bend to kiss the top of his head and walk toward the stairs that lead up to the bedrooms. Mine, the master, is the entire third floor. My sister and Mallory are talking together at the island. I'm about to shut my phone off when I see the video notification from weeks ago in the chain from Christine.

"I'm going to take my pre-game nap," I tell them and stupidly hit play. To be fair the majority of videos Christine has sent me over the two years she's been working for the Quake have been either team footage or funny TikToks. But this isn't funny. It isn't a social media video. Or Quake footage.

It's a video that starts off black and then as the camera pulls back it's black lace panties, with a red manicured hand in them. The camera flips and there's Christine. She's sitting on her bed, legs spread in nothing but those undies and matching bra and she's masturbating, smiling at me in the mirror, and then she lets out a throaty moan. She's coming. I know the sound. And of course, my phone volume is so high everyone in the room hears it. Hears her moan *my* name.

Chapter 19

Tate

Tenley and Mallory stop speaking. I look up, eyes wide with embarrassment, which I know must make me look guilty as hell. "Sorry."

Mallory looks away and immediately goes back to the contents of the box on the island, turning her back to me. Tenley glares with the heat of a thousand suns. I bolt all the way upstairs until I'm alone in my new bedroom. I close the door, tip my head back, and close my eyes. That was a nightmare.

Fuck, I can't believe that happened in front of my sister, and right after Mallory basically asked me if we're exclusive. And I didn't really answer. Double fuck.

I open my eyes and look around the room. It's all my stuff but it doesn't feel like it. My bed, my dresser, and my night tables all look ridiculously tiny, like doll furniture, because this room is way bigger than my other bedroom. The bed is against a false wall, facing the bifold doors that open onto the balcony that overlooks the canal. Behind the false wall is a closet which you walk through to get to the massive slate and stone bathroom.

I walk over toss my phone on the charging pad on the nightstand and drop onto the bed. At least it feels familiar. The California sun is spilling into the room, illuminating everything. It's great but not when I'm supposed to nap. I roll over to get up but I see the little remote on the other night table, grab it, and hit the button marked close. There's a hum and black-out blinds slowly descend on the windows.

Once the room is submerged in darkness I peel out of everything and slip under the sheets. Sleep evades me for way too long because all I can think about is that blunder. I finally doze off but it doesn't last long because I'm suddenly being shoved awake.

I know that shove all too well. I remember it from childhood. The rough shake on my shoulder on Christmas mornings or school days when I slept through my alarm. And it's always followed by a small but hard smack to the side of my head.

I lift my arm, blocking the impending slap with my forearm. "Tenley get the fuck out of my room."

"Nope."

"Oh my God, why didn't Mom and Dad stop with one kid?" I groan and sit up. I'm groggy and grumpy. "I have a game to play tonight. Come on. You know better than to be a menace on game night."

"You were watching sexting videos in front of Mallory and your son!" Tenley announces in a hiss and then she shoves my shoulder again. I don't expect it and kind of rock, almost tipping over in the bed.

"It was an accident."

I reach for the remote for the blackout blinds. I need light to defend myself. As the blinds slowly raise her angry face comes into view and she takes in my naked torso with the covers bunched at my waist. "Are you naked?"

"Yes. It's my bedroom and I sleep naked."

Tenley steps back from the bed and spins to face the wall. "Gross. Get up. Put on something so I can yell at you."

"How about you get the fuck out of my room," I growl. "Game day, Ten. Damnit!"

I grab the pants I dropped to the floor earlier and tug them on without underwear. Tenley, still facing the wall, says, "In all seriousness Tate, I don't know who you are anymore and I don't like it."

"What the hell does that mean? Why don't you think you know me?" I question. "You can turn around."

She faces me again, pushing her long blonde hair back over her shoulders before folding her arms over her chest, which is covered in a black t-shirt with simple white lettering that says Not Photoshopped. "You aren't going to beat Dad's record, are you?"

I sigh and walk into the closet so I can find a suit that Christine will approve of. I don't know what my 'best suit' is. "I have no idea how it's going to go, Ten."

She appears in my closet. "I think you do. I saw the way you averted your eyes when the topic came up and the vague answer. This is all you've wanted since you picked up a damn hockey stick as a toddler. To beat Daddy."

I make a face. "Don't call him Daddy. That's so fucking weird."

"You're not even going to try to score anymore, are you?" Tenley looks furious. Like this is some kind of personal offense. "Because you're trying to hide Dylan?"

"Tenley just shut up and mind your own business for once!" I bark.

"He's my nephew. He is my business!" she snaps. "I may never have kids, okay? You having some one day was my only hope."

Whoa. I did not expect that to come out of her mouth or for her eyes to start filling with tears. Tenley turns away from me, wiping at her eyes, but she continues talking. "I didn't expect you to have one now, while I was in college, and you still have the emotional intelligence of a potato, but hey. Whatever. Dylan is here and Mom and Dad will love him, like I do. To pieces. The whole family will if you fucking let them!"

"I just need the paternity results, Ten. And then to tell the coach and PR."

"He's had more trauma than any kid should have already, so don't make it worse by hiding him from the world and being a dad who fails on purpose," Tenley barks at me, hands on her tiny hips. "What the fuck, Tate. You're a Garrison. We don't fail. Especially not on purpose."

"Stop with your melodramatics." I sigh. "For the record, you constantly on my ass about everything is not helping."

"Are you going to stop trying to score? Are you going to miss the net on purpose?"

I stare at my perfectly hung suits. "Yes. Okay? If the lawyer can't get the birth certificate sorted before the end of the season, then yes."

"Why?"

I sigh, close my eyes, and turn to face her. She's standing by the built-in dresser. Her glare has softened and she just looks confused more than irate. "They want to do this big ceremony, even if I just tie the stupid record and bring Mom and Dad here and it will be a thing. I can't risk that so... I can't break the record."

"I know. Someone named Christine already contacted me about it all," Tenley replies. "She wants me at the last game of the season. I called Mom and they've been invited too. It's supposed to be a surprise."

"What?" I shake my head. "No. No. I said fucking no!"

"Deep breaths," Tenley reaches out and grips my bare shoulders firmly. "You should have the DNA results soon and then the lawyer can work overtime to get the new birth certificate. And besides, Tate, Mom and Dad aren't going to care about all that shit."

"Fuck. I have to tell the coach tonight." I start to pace. "And Christine or Adam, her boss. Both. Probably both. She is the one who sent me the video by the way."

"You're sleeping with a Quake employee?" Tenley asks. "Even I know that's not smart."

"I'm not. I haven't in a while, but we don't have a fraternization policy so it's not like it's wrong," I reply. "Ten, can you leave now? I have a lot to deal with."

She hesitates but turns and starts to leave. I grab the pieces of my favorite suit, a charcoal and navy one with muted checks, a white shirt, and a navy tie. When I move back into the bedroom to lay it out before my shower, Tenley is still standing by the door. I'm about to bark at her to leave again, but she levels me with a serious stare. "She's not one of your bed buddies, Tate. She may be playing the part but she wants more than that. And if you break her heart, you're a total asshole."

And then she leaves before I can ask what the hell she's going on about. But the fact is, I know. It's Mallory. But Mallory knows what we're doing. We've talked about it and she's been a willing participant.

Well, I'll add having a talk with Mal to my long list of uncomfortable things I need to do. And I'm sure it will be as painful as missing the net on purpose, which I'll also have to do tonight if someone slides me the puck on a power play.

I head into the shower filled with stress and a little rage. Why are things getting worse instead of better?

* * *

I'm late so the glare from Christine isn't unexpected. The ESPN crew is looking a little miffed too. I give them all a sheepish smile. "Sorry. There was an accident on the 10 so I had to take surface streets."

Total lie but this is a sports station, not a news station. They're not going to know. Christine's frown lessens a little as I immediately drop onto the stool they have set up for me. "Where's the interviewer?"

I glance around. We're doing this in the hallway, halfway between the home and visitor locker rooms, and if we don't get to it, the teams will be arriving and we won't get the quiet we need. "He went to the bathroom. He'll be here in a minute. Let's do a lighting and sound test, okay?"

I nod at the guy talking and he walks over and mics me up. Usually, the interviewer just holds a big mic for these things, but they're putting a tiny one on my lapel instead. It doesn't raise a red flag but there's a weird look on the camera guy's face when a moment later he says. "So I'm gonna shoot some footage, just to get the angles and the lighting right. You can ignore me."

Okay... I do. I pull out my phone and send Mallory a text. When I got downstairs after my shower I found a note that she was on a grocery run and would be back. I waited as long as I could for her to return, and then even took the long way here, driving by the closest Trader Joe's and the closest Ralph's to see if I could see the new SUV in the parking lot. I was fully ready to stop and run into the store and talk to her, even if it meant I was super late. But I didn't see the car.

> Hey. I need to explain that video. And I will. Don't worry.

> Please wait up for me tonight. I want to see you.

I close my WhatsApp and a picture of Dylan fills my screen. He's standing in the old townhouse. Well, standing is a stretch. He's holding himself up by gripping the edge of the sofa but the smile on his face is so big and proud. Mallory says he may start walking any day now. I hope I'm home for it.

"So, Tater Tot Garrison, how does it feel to be on the verge of crushing your dad's ego?"

The voice is deep, jovial, confident, and one I've been hearing as long as I've heard my own parents' voices. My head snaps up and walking toward me is my uncle Devin.

He's dressed in a light gray suit with a mic clipped to his lapel too. I stand up, dropping my phone onto the chair and trying not to let my jaw hit the concrete floor. The floor feels like it's wobbling because my knees are on the verge of buckling from surprise—and fear.

He doesn't notice and, grinning, pulls me into a bear hug. I wrap my arms around him too, because what the hell else can I do? Faint? Yeah, that feels like something I want to do, but I can't. I shoot a glare at Christine over Uncle Devin's shoulder. "Hey! Wow!" I say, hoping my voice isn't as clogged with terror as my heart is. "If I'd known you were the one doing the interview I would have been later, and I wouldn't have bothered with my best suit."

"If that's your best, then you need a new stylist," Devin jokes and ruffles my hair like I'm six again. I swat his hand away good naturally and he hugs me again.

Oh God. Oh fuck. I step back from the hug and mentally give my head a shake. It's fine. It's just an interview. I can handle this. Devin grins. "When they asked me to do this, I couldn't wait. You know your dad still gloats about that record but when we were playing together it was his constant dig. He knew I was horrible at killing power plays, so it was the one record that I wouldn't be able to beat."

"Well, you did pretty good being the Barons' Captain and getting your name on the Cup three times," I remind him.

He grins. "You think you might be the next Garrison to add your name to that trophy?"

He moves toward the chairs and so I follow beside him. The cameras are rolling and have been since before he walked down the hall. I realize the 'test' was them setting up this little surprise. I wonder, irrationally, if they could see my screen while I was typing.

"I'm not the only Garrison who is going to be in the play-offs," I remind my uncle AKA the ESPN reporter, as I reach for my phone, which I carelessly put on his stool not my own. "Conner, Grady, and Theo will also probably be in the first round this year."

"You'll have to face Grady in the first round," Devin grabs my phone before I can. He passes it to me, casually, like it's no big deal. But he looks down and sees Dylan's photo. His eyes fly up to mine and he grins. "Wait... do you have your own baby picture as your screen saver?"

Oh fuck.

I swallow but my throat is closing like I'm in some kind of anaphylactic shock. I cough a little. Devin laughs. "I haven't seen this one. It's adorable, but I'm surprised there isn't a hockey stick in it. You used to carry around this plastic one everywhere you went."

He starts to hold it up toward the camera. I try and grab it from his hand, but he still has quick reflexes and manages to keep it from me. So I plaster a wooden smile on my face. "No one needs to see my goofy baby face."

"Want to? They need to!" Devin grins and I want to punch him, which is unfair. He's a great uncle and he's just doing his job. He starts to turn my phone to the screen again but I manage to grab it this time, covering it with my palm ripping it from his grip, and sliding it into my pocket.

I turn to the camera "You better be splashing a picture of

baby Grady on national television too if you interview him. Maybe that will throw him off his game if we face him in round one."

I watch my uncle's hazel eyes flicker with something that breaks through his sportscaster face, but it's gone before anyone registers it. He motions for us to both finally sit down. "I know before we all ended up on the same team it was a mixed bag of emotions when I had to face your dad or your Uncle Luc. I wanted to win, but I hated to beat them. Is it the same with your cousins?"

I nod. "Yeah, I mean, ultimately I want us all to have our names on the Cup. I know they feel the same, but... one of us has to be first. Might as well be me."

Devin laughs. Hell, the whole crew and even Christine laugh. The interview is back on track. It goes on for another ten minutes, and we talk about the short-handed goals record and growing up with my dad playing, and pond hockey with the cousins. It's a perfect interview, on the outside. Fans love the family dynasty thing and Devin is a charismatic interviewer.

But every moment is a vortex of misery for me because all I can think about is that picture of Dylan on national television. How clear was it? Who will see it? I mean, my family will because I'd bet all I own that they're all watching. They all knew about this surprise interview before I did. Maybe not Tenley. She wouldn't have hidden this from me, but my uncles and aunts would have known. And my parents.

Finally, Devin wraps it up, wishing me luck for the shorty record and the impending playoffs and we hug instead of shaking hands. "Cut!" the cameraman calls out.

Devin turns to him. "You guys get that footage straight to head office. They want to run it tonight after the game."

"Can you cut the baby photo stuff out?"

"No! It was adorable!" Christine argues and her bright red

lips are parted in a grin. "Can I see the photo again? We can put it on our website when we link to the piece. In fact, it gave me an idea to do a whole baby photo thing with the entire team."

"I wish Conner played for you guys. I have a great one of him covered in birthday cake," Devin chuckles.

"I'll send you a copy or something," I mutter to Christine. I grab my uncle's arm. "Can we talk? Do you have a second? Alone."

He nods and we start down the hall. The problem is we aren't in a private area. The guys on both teams have started wandering in so there are people at both ends of the curving hallway. I walk to the medical room. It's used when someone gets a hit to the head during the game as the concussion protocol space. Or if someone needs stitches. I pull Devin into the room and close the door.

"You can't show that photo."

He blinks and really looks at me. I can feel him taking in my panic and agitation. He cocks his head to one side. "Okay. Why?"

"Because."

"Tate. I don't have any control over the back end of interviews," Devin tells me.

"Uncle Devin, please. You can't. It's not me," I finally confess.

Something feels inherently, intensely wrong about telling my uncle before my parents. Like this will just make the whole situation worse. He narrows his eyes and then he gets this look of understanding, and he smiles. "Was that Tenley? You guys did almost look like twins as kids. You were a blond too for the first couple of years."

"What? No. We didn't." It's my automatic reaction anytime someone says I look like my sister. But I realize he's given me an out on this and I have to take it. "I mean, if you all thought it was me, I guess we did. Thankfully we don't anymore."

He makes a face like I'm an idiot. "Why do you have a pic of your sister as your wallpaper?"

"Because it annoys her," I say like it's the most obvious answer in the world.

Devin laughs. "I am so happy that there is no sibling rivalry between Liv, Mae, and Conner. You and Tenley have enough for the entire family anyway."

"Yeah. We do," I mutter. "Can you have them cut it? If not, my life will be hell from now until the end of time."

Uncle Devin shoots me a sympathetic smile and squeezes my shoulder. "Should be doable. But that PR lady seems to have her own ideas now."

"I can give her a real baby photo and she can do what she wants on the Quake site," I promise him and he nods.

I open the door, because I have to get to the locker room and change now. "Tater, we're all cheering you on. Even your dad."

"I know. Thanks."

"Maybe rejoin the family group chat and acknowledge our existence once in a while?" Uncle Devin gently suggests and I nod.

"Yeah. Sorry. I'm still there, just muted you guys," I admit with a sheepish grin.

"Conner is the muter, not you."

"Fine. I'll pop in this week and say something to piss you all off, so you know I'm doing fine," I joke and he laughs.

I wave goodbye and bolt into the locker room. I want to believe I dodged a bullet, but I'm shaky and almost nauseous as I change into my gear. It still feels like there's a bullet with my name on it.

Chapter 20

Tate

It's the third period. We have four minutes left and Spike Adams, our resident pest, got a little too pesky. He's in the box. I'm on the ice for the penalty kill. We have forty-two seconds left to kill this. Coach breaks up Nash and Crew on penalty kills because it's where Nash excels and Crew doesn't, so Nash is on the ice with me.

We've managed to clear the puck twice. Collingwood blocked a shot, but it was a close one and to be honest, the post did most of the work. We need to keep this clean and simple because we're only ahead by one goal. If San Diego scores on this, we're tied and there's not much time left to change that in regulation.

San Diego's star forward gets a pass, but Nash is on him, making his view of the net impossible. He winds up like he's going to shoot it anyway, but I notice his eyes through his visor dart left. I remember this play from the game tape we were watching in practice. He's gonna fake a shot on goal and slide the puck over to his wingman. I leave my position guarding the left winger so I can double-team the guy on the right wing with my teammate Landon Casco.

"What the fuck you doing?" Landon asks when I get there, but I don't have time to remind him because the puck is sailing right across the ice. Right toward us. Toward me.

"Go!" Landon bellows and gives me a little shove. I skate up, managing to get to it a millisecond before the San Diego winger.

The crowd roars. The Quake bench is on its feet, but they're all a blur as my thighs pump, moving me down the ice at a blinding pace. Toward their goal and their panicked goalie. I'm alone. It's a breakaway.

But I can't score. I can't inch closer to my dad's record. I can't bring that level of attention into my life right now. I can't...

My sister's voice echoes in my ears.

You're a Garrison. We don't fail. Especially not on purpose.

Tenley is right. My brain may think that the logical thing to do is whiff the shot. Purposely shoot wide or otherwise fuck it up, and maybe it is the only way to keep my secrets, but... I'm a Garrison. I was born to win.

My stick rears back, my eyes hone in on the narrow space between the goalie's leg pads, and I shoot. The puck sails hard and fast, right through his five-hole with such force the back of the net whooshes out so far even I can see it.

The crowd is deafening. I glide around the net, stick in the air in victory, and let out a howl of celebration. People bang the glass. The Quake bench all pile on me as I skate over, slapping my back and tapping my helmet, screaming celebratory words into my ears.

I hop over the boards. Coach Braddock walks up behind me as I sit down and grabs me by both shoulders. He leans in. "I knew it."

I glance up at him and he grins and winks before I turn my focus back to the ice. Everyone is looking up at the Jumbotron as the refs get ready to set the face-off at center ice. The screen is showing Uncle Devin's face where he sits in the press box. He's grinning and he turns his phone toward the screen. It's a video chat and my dad's face is there, grinning wildly. I can see the pride. So can everyone else. I give the screen a thumbs up as best I can with my gloves on.

Then I look away and focus my eyes on my skates to rein in the emotions running through me. I still have a game to finish and consequences to deal with after this. I am not going to back down on breaking this record, so I need to tell everyone about Dylan ASAP.

Chapter 21

Mallory

I'm happy for him. I really am. But I'm also still humiliated. I know Tenley knows about me and Tate. She hasn't said a word but the girl is ridiculously intelligent and she has read the signs. She also knows her brother. She wasn't at all shocked when that horny video got played. She looked upset but not shocked.

I was shocked. It felt like I had been whacked in the face with the frying pan I was holding. That's why as soon as Tenley left, and Tate was still upstairs, I left too. I wasn't ready to talk about it with him. To admit I not only want to be his only 'bed buddy' but I need to be. So instead I went to the beach with Dylan. I sat there and watched him play in the sand and tried to run through every possible conversation we might have about this.

The first was he would say sorry but it wasn't like we were exclusive. Only people in a relationship are exclusive. We're in an agreement. I'm cool, right? If not, let's just end this now so we can stay friends.

The next version was that he told me it was from an older lover, not a current one. He was going to tell her he was involved with someone and he would promise it wouldn't happen again. Because I was all he wanted. This thing, me and him, was enough for him.

I felt tears prick my eyes as that second scenario ran through my brain because it was such a pathetic fantasy.

After I was sure he would be gone to the arena, I collected Dylan and drove home after breaking down and stopping at Trader Joe's for some pre-made meals because cooking was the last thing I wanted to do. And after Dylan was bathed and in bed, I Door Dashed a pint of Cold Stones Birthday Cake Remix and when it arrived I settled in and watched his game in the yard overlooking the canal because Crew had a TV built into the outdoor fireplace there.

With the Canal water lapping beyond the rod iron fence and the warm California air blowing in my hair, I watched Tate Garrison inch ever closer to beating his dad's record. I also noticed his uncle on the Jumbotron. The TV announcer proclaimed, "This family is wild. I feel like they should do genetic testing on them. They get more and more talented each generation."

To which the other announcer added, "Did you know Silver Bay, Maine, produces more hockey players, per capita, than any other place in the United States. They're only beat globally by Thunder Bay, Ontario, Canada."

"Yeah. I know," I mutter and shovel the last of the Cold Stones into my mouth.

"Must be something in the water supply over there." The first announcer chuckles but I stop listening to their banter because the screen is now just Tate's face on the bench.

His coach leans in from behind and whispers something to him and he smiles. His face is red from exertion and damp with sweat, which you can see through his visor, but his eyes twinkle. His mouth is spread in a wide, proud grin. He looks so devastatingly handsome all I can do is stare longingly. Because I may get to be naked with him just about every night, but he's not really mine. And that hurts.

The Quake win the game. I pull up my phone and re-read Tate's message asking me to stay up. I don't want to but I know I'm going to have to have this conversation with him at some point. Might as well stop avoiding the inevitable.

I head back into the house and wait for him on the couch in the living room. I stretch out and play Wordle on my phone to distract myself and keep my mind from anxiously predicting how this conversation will go again. He must take longer than normal to get home because I end up falling asleep.

I wake up to the feeling of being lifted into his arms. My eyes flutter open and I see him looking down at me with a soft smile. "Sorry baby girl. The press was relentless tonight. Everyone wanted to talk to me. I got home as soon as could."

"We need to talk," I mumble as I lift my left arm and rub the sleep from my eyes. "Put me down. Let's do this."

He lets out a rough chuckle, probably at the unenthusiastic tone in my voice. Like I would rather be picking porcupine quills off an alligator. If that was an option, I might take it. We reach the landing of the second floor, the one where both my and Dylan's bedrooms are located, and he pauses. I expect to be let down, kissed on the cheek, and sent to my room.

"Is he adapting to his new room?" Tate asked. "Or did he freak out?"

I shake my head. "He did just fine. He had his own room in England so I think he remembers what it was like to sleep alone. Plus that new crib you ordered is great. He is so comfy in it I almost wanted to crawl in there with him."

Tate smiles. "If your mattress sucks, I can get you a new one."

He starts up the last set of stairs to his bedroom. Without

putting me down. Okay, I'm wide awake now. "No. I mean, it's fine. What are you doing?"

"Taking you to bed," Tate replies. "My bed. My mattress is admittedly better. I ordered it from the Four Seasons."

"The place we stayed that time?" I stutter out the words.

"Yeah. But we almost always stay in Four Seasons on the road. It's why I picked the Beverly Wilshire when we were too drunk to drive," Tate explains as we mount the last stair and he uses his elbow to flip on the light in his room. "I know they're a Four Seasons and their beds are the best. You can order their bedding and mattresses online, directly from their supplier, which is what I did when I bought the townhouse. For me, not the guest room. But I'll order you one tomorrow."

"You don't have to. I swear my mattress is fine."

He walks right over to his own bed and bends, laying me down in the middle of it. He hovers over me for a second, just long enough to press a chaste kiss to my lips. "You deserve better than fine."

Shut up, I internally chastise my heart, which seems to be doing some kind of waltz in my chest. I sit up as soon as he steps away and starts pulling off his suit. "So I'm up. Now. You wanted to talk, so let's get this over with."

Tate is yanking on his tie, pulling it loose from his neck. He walks to the side of the bed and stares down at me. "I didn't say I wanted to talk. I said I wanted to see you."

"Well, hi!" I wave up at him, feeling even smaller than I am because he looks so big hovering over me. "I'm here. You saw me."

He grins. It's feral. "I haven't seen all of you. Yet."

He wants to have sex? Umm... well... okay. Yeah. I will. I'm weak and I know it. But I need to know if this is goodbye sex or not. If he's still sleeping with the woman in the video, then this is goodbye sex. "Listen, about that video."

"It's old," Tate replies. "Someone I used to have an arrangement with... she sent it a couple weeks ago but I never bothered to open it and I just didn't... I didn't know it would be that. I'm sorry you heard it."

"Okay." I mentally stamp down the hope in my chest because this isn't exactly what I wished for. It's still short of what my heart longs for. "So... is there anyone else you're currently also in an arrangement with? Besides me?"

"Nope. Just you," Tate replies and continues to undo his tie. "I scored a shorty tonight."

"I saw."

"I'm one goal from tying my dad's record."

"I know."

He's working on the buttons to his shirt now, one after the other, unveiling his buff chest little by little to my eager gaze. His hair is hanging over his forehead as he looks down at me. I'm in the same shorts and tank I've been in all day but he's looking at me like it's sexy lingerie. "And my uncle was there tonight. The PR team wants to have my dad there at the next game because they're sure I'm gonna tie him then."

"Are you sure?"

"Yeah. I think it's gonna happen." Tate grins at me, but there's a nervous glint in his eye. "So I've got a meeting scheduled tomorrow afternoon with my coach and the head of PR. So I can tell them about Dylan. But first I'm calling my parents in the morning. Video chat so they can meet him after I tell them."

I sit up straighter, tucking my legs under me. "Oh my God, Tate, this is actually happening?"

"Yeah. The lawyer is still waiting on the birth certificate but he says I can go ahead." Tate yanks off his shirt. "Can you help me get undressed? My pants seem a little tight and I might need help with the zipper."

I drop my gaze and there, right in front of me, is his erection straining the expensive fabric of his suit pants. I bite back a grin at his cheeky behavior and force myself to look him in the eye. "Tate, this is a big emotional deal. You can't be thinking about sex right now."

"I think about sex every time you're in the room with me," Tate tells me and when I don't reach for his pants he does. First, he starts to undo his belt. "I think about how wet you always are for me. How ready. How good you taste. How you let me look at you spread and swollen with need and you don't even blush. You like my eyes on your pussy. I think about how much I love to watch you come."

His pants drop to his ankles and I stare at that bulge in the front of his charcoal boxer-briefs. My God... I am so wet I'll be surprised if there isn't a damp spot on my jean shorts. "Tate..."

He bends down again, roughly putting a hand under my chin and tipping my head up so he can capture my lips with his own. The kiss is powerful. Raw. Perfect.

I have to give in. My body has hit the override switch on my mind and I reach down and pull my tank top over my head. "Good girl," he whispers as his hands reach for the button on my shorts.

Moments later, after he rolls on a condom, I'm naked on the bed with Tate on top of me sliding his cock into me with a steady swing. It isn't a struggle. "You make me so wet," I confess. "I can't even watch you play hockey without my clit tingling."

"Has it always been like that?"

"Since I was a teenager," I admit.

He nips on the side of my neck before groaning in satisfaction, like my words are bringing him closer to climax. He cants his hips and I wrap my legs around his waist. Missionary is my least favorite position because I never come this way, but I know that's about to change. It's impossible for me not to orgasm with Tate. His left knee bends and he lifts his torso with his arms on either side of my head and he bucks again. He manages to hit that secret spot with the tip of his dick. The one that makes my limbs prickle with pleasure and my stomach quiver.

"Oh God..." I pant.

"I will never stop wanting you, Mallory," he whispers into my ear, his rhythm as shaky as his confession. "It's like I'm addicted to you."

He can't really be saying this. Not to me. This goes beyond everything I dared to dream about him. I arch my back and press the heels of my feet into that round, hard ass of his. "Tate... I... God..."

"Come baby girl," Tate begs me. "Come all over my dick."

And then I do.

And he follows me moments later and then collapses on me. When we find our way back into our bodies, he slowly pulls out and disappears behind the false wall into the bathroom. I turn my head into his pillow, take one last deep breath of his scent, and slowly sit up. The euphoria is replaced by melancholy as I do it.

I don't want to go back to my room, but I know he expects me to. He wants me to. I'm holding the duvet to my chest and leaning over to grab my clothes from the floor when he appears again. He's naked, and not hiding a thing. His dick is soft but still formidable as it hangs between his legs. His skin is still flushed and his muscles still taut from exertion.

He walks around the bed, crawls under the covers on the other side, and wraps his arms around my waist. He pulls me backward, towards the center of the bed and him.

"What are you doing?" I ask, fighting the smile that wants to bloom on my face.

He nestles against me like the big spoon and I have no choice but to lie there with my head on his bicep because he still has a bulky arm around my waist holding me in place. "Cuddling before we fall asleep. I'm new at this so if I'm doing it wrong, help me out."

"You're doing it right," I reply and let that smile bloom. "Where is Tate? What have you done with him?"

"Shut up." His laugh tickles the back of my neck. "Listen, I want you to be there with me. When I call my parents."

"You do?"

"Yeah. You are part of this. My life. Dylan's." He pauses and tugs me in a little closer. "I need you."

"Okay."

"Thank you, baby girl." I feel his lips press to my shoulder.

We lie there in silence for a long time. I feel his muscles soften, and his grip around my belly loosens. His breathing gets deeper. My eyelids get heavy, my mind stops running, my limbs get loose. But... when I drift off it's not a deep sleep. I'm still on alert, waiting for the switch to flip. For old Tate to turn back on. To be asked to leave. To be told I'm just the nanny with benefits.

Hours later when I slip out of bed to pee, he grabs my wrist. "Don't go."

"Bathroom."

"But you'll come back to bed? This bed?"

"If you want me to."

"I want you. Here. With me."

"Then I'll be back."

And when I come back from the bathroom, he holds the covers open for me and I crawl right in, resting my head on his chest, and drift off. I don't dream for the rest of the night. My subconscious knows it can't compete with real life now.

Chapter 22

Tate

I am freaking the fuck out. There is no point in trying to hide it. It's barely seven in the morning but Dylan woke up earlier than normal. Mallory thinks it's just the new environment, not more sleep regression, which is good. She offered to take him downstairs alone but I got up with her because the impending weight of what I have to do today would make more sleep impossible.

"When are you calling them?" Mallory asks me as she chops up a banana onto the tray on Dylan's new, proper high chair.

He's fisting the pieces and putting them in his mouth as soon as they drop. He's also already eaten one of my protein pancakes and loved it. I watch him as I pour Mallory and me fresh cups of coffee. "Nine our time. That's noon in Maine and Dad usually gets home from his morning gym session by then. ."

She nods and shoots me a confident smile. "You're doing the right thing and it will be fine."

I nod and sip my coffee taking too big a gulp and burning my tongue. "Fuck!"

"Fuuu! Fuuu! Fuuu!" Dylan tries repeating and my eyes flare.

Mallory's are wide too as she says, "We should start watching our language. If his first word is an F-bomb, I will die."

"Me too," I reply. "Tenley will laugh her as—butt off though."

"Have you told her you're telling them?" Mallory wants to know.

"No. She'll want to be here, and I appreciate that but I need to do this on my own," I inform her and then add, "With you. You're the only one I want here."

She nods and smiles but says nothing and keeps her eyes on Dylan. She's been weirdly quiet since we had sex last night. I watch her now. She's wearing a navy jumpsuit with white buttons. Her hair is down but she only finger combed it so it's wavy and a little messy in that perfect way. She threw water on her face this morning after she brushed her teeth. I watched her from the bedroom as I changed Dylan, and she threw on some mascara and blush, I think because of the upcoming video call with my parents. Anyway, she looks beautiful, but also like a skittish kitten.

"Mallory?" She looks up. "Since I'm having big conversations today I thought I would tell you that... I don't think this is an arrangement anymore. Or an agreement. Or anything resembling anything I've ever had before."

"Oh."

We stare at each other. Her in the dining room, by the table. Me in the kitchen, by the island. Dylan ignoring both of us and concentrating on his banana. Finally, I break the stare and look down into my coffee as I lift the other cup I filled and bring it to her. "I don't know what to say next."

She takes the mug from me and looks up into my eyes. Her expression is startlingly clear, glinting with gold in the morning sunlight. "Tell me what I am if I'm not like the other girls."

It sounds so simple. So why is my heart running like it's

being chased by a serial killer? I brush my fingers over her hair. "You're—"

The doorbell rings.

We both startle. "Who the heck is here at this hour?"

I shrug at her question and make my way to the door. The only thing I can think is that it's Tenley because her schedule is that of a Vampire with ADHD. Or it's Crew because he forgot something here.

Holding my coffee, dressed in nothing but sweatpants and a ratty old T-shirt, I open the door and come face-to-face with Jordan and Jessie Garrison.

"What?" I blink. "I... How?" I swallow and choke.

"Westwood said you swapped houses with his son," Dad informs me. "Yet another red flag in a series you've been waving lately."

Fuck. Of course, Crew told his parents he moved. Of course Avery Westwood mentioned it to Dad, they're friends. How did I not see this coming? Dad gently pushes me aside and steps into the hall. Mom follows and stops to give me a hug. "We love you, Tate Henry Garrison. You need to know that we love you."

"Okay."

Mallory and Dylan are out of view, the dining room table is just on the other side of the wall that separates the entrance. All my parents can see is the living room and the open bi-fold doors that lead to the backyard.

What do I do? What the fuck do I do?

Dad looks down the hall into the living room then turns back to me. "We love you. Like your mother said. Now do you mind telling us why the fuck you have a picture of a kid on your phone that isn't you?"

"But looks exactly like you," Mom adds, her voice shaking.

"And don't tell us the same lies you told your Uncle Devin," Dad warns, his blue eyes narrowed so harshly that his crow's feet deepen like canyons on the sides of his eyes. "Your mother knows every baby picture ever taken of you and your sister, and that's not one of them."

"He showed you the footage?" I ask, feeling a bit bitter about a betrayal by my uncle.

"The whole world saw the footage, Tate," Dad replies tersely. "They aired it as part of your segment after the game."

"I told them not to!"

"There was a cell phone on the corner of the couch," Mom interjects, her eyes also darting around the house. "An iPhone. That kid is under a year and the iPhone came out when you were four and Tenley was three. So I'm not the only one who might figure out that isn't you or your sister."

Now I know where Tenley gets her investigative skills from. I could say that out loud, to lighten the mood, but I doubt it would work. So instead, I take a deep breath and try to remain calm when I say. "Come in. I have someone you have to meet."

"Oh my God..." Mom whispers and Dad takes her hand and side-by-side they follow me into the living room.

I turn to the dining room, motioning grandly with my arm only to look over my shoulder and find it empty. The entire first floor, that I can see, appears to be empty.

She ran. I can't help but smile at that. Mallory Echolls would do anything for me. It's like... she loves me.

"Tate?" Dad snaps and I can tell he's on his last ounce of patience. My father is a kind, sympathetic, and compassionate man but he has buttons like anyone else and if you push them enough... he will let you know. And you will regret it. "What the hell kind of bullshit are you pulling here? Why are you living in this big house? Why is there a fucking high chair?"

"We're trying not to say the F word here anymore," I warn.

"Tate!" my mother barks. If she's mad I'm in real trouble.

"Mallory, it's okay. Come here," I call out. "It's not the video call I'd planned but... maybe it's better."

Surely they'll be less likely to keep getting angrier if they see Dylan in person. Or, you know, they both just have heart attacks.

"Mallory Echolls? *That* Mallory?" Dad asks, his tone confused, not annoyed.

The door to the powder room at the end of the small hall off the kitchen opens and she steps out. She's holding Dylan. My parents are watching like it's the big reveal on a suspenseful television show or something. They're also holding hands and my mom has her other hand wrapped around Dad's bicep.

Mallory walks slowly into the kitchen with Dylan on her hip. He's been cleaned up from breakfast and he's blinking, looking tentatively at the new additions to the house. "Who..." Dad swallows. "Who is this?"

"Mom, Dad, this is Dylan. Your grandson."

It was shockingly simple to say those words out loud.

My mother lets go of my dad and walks right up to Dylan and touches his cheek. "Oh my God, you are the most perfect lil thing. I love you, baby boy," she whispers.

Mallory looks over at me, her eyes swimming in tears. "Would you like to hold him, Mrs. Garrison?"

"If you'd let me," Mom says in a trembling voice.

"Take him, Ma," I encourage before Mallory can say anything.

My dad is still rooted to the floor in the living room like the soles of his shoes are made of wet cement. My mom lifts Dylan from Mallory and cradles him to her chest. He wiggles a second and then reaches for her hair and fists it, staring at the copper color like he's mesmerized. "Bah. Boo. Da. Ba."

I have no idea what that means but he seems to approve of her because he doesn't cry. Their eyes lock and he grins and my mom bites her trembling bottom lip and hugs him. "Tate... you have so much explaining to do."

Her tone is gentle. Tired, even.

I look at my dad. Holy shit... is that... a tear. His left cheek is wet. "Dad...?"

He glances over at me and then away just as quickly. He clears his throat and moves away from me, stopping behind my mom to peer at Dylan's little face. "Hey, kiddo. I'm your... Jesus, I'm barely fifty. I can't say gramps."

Mallory smiles. "Pops and Nan? That's what I call my grandparents on my mom's side."

"Pops and Nan..." Dad repeats like he's testing them out. He reaches up and runs a hand over Dylan's head. "I'm your Pops, kiddo."

"Dylan," I say. "His name is Dylan."

"Dylan," Mom whispers. "Good name."

"Mal calls him Dyllie Bear," I admit and Mom looks over her shoulder at me with a grin. "I like that too."

"Maybe you should all sit down and chat?" Mallory suggests, motioning toward the living room. "I'll make more coffee and I think I have some Trader Joe's croissants in the freezer I can heat up."

"No, no," Dad says and takes my coffee cup from my hand. "I'll just drink his coffee. You sit down and join us, Mallory. You're his mother and we'd like to get to know you too."

"You're a part of this family now too," my mother says without a snag of hesitation in her voice. I guess a baby completely erases the fact that Mallory's mother "bullied the hell out of her when she was in high school" —Aunt Callie's words.

"Oh no." Mallory starts waving her hands in front of her. "I'm not. He's not. I'm just the nanny."

"She's not *just* the nanny," I blurt out. Now everyone is

looking right at me, including my son. He's literally staring at me like, okay then Daddio, let's hear it. I look over at her, holding her pretty eyes with my own. "She's my rock. She's my best friend and my girlfriend. But no, Dylan isn't hers biologically."

"Oh." My mom is utterly baffled.

"So the mom is...?"

"Mallory's right," I say gently. "We should all sit down."

"I'll get fresh coffee for everyone. And those croissants," Mallory says, and I give her a smile and wink. She flashes me a brief but dazzling smile, which I take to mean announcing she's my girlfriend was okay by her.

I follow my parents, who are still holding Dylan, into the living room, sit down on the couch across from the one they're on, and take a deep breath.

The next two and a half hours are spent talking with my parents about everything that's happened over the last couple of months. They both take it pretty well. There are tears about Diana dying, and anger that she was going to keep Dylan from me. But the only disappointment they have is directed at the fact I didn't tell them immediately.

"We had to find out by watching an interview with you," Dad grumbled. "And then book a last-minute red-eye to force the truth out of you."

"I was going to tell you today," I promise, but I know the damage is done. They're taking it personally.

I was so absorbed in myself, and trying to be the responsible adult no one thinks I am, that I completely missed that cutting them out would make them feel like they'd failed me. Like I didn't trust them or love them enough to let them help me. I feel sick with guilt over that.

Mallory stays quiet most of the conversation, sitting in the reading chair over by the folding doors, tending to Dylan, and refilling the coffee and the croissant plate as needed. She does reassure my parents that I'm doing a great job with Dylan and that he's a really good kid who has taken all these life changes in stride.

Mom really can't stop staring at him. Her eyes flood with tears on occasion, without any real reason I can discern, and she wipes them away smiling. "I'm not sad," she clarifies at one point. "I'm just so in love with him."

"Your mother is going to visit all the time now," Dad tells me. "I have a feeling we're going to have to buy an apartment here for longer visits."

"I'm going to call a real estate agent this afternoon," Mom confirms, and I have a flash of panic. Because it's Old Tate. The loner playboy reacting out of habit. But then I realize that dude is pretty much dead. And Dad Tate would love to have his parents hang out with his kid as much as possible.

"That would be cool," I admit. "It takes a village after all and you guys are the best villagers ever."

"Yeah, and I've got to teach him how to skate," Dad remarks.

"I think that's something I can manage," I reply and he looks at me with a skeptical expression.

"You can't even beat my record, kid," he teases. "So let him learn from the best."

"Dyllie Bear you are gonna need some warm clothes for all the ice rinks your pops and dada will have you on," Mom says to Dylan, and damn if I don't feel like blubbering watching her talk to my son. "I promise to always have hot chocolate ready to warm you up after hockey practice."

"Ahbkey," Dylan says.

We all freeze. "Did he just say hockey?"

Mallory gets out of the chair and walks over, her eyes wide.

"Is that his first word?" My father wants to know.

"I mean... kind of. He says babees which I think is berries, but this was definitely more articulated," Mallory explains and kneels down in front of Dylan.

"Hockey?" I say.

"Ahbkey!" he mimics. "Babee. Duhbber."

"Yeah, so we might be overthinking this," Dad grins. "He's just babbling."

"He'll get there," Mom assures everyone.

Mallory puts a hand on my shoulder. "You have practice."

"Right. Sh...sugar." I stop myself from swearing and get up off the couch. I stare at my parents and then at Mallory.

"You two have a place to stay? I can drop you somewhere," I say.

"Or you can stay in the guest room here," Mallory suggests and it's another panic moment. But she's right. I should want them to stay here and bond with Dylan.

My parents look at me. "Yeah."

"I want to be near him every waking hour," Mom announces. "You can go on a date with Mallory. I'll babysit."

A date? Wow. I... Mallory looks so excited. "Yeah okay. Tonight. Let's go out, Mal. We'll figure out the details when I get back. I'm off to practice. And I have a meeting afterward."

My parents barely even say goodbye. They're still staring at Dylan. Mom is making gurgling sounds and Dad is making faces at him so he'll smile and laugh.

I walk to the front door. Mallory shuffles along beside me. "Are you sure it's okay I offered my room? I don't have to spend the nights with you. There's a couch in the office."

"If you think I'm letting you stay on a couch," I lean in and kiss her, "maybe you missed it but I just told my parents I have a girlfriend."

"I didn't miss it," she replies. "I may be in shock, but I heard it."

"Yeah, I'll be honest, I'm a little stunned myself." I laugh. "And now we're going on a date."

"We don't have—"

I lean down and kiss her. "We're going on a date. My parents won't be here forever. Even if they buy a place, they'll only be here occasionally so let's take advantage of the built-in babysitter while we have it."

I kiss her again and then leave. I'm still feeling a little disoriented. Like I'm in an entirely different world than the one I woke up in, but it's not over yet. I have the team management to handle next.

Chapter 23

Mallory

I feel a little lost. I haven't had a free afternoon since I got here. But Mr. and Mrs. Garrison insisted I take the afternoon and do things for myself. They wanted some time with Dylan. I couldn't say no. They were handling this better than I'd expected and if they wanted to bond with their grandson, I would let them. So although I had no idea what to do, I left the house. I could stick around, but it was still a little weird.

I had never really spoken much to either of Tate's parents. My family and their family were forced together at town events because everyone wanted to see the famous hockey players together, but my family and Tate's liked to pretend the other didn't exist. I remember being about ten at the grocery store with my mom and she literally got out of a short line and into a very long one just to avoid standing directly behind Jessie Garrison.

But for me personally, I've never had any reason to dislike Jordan or Jessie Garrison. Because I've never really met them until today. And the way they accepted Dylan so openly, and were ready to accept me when they thought I was his mom, definitely doesn't make me hate them. They seem like good people.

But now that they know I'm not the mom, and they've been told I'm the girlfriend, there's a slight shift in the dynamic. They're cordial with me, but thank God we have Dylan as a distraction. Otherwise, we would be struggling to make small talk all day and ignoring the elephant in the room, which is whatever the hell went down between them and my parents when they were my age.

So now, I'm walking leisurely through the Third Street promenade in Santa Monica. I have an iced caramel latte in my hand and a shopping bag in the other. I spent forty minutes in a store convincing myself to buy a new outfit for my first official date with Tate. It's a pretty, snug cocktail dress in a dark jewel-tone green. It's like nothing I've ever owned before and I'm probably insane for buying it, and the two hundred dollar heels the sales clerk said were the only shoes in the world that went with it, but... this is a big deal for me.

I'm dating my dream man. I should splurge on something pretty. And lord knows I have the money. Tate's been paying me and I don't have a single living expense. My phone starts to buzz in my purse so I dig it out and take a seat on a bench facing one of the dinosaur topiaries that pepper the outdoor walkways. My brother Beckett's name is on the screen and for the first time in a long time, I smile when looking at it. He's called me at least once a week since I got here, but I've started to avoid his calls. He is digging for information for my parents, who still want me to come home.

"Hi, Beck."

"Hey yourself," he replies. "You sound... happy?"

I smile. "Yeah. You could say that. How are you? How's the wedding planning coming?"

"I don't know. Ask Heather. She's the one handling every-thing," he replies and there's a tension in his voice that I know well. "And before you give me attitude like Ma does for not helping organize this debacle, I'll tell you she won't let me do a thing. She says I will fuck it up and waste time."

He sounded like that all through high school too. I thought it was because he was stressed out trying to get the grades to get into a good school. After all, he knew even then that he wanted to be a doctor. Or maybe the pressure from our dad to keep playing hockey, which he gave up in junior year. But now I know it was dating Heather that stressed him out. He didn't sound like this after they broke up. Not when he was in college or when he was dating Mackenzie Larue.

"Brides will be brides, I guess," I say because what do I know? I'm not a bride. Tate flashes through my brain, in one of his fancy suits, standing at the edge of Silver Bay Lake, in front of an archway of wildflowers and a minister, with Dylan in a teeny suit by his side.

Whoa. Chill out brain. We are *so* not there yet.

"Mal? Hello!"

"Sorry. What?"

"I said when are you coming back?" he barks, a little annoyed I zoned out. "Heather is worried you'll bail on the wedding. Mom and Dad are worried you met some granola-eating hippie in Oregon or joined a cult."

I laugh so loud passersby glance over. I quiet down and take a sip of my latte. "Let me guess, Dad is worried about the hippie, Mom about the cult."

"Yes," Beckett replies. "And I'm worried about you. How are you supporting yourself? How are your injuries? And your mental health?"

"I'm healing both mentally and physically." I stare out at the busy promenade and up at the blue skies above. The gentle ocean breeze dances through my hair. "I'm happy like you said. And I'm going to be okay. I will be home for the wedding but... I think this is where I'm going to stay. For a while."

"In Oregon?" He says it like it's a steaming pile of dog poo.

"I have to go, Beck," I tell him. "I have a date tonight. But don't worry you can tell Mom and Dad it's not with a granola-eating hippie or a cult member."

"Well who is it—"

"Bye Beck!"

I hit end on the call and shove the phone back in my purse. I get up. Obviously Mr. and Mrs. Garrison know how to take care of a toddler but I still feel like I've been gone long enough. I should go home and make sure everything is okay.

I stand up and start toward the parking garage off Third Street where I left the new Mercedes SUV Tate bought for Dylan and me to use. I wonder how his meeting with management is going. I know it's going to be a weird conversation, but I'm glad that Dylan won't be a secret anymore. If Tate actually wins the Cup this year, I want Dylan there with him.

"Mal?"

I stop walking.

"Mallory?"

I know that voice. I turn around and there, in front of the Gap Store, is my younger brother Emmett and two guys I don't know. I can tell by their hulking size they're likely also hockey players from his team. Emmett lumbers over with a friendly but surprised grin. He pulls me into a hug. "What are you doing in California? Mom and Dad said you were in Oregon."

I'm on vacation. I am visiting a friend. I'm not Mallory, I must just look like your sister sorry strange man, have a good day. All of these lies run through my head but none of them come out of my mouth. Emmett is the sibling I'm closest to, but that doesn't mean much. Still, I really don't have a reason to keep lying. Tate is talking to his team right now. His parents know. Dylan's birth certificate, with Tate's name on it, is being processed.

"I live here."

Emmett pulls back from the hug and stares at me with his eyes that match my own. "You live here? In Santa Monica, California?"

"Well, in Venice actually," I reply and stare at his teammates. "Hi. I'm his sister."

"Echolls, you didn't mention you had a beautiful sister," one of them says with a broad flirty smile.

"I'll catch up with you two later," Emmett replies and starts pulling me away from his horny teammates.

When we're across the walkway near an overly fragrant candle shop, he turns back to me. "What the fuck, Mal? Why does everyone think you're in Oregon."

"Because I lied to them," I admit. "Em, look, I was dealing with a lot when Diana died. And you know how Mom and Dad are. If I went back to Silver Bay, my situation would have been more complicated."

He stares down at me, his expression contemplative. He gets how overbearing our parents can be. How Dad loves to make everything about him and Mom isn't happy unless she's miserable. Beckett is a lot like them, so he doesn't see it. But Emmett does. He's a hockey player, which automatically makes him Dad's favorite but he's not like Dad. On or off the ice.

He grips my shoulders and gives them a squeeze. "I'm just glad you seem to be okay. You look good Mallory."

"I am good." I give him a quick smile. "I guess you're here to play the Quake?"

"Yeah." He tilts his head. "You don't follow my career at all, do you?"

"I do!" I feel like shit. "I just... I have been busy, Em."

He leans down a bit so he can grab one of my hands. He's so tall that I'm a literal munchkin beside him. Emmett is a towering six-foot-five. In high school, he played both basketball and hockey, much to my father's dismay.

"I haven't called because Mom, Dad, and Beckett all say you barely ever pick up anyway, but I want you to know how sorry I am about Diana." The sadness in Emmett's hazel eyes is genuine. "And I'm glad to see you're okay. Your injuries have obviously healed."

"Yes. I'm good and I've been cleared by a doctor here so you can tell Mom and Dad that," I reply and squeeze his hand before pulling my own back. "I should go though. And I'm sure you want to rejoin your teammates. Good luck tonight."

"Wait one minute!" Emmett says firmly before I can start to walk away. I turn back and stare at him. He cocks his head again. "Why did you pick Los Angeles, Mal? Of all the places to start over, why L.A.?"

"I mean..." I hold up my hands and kind of wave them around. "Look at this place. It's sunny all the time. It's warm. There's a beach every five miles. And lots of nanny work."

"So you have a job?"

"I... yeah. I have a job."

Emmett stares at me like he's waiting for me to elaborate, but I don't want to. He lifts an eyebrow. I look away, concentrating on the ridiculous topiary. "What happened to Diana's kid?"

"He's with his father."

Emmett nods his head. I see it in his shadow because I still won't look at him. "So not that dude she was engaged to? The actual father?"

I nod.

"Tate Garrison?" Emmett says his name and I flinch. I don't mean to, it's an involuntary act but it's a tell as obvious as a neon sign.

I slowly bring my eyes up to my younger brother's. I blink. He lets out a long slow breath. "Shit. I fucking knew it."

"How did you know it?"

Emmett chuffs out a confident laugh. "Mal, I can do math. She would have had to get knocked up the second she got off the plane to have it be the British dude's baby. And Garrison was her constant bed buddy for like two years. Everyone in Silver Bay knew that."

"Emmett, you cannot tell Mom and Dad!" I whisper as if we're being eavesdropped on. "You can't tell *anyone*. Tate is just now able to tell his parents and his team."

"So you came here to deliver the kid to Garrison?" Emmett replies, ignoring my pleas. "And now you're staying?"

"I like California and I'm... I'm staying with Dylan, as his nanny." I can't bring myself to say I'm dating Tate. I don't know why.

Emmett looks shocked and his jaw drops for a second. "You are Garrison's nanny?"

"No. I'm Dylan's nanny."

"You're working for your bestie's bed buddy? The dude you had a crush on in junior high?" Emmett is laughing at me. Not outwardly, but inwardly. I can see it in his eyes and the way he's smirking. "Between Beck taking back that nightmare Heather and you setting yourself up for heartbreak over here, it's finally official. I'm the only well-adjusted Echolls kid."

"Shut up," I snap, feeling like the little girl who used to get teased by both her brothers all the time growing up. "I'm not some lovesick stalker girl chasing her childhood crush across the country! I owed it to Diana to get Dylan to his dad. The only person who wanted him, by the way. And Tate and I are—"

"Friends." Emmett rolls his eyes at the word. "Yeah. I know. You have been saying that for years. But Mal, you aren't supposed to want to bang your friends."

I blush and Emmett laughs, taking it as a sign of guilt. He puts a hand on my shoulder again but this time it feels condescending, not compassionate. I shrug it off. "Nice seeing you, Emmett. I hope Tate wipes the ice with your team."

I turn and start to stomp off. "Mal, wait!"

I only make it a few feet and then he's a wall in front of me. His dark curly hair rustling in the breeze and his expression contrite. "I'm sorry. I promise I'm not making fun of you."

"Spoiler alert: It feels like you are."

He smiles guiltily. "I'm sorry. I'm just protective of you. Honestly, that's all it is."

"I'm a big girl, Em," I promise him. "I know exactly what I'm doing. I'm not going to get hurt."

I'm not. Tate and I are on the same page. And in a couple months, we'll head home together, as a couple, for the hockey summer break—hopefully with a Stanley Cup ring on his finger —and they'll all see how happy we are. Then maybe everyone will stop treating me like a confused child.

"Just don't let Garrison take advantage, Mal," Emmett warns. "The guy doesn't make it a secret he's not into commitment, and that's fine, but don't fool yourself into thinking he's gonna be different with you if he hits on you."

"Don't worry about me." I just want this conversation to end.

He stares at me for a heartbeat and then nods and pulls me into a hug. "You're right. I'm being one of those overprotective jackass brothers I hate. I know you can handle yourself. And besides, you wouldn't want Diana's leftovers. That would be weird."

Ouch.

He lets go of me and takes a step back. "Bye Em."

"Later, Mal." He starts walking backward slowly, away from

me in the direction his teammates disappeared. "Will you pick up the phone if I call now?"

I nod give him a wave and watch him disappear into the crowd. My walk to the car is decidedly less upbeat than it would have been had I not run into my brother. I want to text Tate and tell him about running into Emmett and ask why he didn't tell me he was playing Emmett. But I know he's dealing with the team management this afternoon and also, I should have known the hockey schedule. And if I picked up any of my parents' calls lately, they'd have likely mentioned Emmett's road trip. They always talk about him, especially Dad.

I get behind the wheel of the SUV tuck my bags onto the passenger seat and pull out of the spot to start my trip home.

At the house, I walk in to find Mr. and Mrs. Garrison relaxing in the backyard. They're stretched out on a couch together. Mrs. Garrison is looking at her phone and Mr. Garrison is watching a sports show on the outdoor television. She looks up from her phone and shoots me a smile as I step outside. "All good?"

"For us, yes," she replies and holds up her phone. "I'm just watching Dyllie Bear sleep on the app you installed for me. This is so much better than the old monitors they had when Tate and Tenley were little."

"It's amazing," I agree.

"Tate's having a harder time of it," Mr. Garrison says and he points to the screen. I look at the headline on the screen under the reporter, who is outside the Quake arena.

Quake forward Landon Casco collapses at practice. Transported to UCLA Medical Center.

"Oh my God," I whisper.

"Tate called," Mr. Garrison says. "No one is sure what it is yet, but he's in stable condition."

"They really shouldn't have given away the hospital he's at," Mrs. Garrison says with a frown. "Fans will swarm the place."

"It's Los Angeles," Mr. Garrison remarks. "If anyone knows how to handle wild fans, it's the security in this town. Celebrities get hospitalized too, you know."

"Come sit down," Mrs. Garrison says and motions to the couch they aren't on. "I promise we don't bite."

"No matter what your parents might have told you," Mr. Garrison adds and she slaps his chest. He grins and gives me a small wink.

"Can I ask what that is all about? Your side," I clarify. "Because I know their side."

"Oh I would love to hear their side," Mr. Garrison remarks acerbically.

"Jordy! Be nice. Last warning," Mrs. Garrison warns. She looks over at me, brushing copper hair out of her face. "I'm sorry. Don't take it personally."

"I don't," I reply. "I love my parents, but I know they aren't everyone's cup of tea."

She reaches out and pats my hand. "Well, I'm glad you're Tate's cup of tea, Mallory. You seem like a very sweet girl and I'm grateful to you for reuniting Dylan and Tate."

"Don't thank me." I shake my head. "I know Diana would have wanted Dylan with Tate."

"Then why didn't she tell him about his son?" Mr. Garrison demands, his voice is gentle but I know he's upset.

"She had reasons, and I didn't totally agree with them," I say. "I was going to make sure Tate knew, even before the accident. Even if it cost me my friendship with Di."

They both nod and Mrs. Garrison looks at her phone again. "He sleeps just like Tate did. Splayed out like a starfish but with his thumb in his mouth. Oh man, this is a trip. I don't think I've fully wrapped my head around this."

"I appreciate how you're handling it, though," I tell her. "You're not acting disappointed."

"I'll be honest with you." Mrs. Garrison looks up from her phone. "I would have loved it if he had been more careful and waited to be a father until he was older. But... well life doesn't always unfold the way you'd hoped. I didn't want to be orphaned at nine years old, but I was and in a way, good things came from it. My sisters and I had to move to Silver Bay, where Donna Garrison took us under her wing, and I met her son and fell in love. So good things can come from unexpected plot twists in life."

"I like that you think of Dylan as a plot twist and not a mistake," I note.

She grins. "No one in this family is a mistake. Even me who was born to a gallivanting hockey player out of wedlock."

"I would call your sister Callie a mistake," Mr. Garrison says and he grins, so I know it's a joke.

"She would call you an abomination," Mrs. Garrison shoots back.

There's a cry and Mrs. Garrison's eyes dart to her phone. "Oh, Dyllie Bear is awake!"

I get up. "I'll go get him."

"Are you sure?"

"Yeah. I've missed him," I admit and both of Tate's parents smile at me as I head into the house and upstairs.

This is strange, and not a development my parents will appreciate, but I really like the Garrisons.

Chapter 24

Tate

I force myself not to look at my phone. Keep my eyes on Mallory. After all, she looks amazing. That dress she has on hugs every curve and shows just a sliver of cleavage at the neck. It's driving me insane. Her long blonde hair is loose and the layers that frame her face hold a delicate wave. She's wearing more makeup than I've ever seen on her, but not in a bad way. Her eyelids shimmer and her skin is kind of glossy. Her eyelashes were thick and dark and they fluttered when I reached down and took her hand as we walked into the restaurant.

I need to focus on her. But when she excuses herself from the table to go to the restroom, between the appetizers and the mains, I yank my phone out of my back pocket and check the avalanche of messages.

There's a team chat, with my friends from the Quake that has forty-two messages, all about Landon. I scan them all only to learn that we don't know anything solid yet. He's awake. They've performed a battery of tests on him. His parents have come into town and so has his uncle and aunt. Landon is another second-generation hockey player. His dad and his uncle played around the time my dad did.

Then I scan the sixty-two messages on the family chat. Sixty-freaking-two. My family is nothing if not chatty. But I get it, I have a child. It's a big deal. And Mom dropped the bomb with a selfie of her, Dylan, and Dad and the words 'Meet Dylan Garrison!' That reminded me, I need to get back to the lawyer with a middle name. Diana never gave him one and I'd like to get one on the birth certificate.

The highlights from the family chat have me smiling despite my concern over Landon.

LIV: Wait. What. Who? HOW?

CALLIE: Honey we had this talk when you were twelve.

LIV: MOM! GOD! I know but TATE?

MOM: It's shocking but happy news.

DAD: I've aged twenty years but, honestly, the kid appears to be worth it.

CON: My mind is blown but congrats Tater.

AUNTIE R: I can't wait to snuggle him and kiss those fat cheeks!

GRADY: No fat shaming Auntie Rose.

GRAMPS: I'm going to the garage to find Tate's old baby skates. Grandma says congrats. She's crying so she can't type.

THEO: He's cute. Must get that from the mom.
And WHO is that?

DAD: That's a long story. Tate will explain more
in person. After he wins a Cup.

And then the next fourteen messages are Grady, Conner, and Theo arguing about who has better odds than the Quake of winning the Stanley Cup.

I grin and finally break my silence because I haven't responded to any of this.

Thanks, everyone. There's a lot to explain,
Mom and Dad (AKA Pops and Nan) will fill you
all in when they get home. Or you can wait until
I get back this summer, with my gf, my son,
and the Cup.

CON: GF? That has to stand for gluten-free not
GIRLFRIEND.

GRADY: He has a girlfriend too? It's the
apocalypse.

THEO: You are NOT getting that Cup before
me, Tater Tot!

"Everything okay?"

I look up and Mallory is sliding into the other side of the booth. I don't know why I picked this restaurant. I mean the appetizer was good enough. But... it's fancy. Way fancy. I'm in an untucked, slightly wrinkled button-down and jeans. Mallory definitely blends in but I don't. And it feels stuffy in here. And too quiet.

"Yeah. Good," I reply. "Family stuff and checking on any updates from the team on Landon."

"Anything?" She looks genuinely concerned and I love her for it... I mean not love-love, but...

"He's awake and they're running tests," I tell her. "Crew says the coach is still at the hospital with Landon's family who has arrived. They live in San Francisco so luckily it was a quick plane ride away."

"That's nice of the coach to stay."

"They're family," I explain. "Coach Braddock played hockey with Landon's dad and his uncle. They won two Cups together and Landon's mom is one of Coach Braddock's sisters."

"Oh crap." Mallory looks stricken. "And he was there when his nephew collapsed."

"Yeah, and so obviously he canceled our afternoon meeting," I explain. "And the PR team is in crisis mode trying to control the press around this, at least until they know what's wrong with Landon. So I decided telling them about Dylan can wait until tomorrow."

"Yeah, I understand." Mallory nods and brushes her hair behind her shoulder. "I hope he's okay? You guys must all be so shaken."

"We are," I admit and it feels really good to have someone to share this with. Mallory is my rock. I didn't know I needed one, but now... I can't imagine my life without her to confide in. "Some of the guys are at our local hangout now, waiting for news together."

"Where's that?" Mallory asks.

"A bar called Musica's down by the beach," I explain. "The owner, Rich, opens it whenever we get home from a road trip, no matter how early or late. He's got a bunch of pool tables, crispy wings in forty flavors, and a bunch of the cheesiest nineties movie memorabilia on the walls."

"Like what?"

"Behind the scenes stuff from movies like *Freddy versus*

Jason and pages from old scripts like *Clueless*," I say that movie, and her whole face lights up like a Christmas tree.

She grips the edge of the fancy table. "*Clueless*? Like Alicia Silverstone and Paul Rudd's timeless classic *Clueless*?"

"I wouldn't exactly call it that, but yes, that *Clueless*."

She gasps. So loudly that a couple of tables nearby turn and stare. She shrinks into herself, cheeks turning pink. I smile at her. "Don't be embarrassed. These people all look like they could use a good gasp moment."

She grins. "It's a very nice place."

"Yeah..." I shrug and catch her eye. "Too nice."

She leans forward. "I agree. They have an attendant in the bathroom and she corrected me when I washed my hands, like I used the wrong soap or something. There were six soaps in there. And she instantly refilled the teeny amount I used from the lime one."

"Lime was the wrong soap?"

"She said I should have used the melon-scented one." Mallory shrugs.

I lean closer too so now we're whispering across the table at each other. "Do you want to go see the *Clueless* script? It has shooting notes on it from the director. And rumor has it Rich also had an outfit worn by the lead. I've never asked because..."

"Because you don't care, because you have horrible taste in movies?" she quips without blinking or a hint of sarcasm.

"Let's go." I start to slide out of the booth and she follows.

I feel so much better as I leave a fifty for the food we won't be consuming and make our way to the front door.

"Tate," she says as we pull out of the parking lot and I turn the car toward Venice and the bar I know and love. "Am I over-dressed? Are your buddies going to be there? Am I going to meet them?"

"No, yes, and yes," I reply. "Is that okay?"

"If it's okay with you."

"Baby girl I am happy to show you off," I assure her. "Especially in that dress. I can barely look at you you're so hot."

I steal a glance and she's smiling. I reach over and take her hand. "I'm sorry I didn't mention Emmett. I can't believe you ran into him."

"I should be paying attention to my brother's schedule. And yours," she replies.

I turn into the parking lot of Musica's. I recognize a ton of the parked cars. I slip into one of the few remaining spots and rush around the car to help Mallory out. I take her hand and keep holding it even after we walk into the place and every set of eyes seems to turn and stare at us.

"Garrison!" Crew calls out, walking up to us while the rest of my teammates just gawk at us like we're exotic zoo animals. Jesus, is it that weird to see me showing a woman affection?

Crew slaps my shoulder and turns to Mallory. "Hi again! Good to see you."

"You too. How is your teammate?"

"Still waiting to hear about test results," Crew replies. "And thanks for asking. And coming here to hang with us. I know it was your first official date."

"Tate and I are doing everything in our own unique way," Mallory announces. "Why should this be any different?"

Crew grins and looks at me. "I like her."

"Of course you do." I tug her closer to my side. "Who doesn't?"

"Hey, pretty lady and Garrison, my round. What are you drinking?" Nash calls out from the corner by the bar.

"Mal, you up for a margarita?" I ask with a wink and then lean down and whisper in her ear. "Like old times?"

She just bites her lip and nods. It's adorable and hot as hell all at the same time. I kiss her, which gets the guys to all make stupid noises. Rich, the owner, laughs. "Leave the kid alone. No wonder he hasn't brought her by here before."

"Rich, you got some *Clueless* stuff to show Mallory?"

He smiles and nods. "Be right back!"

Two hours later, Mallory is tipsy and happily explaining every single aspect of *Clueless* to Nash who for some insane reason actually seems interested in it. I'm humiliating Collingwood at a game of pool. My parents have sent fourteen photos of Dylan, the last five are of him sleeping. I finally had to text my mom back and tell her to leave him to sleep and just stare at him on her phone app instead. I love the way she's already obsessed with him though.

"Look, they're talking about Casco!" Nash calls out and points to the muted TV above the bar. "Rich, turn it up!"

We all turn to the television and Rich grabs the remote and pumps up the volume. It's a reporter standing outside the arena with a somber look on her face. "The Quake is at the top of their division, guaranteed a playoff spot but off the ice, the team seems to be in turmoil."

"That's a bit dramatic," Crew grumbles.

"Forward Landon Casco collapsed on the ice during practice today, just one day before the last game of the year against the San Francisco Thunder," she goes on. "The cause is still unknown but we're told he is in stable condition now. And just an hour ago, TMZ Sports broke a story that star forward Tate Garrison has a secret baby."

"What?" Collingwood balks and starts to laugh. Loudly. He looks over at Mallory. "You're a tiny woman and not that tall, but surely they don't think you're a *baby*."

It's a joke. It's not funny.

I stare at the television, my body frozen in shock. I hear

Mallory say my name but I just keep staring. The image changes from the reporter outside the medical center to a picture of me and Mallory outside the townhouse, I'm carrying the stroller down the front steps and she's standing there with Dylan in her arms. Her face is blocked by her hair. Dylan's face is in full view and a wave of rage washes over. He's a kid and he didn't agree to have his face plastered everywhere.

"The mother is unknown. According to sources who live in the same complex as Garrison in Venice Beach and supplied this exclusive photo. Garrison is not only keeping the child secret, he's leaving it to be raised by nanny Mallory Echolls, who is also the sister of San Francisco Thunder defensemen Emmett Echolls."

"How...?"

I finally look at Mallory, but I don't have time to say anything as my phone is blowing up. Text message alerts and telephone calls. Coach Braddock, Adam from Communications, Christine. Crew exhales loudly beside me. "I thought you told the team? And your parents?"

"Parents yeah, they're with Dylan now. But my meeting with the team management was canceled when Landon collapsed," I mutter.

"Wait... this is true?" Collingwood balks.

"You knew?" Nash says, staring at his twin with a shocked expression.

"I don't tell you everything," Crew snaps at him. "Just like you don't tell me everything."

Crew turns away from Nash and back to me. "The townhouse complex is going to be swimming with paparazzi. Good thing we switched houses."

I nod. I grab my phone and call the person I know is the source, my neighbor Tara. She works for TMZ. She answers on the first ring. "Hey. Do you want to make an official statement?"

"How about fuck you," I snap at her. "I thought we were friends but you just wanted a story."

"Oh come on, Tate, we were never friends," Tara replies, her voice carefree because she gives zero shits she just complicated the hell out of my life just as things were finally on the verge of getting easier. "You were nice to me because you wanted to fuck me. And that's still on the table. But I can't sacrifice a good scoop for a potentially good lay. And he contacted me."

"Who?" I demand.

"The nanny's brother," Tara replies. "Anyway, you're a hockey player. This will blow over quick. L.A. is a basketball town. Relax. Now do you want to tell me your side? Clarify any of this?"

I hang up. Mallory has moved and is standing directly in front of me. I look down at her, but I don't really see her. I'm just furious. "You told your brother."

"What?" She blinks and her whole face changes. Her eyes are heavy with guilt. "I..."

"You told your family and they told the tabloids," I tell her and run my hands into my hair, frustrated. I start walking toward the door. "Fuck, Mallory! You knew this was private!"

"I told Emmett. I mean, he figured it out on his own, but you had already told your parents," Mallory explains, her voice high and wavering. "And you were supposed to have already told the team. I didn't think—"

"No, you definitely didn't." I start towards the door. "We have to get home. I have to call Coach and Adam back and—"

The door flies open and Christine is standing there. She is still in her work clothes, and her expression radiates fury even from across the room. Her eyes hone in on me immediately and I walk toward her. Mallory, I realize, is scurrying along behind me. "Christine, I asked for that meeting today so I could tell you."

"A kid?" Christine says, her voice hard but also confused. "You? Jesus Christ Tate, you should have told us the second you found out."

"It was complicated at first and I had to sort some stuff out," I explain. She shakes her head.

"All you had to do was tell us. Do you think this is what we want now? One game from the end of the season, when we should all be focused on Landon and the playoffs, we have to deal with your trailer park drama."

"Christine..." Crew says warning her of the lines she's crossing.

"No one asked you, Crew." She holds up a hand in his direction. Then her eyes land on Mallory. "You proud of yourself?"

"Me? I..." Mallory sputters. "I didn't want this to happen."

"Then maybe you should have kept your mouth shut," Christine snaps at her. "And your legs. Because I'm guessing you aren't just in this for the baby."

"Whoa." Nash walks up. "That's uncalled for."

"She's the reason we're in this mess," Christine replies without an ounce of remorse in her tone. "And FYI, my source at TMZ says this was a paid tip. They paid someone to spill this shit. How much did you get?"

Mallory shakes her head. I turn to Crew. "Can you take her home? Can she stay with you for a night? I have a lot to deal with."

"I don't... Tate. I can't stay with Crew," Mallory replies, her voice is shaky now. Her eyes wide with fear or confusion, but I'm drowning in a lot of very hard, horrible emotions myself and I can't. I just can't.

"I have to get home to Dylan," I reply. "And I have to sort

out a statement and stuff with Christine and... I just can't with you right now."

"I..." She blinks and tears flood her eyes.

Crew puts a hand on her shoulder. "Come on."

Mallory looks devastated. "I didn't do this on purpose."

"But you did do it," Christine points out and grabs my arm. "Let's go, Tate."

"Tate!" Mallory says, her tone pleading.

"I'll talk to you later," I say, my tone ice cold. Everything in me is running cold, my blood, my thoughts, my mood. I want nothing to do with anyone. I just want to go home and see my son but instead, I have to deal with this and then maybe I will be able to thaw my heart and handle whatever is left between Mallory and me.

Chapter 25

Mallory

Crew watches me as he shrugs into his suit jacket. His eyes are kind and soft, looking at me curled up in the corner of his couch like I'm a wounded puppy at a shelter. "You really should come with me."

"Nope," I reply and tuck my knees under the hoodie I'm wearing. It's Crew's, since I came here in nothing but the dress I was wearing last night, and you could fit four of me in it.

"He told me to bring you."

"He can fuck off."

"Mallory," Crew sighs. "I know he's sorry. He told you he was sorry."

"He texted me he was sorry. He knows where I am. He could drive his ass over here. It's less than ten minutes from his house," I remind him.

"He hasn't had a chance to breathe let alone come here," Crew defends his teammate like it's his job. I guess, as co-captain with his brother, it is his job. "He did three print interviews this morning and one TV interview is scheduled for before the game with his dad."

"Well then it's best I stay out of his way." I don't move off the couch as he adjusts the cuffs on his shirt, twisting the cuff-links and giving me his best puppy dog eyes.

"I'm sure Dylan misses you."

"Low blow."

Crew's mouth lifts a little in the corners. "I didn't say I would fight fair."

"Dylan has his grandparents," I say, trying not to give in to that ache in my chest. "And if I was so important to his son, he wouldn't have dumped me on you last night. Which made things worse, need I remind you."

"No, you don't need to remind me." Crew's rugged face grimaces.

Because this is the address the world still thinks Tate lives at, there were four photographers and one videographer outside the gates when Crew and I drove in. He gave me his jacket to cover myself from their lenses since the only way from the parking to the house is to walk by the gate.

I haven't slept a wink. I laid awake in that guest room all night, my eyes wet with tears, my heart aching and my brain growing angrier with every hour that passed. Now, as Crew gets ready to leave for the arena for their afternoon game against the Thunder, I have no more tears. I'm just plain angry.

"Okay well if you insist on staying here, I'll make sure the gate dude is aware. I don't trust those cockroaches to not try and sneak in," Crew tells me. "If they find out the mystery woman I came home with is also Tate's girlfriend, then we'll make the whole thing way worse."

"I'm not his girlfriend," I say. "I'm just the nanny."

"No, you're not," Crew replies simply like there's no room for debate on this. "Anyway, lock the door behind me."

He heads to the entry and I follow behind and lock the door after he leaves. Then I move back to the couch, grab my phone, and look up the only interview Tate's given that's made it online already. It's the Quake's official team website. He talks about how he assumed custody of Dylan after the mother, who lived in England, died in an accident. How he wasn't hiding the child, just trying to ease him into his new life without more unnecessary trauma.

He doesn't mention that he didn't know about Dylan. He doesn't mention that Diana was a bed buddy and not a girlfriend. He says he wasn't with the mother anymore when Dylan was born but he "very much takes responsibility for his son and is a proud dad." He says that "the nanny" is a close personal friend and he trusts Dylan with her "despite the leak coming from her family."

It's the fifteenth time I've read the article since it went live at two in the morning. And the same painful thought hits me hard every time I read it. It isn't Dylan who is Tate's dirty little secret. It's me. And I think I've finally reached the point where I love me more than I love the idea of being Tate Garrison's anything.

Tears well up in my eyes again, but I brush them away. I will not cry over a lesson that I refused to learn any other way but the hard way. My phone rings on the coffee table. It's a video call from my mom's cell. I have been avoiding calls from every single member of my family since the news broke last night but I know it's not something I can do forever.

I reach for the phone and swipe the green button. My mom's face appears on my screen. Her blue eyes are narrowed with concern and her mouth is set in a hard line. "Mallory! Thank you for finally answering."

"If you start to yell at me or lecture me I will hang up," I warn as I settle back into Crew's massive white couch. It's so big it goes from one corner of the living room to the other. His furniture is all too big for this place but he doesn't seem to care. "But don't worry you can do it in person soon enough. I think I'm going to come home. Soon."

"I will buy you a ticket for the next plane out if you want baby," Mom says and she shoots me a small, supportive smile. "And I won't lecture you. I won't yell. Believe it or not, I feel closer to you now than I ever have."

"What? Why?"

She smiles again, this time it's sheepish. "If anyone knows about losing yourself for a Garrison man, it's your mother."

"Mom, I have spent a little time with Mr. and Mrs. Garrison over the past twenty-four hours and, although I might be having some massive issues with Tate at the moment, I can tell you that Jessie and Jordan Garrison have been nothing but kind to me." I watch her face twist a little like she just inhaled an unpleasant smell, but she doesn't argue with me.

"I don't like them," she says flatly. "But I understand why other people do."

Oh. Well, that's new.

Mom's eyes dart to something past the phone and then land back on me through the screen. Judging by the painting behind her she's in her bedroom, sitting on her bed. She's likely looking at the door to make sure Dad is nowhere nearby. He likes the Garrisons even less than she does. "Look, when I fell for Jordan I was fourteen. I was also being raised by a functioning alcoholic and a narcissist. It was a toxic home life, to say the least."

I know this. My mom has never sugar-coated her relationship with my grandparents, who I have never met. Mom cut them out of her life before I was born. Only Beckett has vague memories of them. "Your grandparents were also dirt poor and Jordan, although from a modest middle-class family, was going places. The whole town knew it, even back then. And he liked me back. I held onto that like it was all I had. Like it was the only thing that mattered. But I also didn't know how to be in a healthy relationship."

"Most teenagers don't," I add, trying to cut her some slack.

She smiles and nods. "Oh, I know. But I was next level. I thought the only way to keep Jordan interested was to keep our relationship in a constant state of up and down. I literally should have worn a tiara I was such a drama queen."

I smile at that and let out a soft chuckle. She has never been this open with me. "Anyway, he was in love with Jessie, not me. I think I realized that before he did so of course I tried to make her life a living hell and I dug my claws into him even deeper. Again, I had no self-worth. I thought he was my only hope of escaping my parents and my fate, which I thought would be to become a waitress or something."

"Mom, you ended up going to a good school and getting a master's degree in physics," I remind her. "On a partial scholarship."

"Hindsight, Mallory," Mom says with a shrug. "Anyway, I just want to say that I understand thinking that a Garrison is the answer to all your prayers. But you will be fine without this turd Tate, I promise you. In fact, you'll likely be better off. And that's why Beckett talked to the media."

"Beckett?" I blink. "You mean Emmett."

Mom tilts her head for a second before she shakes it. "No. Beckett is the one who talked to TLC."

"TMZ."

"Whatever."

"How the hell did Beckett know about Dylan?" I demand.

"Emmett told him. In confidence," Mom explains. "And now Emmett's furious and told your brother he won't be in the wedding."

So Emmett didn't screw me over. It was Beckett who screwed over me *and* Emmett. "Fucking hell."

"Mallory! Language."

"Oh come on Mom, this is swear-worthy."

She sighs. "I guess it is. Your brother really fucked the whole family with this one."

"Why would Beckett do this?" I want to know.

Mom shrugs. "He says it was because the tabloid was willing to pay him and the costs for Heather's dream wedding have grown out of control. But I suspect he just wanted to hurt the Garrisons because of that Larue girl."

"Mac," I say and shoot my mom a withering stare. Beckett and Mac dated for years, my mother never liked her. But to call her 'that Larue girl' is a bit much. "But Beckett cheated on Mac. Why does he care if she moved on? Or with who?"

"Because your brother is petty," Mom declares. "And you know how Silver Bay is, everyone talks and the talk is that Mac Larue traded up. She landed the Golden Boy."

"Tate's the Golden Boy," I correct.

Mom rolls her big blue eyes. "All the Garrisons are golden. Do you see why it's annoying?"

"No," I confess. "I mean if they weren't good people then maybe. But... I like them."

"So then why are you talking about coming home?" Mom counters and I sigh.

"Because..." I don't finish the sentence.

And then the doorbell rings. I stiffen because I'm not expecting anyone and I'm worried that Crew's prediction is right and a reporter or photographer has breached the gate.

"Is someone there?" Mom asks.

"Yeah. I have to go," I say and start to rise up off the couch.

"Let me know when your flight is booked baby, or if you want me to book you one," Mom says.

"I'll get back to you," I say as I move one of the curtains on the front living room window to see if I can see who is on the front porch. "Bye Mom. Love you."

"Love you too," she says before I end the call.

I catch a glimpse of the tall lean frame of a man. And a chubby jean clad tiny leg dangling from the front of the man. I walk over to the door and crack it slightly. Jordan Garrison is standing there, Dylan strapped to his chest, and a canvas bag in one hand. He gives me a tentative smile. "Hi."

"Hi, Mr. Garrison. Is Dylan okay?" I swing the door wider.

Dylan looks at me and grins. His chubby hands fly toward me. I reach out and let him wrap his pudgy fingers around my hand. Jordan nods. "Please call me Jordan, and my wife Jessie. And yes, he's good, but he misses you, we can tell."

"Oh." I smile at Dylan. "It's okay Dyllie Bear. I'll always be your bestest bud."

"Jessie thought I should bring you some clothes," Jordan explains and hands me the bag he's carrying. "She picked out stuff from your dresser. I hope that's okay."

I look down at the oversized sweatshirt I'm wearing and the pajama bottoms that are cinched as tight as possible but are still swimming on me. "Yeah. At this point any clothes are great. But I was going to arrange to head home tomorrow and pack my stuff. When Tate was at the arena for practice."

"You're quitting?" Jordan looks crestfallen. "You're leaving?"

"I think it's best," I reply quietly. I can't look him in the eye. "It was my brother Beckett that leaked the story about Dylan. I had nothing to do with it, but if I hadn't told my brother Emmett, then none of this would have happened."

"Well, it did and he doesn't blame you," Jordan says.

"He sure seems like he does," I can't help but share.

"My son is a bit of an idiot when it comes to relationships," Jordan says simply with a sheepish smile. "Mainly because you're the first real one he's ever had."

"Maybe we will be able to talk this out, but..." I can't express to Jordan how complicated my feelings are. It's personal and I'm not even sure I understand it all myself just yet. But I feel betrayed by Tate. And hurt. And... like we ended before we began. "Right now I think I just need some space. I don't want to leave Dylan high and dry when his dad is going to hunker down for playoffs but we had started the interview process and I know there are some good candidates out there who can take over for me."

"Don't worry about that. My wife will likely insist we stay," Jordan explains. "And I don't have any issue being able to attend all my son's home playoff games. Or do unscheduled drop-ins on that daughter of mine either."

He grins, like the idea of surprising Tenley whenever he wants brings him joy. I smile back and nod before running my hand over Dylan's downy blond head one last time. "Well, then... thanks for the clothes."

"Oh I'm not just here for that," Jordan says. "I'm here to drive you to the game."

"The game?"

"Thunder versus Quake," he says. "Your brother versus my son. Last game of the regular season."

"Oh, I'm not going to the game."

"I hate to break it to you but my wife said if I didn't come back with you, she was going to come over here, with Tenley, and kidnap you," Jordan explains and he gets this ridiculously serious look on his face. "My daughter watches enough true crime documentaries that I'm sure she isn't kidding. And she'll have you hog-tied and in the back of her trunk before you know what hit you."

Sadly, I don't think he's exaggerating. I look down at my bag of clothes and back up at Mr. Garrison and Dylan. I give

Dylan's chin a quick tickle and he giggles. "Okay. Come have a seat. I'll go upstairs and change real quick."

* * *

Forty minutes later I've got a VIP lanyard around my neck, sitting on the edge of my seat watching the opening face-off from the Quake team box. Jessie is on one side of me and Tenley is on the other. Jordan is next to his wife and Dylan is asleep in his Baby Bjorn totally unaware his daddy is on the ice below. But I can't take my eyes off Tate. Because he's Tate, and also because he's staring across the ice at my brother who is staring back.

"They are going to tear each other's heads off on puck drop aren't they?" Tenley asks no one in particular.

"They'd have done it in warm-up, but it would have got them booted for the entire game," Jordan says.

There was a moment when both teams were on the ice for warm-up and Emmett and Tate skated down the center of the ice, shoulder-to-shoulder, exchanging what looked like heated words. I held my breath until I thought I would pass out but Crew skated over and pulled Tate away.

"Thank God Dyllie Bear is asleep." Jessie sighs. "I don't want him to see this."

"I don't want to see this," I mutter.

The puck drops. Crew and the Thunder centreman battle for it. But no one is paying attention. It's Emmett who skates across the ice and gets in Tate's face. Emmett drops his stick and his gloves. Tate drops his stick but his gloves remain on and he doesn't raise his arms. Nash and Crew ignore the puck and skate over to Tate but another Thunder player skates in to intercept them.

The ref's whistle blows as Emmett grabs the front of Tate's

jersey and the fans start yelling and hollering. My fists clench in my lap. "What the hell is my brother doing?"

"Well it doesn't matter, Tate's not engaging," Tenley remarks and she looks disappointed about it.

The first period goes on after that without a hitch. The Quake score and then the Thunder score. In the second period, the Thunder score early, and later in the period, Nash Westwood takes a penalty for a slash on my brother, who fucking deserved it if you ask me. And that's when it happens. With thirty-four seconds left on the penalty, Tate intercepts a Thunder pass and makes it halfway down the ice before getting slammed into the boards. He somehow manages to hold onto the puck, break away, and take a shot. It sails past the Thunder goalie's left shoulder and into the net.

Everyone is on their feet in the entire arena. Jessie squeals and claps. Tenley punches her fist into the air. Jordan is grinning. He looks down at Dylan who is startled awake by the noise even with his little noise-canceling headphones on. "Dylan, your daddy just beat my record."

I am still sitting, stunned. Tenley grabs my arms and yanks up to my feet. She hugs me. "He did it! He freaking did it!"

I stare down at the ice. The whole Quake bench is on its feet, leaning over and grabbing Tate's jersey, hugging him and shaking him, high-fiving him. He's smiling but he looks as stunned as I am.

They break to a commercial, you can tell because the red lights go on by the benches. On the Jumbotron, they flash to our box. Jordan grins and gives a thumbs-up. I blink when I see myself on the giant screen, Tenley's arm wrapped around me. My eyes dart to the ice. Tate is looking up at the screen. His grin gets deep and he turns, pulls off his helmet, and squints up at the box. I swear he is looking right at me. And his grin deepens.

Chapter 26

Tate

Holy shit I did it. I fucking did it. It feels pretty fucking great. But there was still a dull ache in my chest until I saw my family on the big screen above center ice and realized Mallory was with them. Holding Dylan.

Then suddenly it all felt so much better. I owed her an apology. I owed her so much more, but I needed to start with an apology. I didn't know if I would get the chance to give her one. Crew had said she was pissed and was talking about going home. And then Emmett tried to get me to punch him, repeatedly. I was furious with him, but I was not going to make this worse by punching him. Even though I desperately wanted to. I knew, in the end, he's Mallory's brother and she loves him so punching him wasn't going to improve my situation with her.

I go into the third period on a high, hoping beyond hope that Mallory's presence here is a sign that she might give me another chance. Nash scores early in the third with an assist from Crew, who can somehow make a perfect pass to his brother anywhere on the ice without even looking. It would be infuriating if they were on the opposing team so I get why the Thunder are irked. They're fired up, still fighting for the last playoff spot in our division. We are fired up because we want to win this for Landon who is still in the hospital.

So things get chippy in the last half of the third. They get a penalty but we can't capitalize on it. And then Crew takes a tripping penalty. He's one of our best penalty killers so having him in the box for one hurts. Coach Braddock points to me as we head out to fight this. "You're not coming off until the kill is over. Can you handle that?"

I nod. He turns to the rest of the penalty killers. "And you all get the puck to Garrison any chance you get. We are not only going to beat these guys, we're going to make sure he leaves his dad's record in the dust. Got it?"

"Coach..." He stares at me, an eyebrow quirked like he's daring me to talk him out of letting me score yet another shorty, which would mean I'm two ahead of my dad's longstanding record. "I've got this."

They all grunt out their support. No pressure, I think nervously. We're only ahead by one goal. If the guys are concentrating on getting me the puck instead of just keeping it away from our zone on a power play, they could get sloppy and the Thunder could tie this up. But Coach has faith I can do this and I should do this so I *will* do this, I tell myself. And I want to do this for Dylan. And Mallory. For the first time in my life, this isn't about my own ego. I want to make my son and Mallory proud. Because I love them.

"Garrison!"

I have been on autopilot, my brain lost in a fog of new emotions. I didn't see Nash get the puck from the Thunder forward, or shoot it across the ice to me at the center line, but it's a foot from me when he calls my name. There's not one but two Thunder players near me, one to the left and one to the right, and both are skating at me with everything they've got, I deke around one.

The puck hits my stick so hard it almost flies over it. But it doesn't and I skate like my whole life depends on it. But I won't make it any closer than I am. I have to take the shot because I know that Thunder player who was on my right is a few short seconds from checking me onto my ass. So just a few feet over the blue line, I narrow my focus on the left top corner of the net, pull my stick back, and let a blistering slap shot go.

It's not the fastest shot I've ever done. It's not the prettiest-looking shot. And I don't even see it cross the goal line because I'm slammed into the boards by the Thunder player and I'm on my back on the ice. But I hear the crowd. They come alive all at once and I swear to God the ice under me shakes.

Someone holds out a hand and hauls me up to my feet. It's Emmett Echolls. He skates away without a word. I look up before the team swarms me, and I see my family. I see my son and I see Mallory. I point at them. At her. I hope she knows it. I hope she knows...

The game ends. We win. And I am Player of the Game. But the announcement isn't the normal one. They bring my family down onto the ice to give me the puck as they announce I got First Star of the Game, and that I just beat my dad's short-handed goal record.

My dad, mom, and Tenley holding Dylan, walk tentatively in a line to center ice and I skate out to meet them. Mallory is at the edge of the ice, against the boards where my parents entered from. I stare at her, she stares back but motions for me to go to my parents. I stop in front of my dad. "Just a sec, okay," I say and pause to kiss Dylan's cheek. He grins at me as I yank off my glove and ruffle his hair.

Then I skate past my family and straight to Mallory. "What are you doing?" she asks, her voice high and squeaky because she knows the cameras have followed me.

"Apologizing," I say. "Look, I will grovel in technicolor as soon as we're home, but for now, just know that I know I fucked up. I handled that whole thing in the worst possible way. I never should have left you at that bar. I'm sorry. I will forever be sorry. And you don't have to forgive me right this minute but if you think you might sometime in the future can you please come out onto the ice right now?"

"They asked for your family to give you the puck," Mallory whispers like we're being eavesdropped on. I have no idea if mics are on us but there is a camera pointed at us over by the boards and I'm sure we're on the Jumbotron. "Just go do your thing."

"You are my family, Mallory," I tell her. "Maybe not on paper but I love you as much as I love them. You matter to me as much as they do so please. I want you there."

"Oh..." She blinks. She smiles. She blinks again.

I take that as a yes so I wrap my arm around her tiny waist and lift her up and skate. She lets out a squeak and wraps her arms around my neck. She buries her head against my neck guard as her legs dangle just above the tops of my skate boot. "You are insane Tate Garrison."

"Maybe," I admit. "I've never been in love before but I guess it makes you crazy."

"Oh my God stop saying that," she whispers.

"Say it back and I will."

"I love you," Mallory says it so easily that it blows my mind. "I have for a very long time, you idiot. But I am still mad at you."

"I'll fix that," I promise as I deposit her next to my sister.

I skate over to my dad. He gives me the game puck and a giant hug while my mom holds Dylan. I hug each of them. And then I kiss Mallory.

As a reporter makes his way over to us, I scoop Dylan out of my Tenley's arms and he comes gladly. I offer him the puck and he holds it in his little hands, staring at it intently, probably contemplating if he can chew on it.

"So, Tate, you sure know how to end a season," the reporter says. "How does it feel to beat your dad's long-standing league record by not one but two goals?"

"Great," I say with a smile. "Almost as great as being a dad."

Dylan squeals something indiscernible and shakes the puck in his hand.

The crowd erupts with laughter and cheers.

* * *

"Are you sure it's okay to kick your parents out?" Mallory asks as I carry a sleeping Dylan upstairs to his room.

"Yes," I say. "And besides, they should spend some time with Tenley. And Liv."

Mallory doesn't answer. I wait for her on the landing and then kiss the top of her head when she comes up the stairs to stand beside me. "Besides, I can't grovel the way I want to with them here."

She raises an eyebrow. "How exactly do you want to grovel?"

"With my tongue. And my dick," I say as I open Dylan's door.

"Please don't say the d-word in front of your son," Mallory warns. "It might end up being his first word."

"Okay well we don't want that," I agree.

She laughs and we both start gently getting him ready for bed, trying desperately not to wake him. It takes a while but we manage to get him out of his clothes and into a onesie. He wakes momentarily but his eyes close as soon as we lay him down.

We turn on his nightlight and sneak out of the room, softly closing the door as we go. Once we're in the hall I stare down at her. She stares up at me, her gaze tentative. "I know you're not over it. I don't expect you to be over it, but will you give me a chance to make it up to you?"

"What happened on the ice with Emmett?"

"He wanted me to fight him," I explain. "He was begging me to punch him. Told me it was his fault the story got out, not yours. He said I was a jackass if I was going to hurt you over this."

"And you wouldn't punch him?"

"I wanted to, but I knew that it would hurt you," I explain and I tuck a lock of her blonde hair behind her left ear. "And I'd hurt you enough."

She looks down, at the small space between us. "Tate, I don't blame you. You freaked out. I might have freaked out too. But what scares me is... I had fallen faster and harder than you. I let that happen. And I felt so... foolish when you left me with Crew. Like I was this burden you had to get rid of. And I won't ever feel like that again. Ever."

"I won't let you. I promise." I cup her face in my hands. "I am so sorry. And for the record, you may have fallen for me first but I fell hard, Mallory. I know I can manage Dylan on my own now. I know I can go on with my life and win this Cup this year and break a million records without you in my life. But I don't want to. I don't want to do anything without you. I don't know when or how it happened but I fell for you, Mallory Echolls. And my life got exponentially better because of it."

She tucks her head and presses her forehead to the center of my chest. I wrap my arms around her and dip my head and whisper, "Was that too much? Not enough? Again, I am absolutely clueless when it comes to this."

"Well just like everything else, Tate, you're pretty perfect at winning a woman back," Mallory tells me and she grabs my waist and giggles before lifting her head. "But I am perfectly fine with you still groveling. With your tongue and your dick."

"Shh!" I hush her and grin. "Don't need Dyllie Bear yelling dick at the Stanley Cup winning game."

She laughs but it's cut short when I pull her into a kiss and then lift her up and carry her to my... *our* bedroom. And half an hour later when she's coming and panting my name I tell her I love her over and over and lose myself inside her. Only for the first time since she walked back into my life, I don't feel lost at all.

Epilogue - Mallory

"I can't believe you would do this to your brother!"

I don't even feel the slightest twinge of guilt as Heather looks at me with big, sad eyes filled with crocodile tears. I smile back at her and lean in so that I'm not making a scene. It's a wedding after all. "Heather, enjoy your day. The fact that I'm leaving a tad early shouldn't phase you."

"We haven't even had the midnight ice cream bar!" Heather whines.

"Babe, Mal not eating ice cream is not going to make or break this wedding," Beckett interjects, his tone not that of an elated groom. More like a disgruntled man who has been in a love-less marriage for years. They've been married less than six hours. "And it will save us some cash, with one less mouth feeding at the trough. No offense."

"Oh yeah, that's not offensive at all." I bite my cheek at Tate's flat, sarcastic tone. "Anyway she needs to keep some room for the ice cream she'll be eating tomorrow. Out of the Cup."

Beckett rolls his eyes. I want to slap him so badly that my fingers tingle. The only reason I attended this stupid wedding is for the sake of my parents. And I even convinced Emmett to attend, who is still furious with Beckett. So am I, but my parents have had a lot to adapt to and it meant a lot to them to have the whole family at this wedding. So Emmett and I came. And now, at almost midnight, I'm trying to make a gracious exit to get home to Dylan. Tate has been nothing short of a perfect date, ignoring Beckett's disdain and my father's out-and-out disgust. But I've reached my limits for him.

"Congratulations to you both," I say with finality as I reach to find Tate's hand.

Our fingers slip together with ease and familiarity. Tate smiles at the newlyweds. "May you be as happy for the rest of your life as you are today."

I turn and lead him across the Silver Bay Golf Club ballroom to the door as fast as possible so no one sees or hears me laughing. As soon as we're in the lobby I let the giggles burst free. Tate yanks me to his side, slinging his big arm over my shoulders and pulling me into him. "I'm going to hell for laughing at that. I truly think that if Beckett wasn't miserable he wouldn't be such a dick."

Tate kisses my bare shoulder. The one good thing that came from the massive family blow-up that happened from Beckett selling me down the river is I could avoid being *in* the actual wedding. Heather picked chartreuse chiffon for bridesmaid dresses. I got to wear a very pretty, simple strapless sundress in a rose color which suits my complexion much better than chartreuse.

"Think they'll figure out we lied?" Tate wants to know as we wander past the front doors and to the doors at the end of the hall that lead to the bungalows that lace the side of the course and are rented out as hotel rooms. "And that my parents have Dylan on a sleepover."

"Ask me if I care?" I counter as he reaches for the door and winces.

"You okay?"

"Worth it," he grunts as I take the heavy oak door from his hand and pull it the rest of the way. Tate broke two ribs in the Stanley Cup final. The whole team, like most teams who achieve the accomplishment, were pretty banged up by the time they hoisted the Cup after sweeping the Barons in four games. That was another reason my dad hated Tate. Oh well. Worth it, as he said. "But damn I'm an asshole for not understanding the pain you must have been living with when you first moved in with me. Holy shit this hurts, like all the time."

"I know. And nothing can fix it but time," I tell him what he already knows.

We're wandering in the sticky night air, down the flagstone path that leads to bungalow four. I lift my hair off my neck and sigh. Silver Bay is in a heat wave and the humidity is cloying. "I hope they fixed the AC in our room."

"Me too," Tate replies. "If you're going to be sweating all night I want it to be from sex, not weather."

I smile. But it quickly falls off my lips when we open the door to the bungalow and the temperature inside is just as gross as outside. I'm about to groan when Tate marches past me and grabs our overnight bags. "Okay then. Plan B."

"I didn't know we had a plan B?"

He grins. "I've always got you covered, baby girl."

He does. I know this now, after living with him through the last couple of months of playoffs. He is everything I dared to dream for Dylan and everything I never dared to dream for myself. I wake up every morning feeling so grateful, but also a little guilty every time I wake up Dylan who is growing like a weed. Diana would be so thrilled to see him thrive. I wish she was here, but my perfect life exists because she isn't. It's tough to think about.

I don't ask questions as Tate leads us back to the lobby and then out the front doors to his car. I have the utmost confidence we're going somewhere lovely until he pulls over next to a field halfway up the hill that overlooks the lake. He turns off the engine and looks over at me excitedly. "I was going to wait until dawn to show you this, but might as well do it now."

"What are you showing me?" I question.

He gets out of the car and I sit there, too confused to move, staring out at the dark blob that is the lake below us. The lights from the park and the nearby houses and streets make the surface shimmer in spots. It's pretty and soothing. So different from Los Angeles and yet I love them both now.

I hear him open the trunk and close it and then there's light. He's holding a camping lantern and rapping on my passenger window. I open the door tentatively. "I don't... I mean I hate to sound diva, but I don't camp Tate."

He chuckles. "Neither do I. We'll head home after this. I just wanted some time and I can't wait to show you."

"What?" I ask as I climb out of the car. He's got a picnic basket with him too. Okay...

He takes my hand, piling everything into his other one, and leads me through the freshly cut grass of this massive aban-doned field. "Who cuts grass in an empty field?"

"The real estate agency selling it. If you ask nicely enough and promise to hoist the Stanley Cup here and give them a shout-out in the paper," Tate says with a smile dancing on his lips.

I trip, even though the ground seems flat and even. Tate catches me, but winces because of his ribs. "Sorry!"

"Are you okay?"

"Yes. I just…" I stop walking. We're almost in the center of the land now anyway. "This property is for sale?"

"Yeah, and I want to buy it." Tate puts the lantern and basket down, opens the basket, and pulls out a blanket. "But I wanted you to check it out first. Make sure you like it."

"Me? Tate… I mean… I would like anywhere you choose to live."

"Enough to live here with us?" Tate asks, his voice getting soft with vulnerability. "Dylan and me? I know that you're with us now, in the apartment above the barn but it's less than ideal. I'm going to build a place here over the season. My own home. Our own home."

God, we are so complicated. "As the nanny?"

"No nanny in the off-season remember?"

Right. We made that agreement when we came back to Silver Bay. His entire family is taking turns helping us out when we need time away from Dylan, but now we're basically co-parenting. He's not paying me anymore. He asked me to stay with him as his girlfriend, instead of getting my own place in Silver Bay and I agreed. But we haven't talked much about the future. I wasn't even sure if I would be moving back to L.A. with him. I assumed but hearing him say it would be nice.

"Mal?" he prods and I blink. When I can't figure out what to say he lowers himself to the blanket and pulls me down too. I sit cross-legged shoulder to shoulder with him and stare at the view again. "so here's what I'm thinking. I'm firing you."

"Excuse me?" I turn to stare. He smiles at me.

"I'm going to hire a nanny in Los Angeles," he turns the other way and digs something out of the picnic basket. He drops a pamphlet onto my knee. "So you can go back to school. You said you wanted to get your master's in childhood education. Long Beach offers that."

"I know. I'm the one that told you."

"So you go back to school. I'll do the hockey superstar thing." I laugh at his fake egotism. He pulls me to him gently and presses a kiss on my lips that's light and sweet. "And everything else stays the same. You live with us. You're my girlfriend. We co-parent Dyllie Bear. Same as now."

"So you still want me." I shouldn't sound stunned and I shouldn't say it out loud. It isn't fair. Tate's never given me any reason to doubt his commitment to me since that stupid tabloid drama.

"Baby girl, I not only want you, I need you," Tate whispers and kisses my neck softly. But then he pulls back and lets out a heavy sigh. "Your dad talked to me tonight. When you left the table to go to the restroom."

Oh shit. "What did he say?"

"That it was convenient of me to pay my girlfriend to raise my kid."

"I'm going to murder him!" I hiss. "I love Dylan. I want to be in his life. I would do it without money."

"And you love me too?"

"I love you too," I confirm.

"So be my partner," Tate whispers. "And nothing more."

"Okay." I feel a jolt of excitement at going back to school. He pulls me to him, cupping the back of my neck and pulling us down to lay on the blanket.

His fingers curl under the hem of my panties. "I was thinking... there's one thing I want to eat out of the Cup more than ice cream."

I think about tomorrow. His day with the Cup and all the fun activities lined up with his family and our friends. "Cereal? Strawberry shortcake? Roscoe's Chicken and Waffles?"

"You..." he breathes as his thumb makes contact with my clit. "You wanna get naked and put that sweet ass of yours in the

Cup and spread those legs and let me lick you until you scream?"

"Oh my God," I shudder out a breath, my head tipping back into the scratchy blanket as his fingers slip into me. "We could never. I mean... that sounds so hot but... you know we can't."

"Then let me have you here," he begs. Tate begging is next-level hot. The Golden Boy begging for me. "Show your pussy to the stars and let me fuck you with my tongue on the land where we'll grow old. Raise Dylan and probably more perfect babies."

I'm turned on by his hand and melting inside at his words. He's got my panties down to my ankles so I slip one foot out of them and spread my legs as I lift my dress. The humid air swirls around my exposed flesh, but only for a second before his tongue claims the space. I tangle my fingers in his silky hair and tug him back so he looks up at me, impatiently. "Only if you let me ride you after."

"Right here?" Tate grins and it's feral. "Under the stars and the moon and the universe."

"Yes. On our land," I pant as his tongue goes back to dance across my pussy. "Where we'll grow old together."

I believe it. It's not just my foolish hopes and dreams anymore.

"I'm still going to do this to you when I'm a hundred."

"God, I hope so."

And then the words stop, as I battle between chasing and running from my release. I come faster than I would like but it's okay because then I ride him, like I promised, and come again. We curl up on the blanket, mussed and sweaty but smiling. He pulls a lock of hair off my cheek and smiles down at me as he props his head on his elbow. "You think Dylan Jordan Garrison will like it here."

"I love that you gave him your dad's name," I tell him. "And yes. He will love it."

"I love you, Mallory," he says, his aquamarine eyes sparkling in the lantern light. "I'd be lost without you."

"You'd do just fine, Golden Boy."

"I don't ever want to find out."

Tate pulls me closer and covers my mouth with his before I can promise him I'm not going anywhere. I guess I'll just have to show him.

Acknowledgments

Thanks to my family, my friends, Brower Literary, my editor Brandi Zelenka, my beta and ARC readers, and my ever-patient puppy Maximus who let me throw his toys with one hand while typing with the other. Thanks to all the readers who have embraced this series, especially the ones who loved Hometown Players and San Francisco Thunder enough to dive in again. Next up, Crew and.... Any guesses?

About the Author

Victoria Denault is an award-winning Canadian romance author. Her book Dauntless won Best Queer Romance in the 2023 Canadian Romance Awards. Victoria writes both MM and MF romance in mostly the sports and small-town genres all with heat, heart and a little snark. She's a nomad at heart and has lived in three different Canadian provinces, as well as California and France. She spends her spare time at the beach, baking, or snuggling her new puppy, Maximus.

www.ingramcontent.com/pod-product-compliance
Lightning Source LLC
Chambersburg PA
CBHW071414200726
48294CB00002B/389